MILKY WAY
REPO

MICHAEL PRELEE

EDGE SCIENCE FICTION AND FANTASY PUBLISHING
An Imprint of HADES PUBLICATIONS, INC.
CALGARY

Milky Way Repo

Copyright © 2016 by Michael Prelee

EDGE SCIENCE FICTION AND FANTASY PUBLISHING
An Imprint of HADES PUBLICATIONS, INC.
P.O. Box 1714, Calgary, Alberta, T2P 2L7, Canada

The EDGE-Lite Team:
Producer: Brian Hades
Editor: Ella Beaumont
Cover Artist: Corey A Ford
Cover Design: Janice Blaine
Book Design: Mark Steele
Publicist: Janice Shoults

ISBN: 978-1-77053-125-3

EDGE Science Fiction and Fantasy Publishing and Hades Publications, Inc. acknowledges the ongoing support of the Alberta Foundation for the Arts and the Canada Council for the Arts for our publishing programme.

Library and Archives Canada Cataloguing in Publication
CIP Data on file with the National Library of Canada
ISBN: 978-1-77053-125-3
(e-Book ISBN: 978-1-77053-092-8)

FIRST EDITION
(20160829)
Printed in USA
www.edgewebsite.com

Publisher's Note:

Thank you for purchasing this book. It began as an idea, was shaped by the creativity of its talented author, and was subsequently molded into the book you have before you by a team of editors and designers.

Like all EDGE books, this book is the result of the creative talents of a dedicated team of individuals who all believe that books (whether in print or pixels) have the magical ability to take you on an adventure to new and wondrous places powered by the author's imagination.

As EDGE's publisher, I hope that you enjoy this book. It is a part of our ongoing quest to discover talented authors and to make their creative writing available to you.

We also hope that you will share your discovery and enjoyment of this novel on social media through Facebook, Twitter, Goodreads, Pinterest, etc., and by posting your opinions and/or reviews on amazon and other review sites and blogs. By doing so, others will be able to share your discovery and passion for this book.

Brian Hades, publisher

Dedications

For Tina, Wyatt & Jacob

Acknowledgments

I would like to thank the following people for their help and assistance.

My beautiful wife Tina, for encouraging me by listening to all my crazy ideas and providing advice, love and support.

My mom and dad, Anna Prelee and Joseph Prelee, for teaching me to read and write and introducing me to science fiction.

My friend Glenn Reed, my first beta reader.

The rest of my family and friends (too numerous to mention by name), for supporting me by being there whenever I needed them.

My editor Ella Beaumont, who provided much needed direction and advice that was spot on. This is a much better book because of her involvement.

Janice Blaine, for putting the cover together.

Janice Shoults, for her marketing assistance.

Finally, Brian Hades at EDGE Science Fiction and Fantasy for taking a chance on me.

Chapter 1

Barrigan Three was a dump of a planet orbiting Alpha Centauri A. Nathan Teller hated visiting this planet but repo agents went where the work led them. This trip out was for a potentially lucrative payday on a cargo vessel that had made its last delivery to Barrigan Three so this was where Nathan and his crew found themselves. The world was habitable only in the sense that there was air to breathe and water to drink. The air smelled of sulfur due to constant volcanic eruptions at the equator and the water had to be filtered to clean out the rotten egg taste. Nathan had spent the past week on the planet and was glad to be high above it now. He was on the orbital shipyards that serviced the ore freighters carrying Barrigan Three's iron and nickel to other planets.

He and his companion were dressed in the dirty gray coveralls of the mechanics that occupied the shipyards. Nathan was the shorter of the two by a few centimeters. A couple of decades of sitting in the pilot's seat had left him with a slight paunch and his short brown hair was just starting to show some gray. Cole Seger was in considerably better shape, leaner and harder than his captain. They approached a hatch leading to a dock. Through a small window they could see a large container ship secured outside. Four hundred meters long and painted a ghastly bright orange, the *Martha Tooey* looked like every other long distance freighter that moved cargo containers full of goods from one planet to another. Nathan double-checked the dock number and looked at his companion. The larger, quieter man gave Nathan a barely perceptible nod and they opened the hatch.

The gangway was long and narrow, ending at an airlock that connected the shipyards to the freighter. A guard sat on a chair outside the airlock snoring loudly. Nathan and Cole walked quietly past him to the small window at the end of the gangway. They stared outside and stole a look back at the guard.

Nathan pulled a bottle out of his coveralls and took a pull on it. He passed it to Cole who did the same. The guard continued to snore.

With a look of exasperation on his face, Nathan looked at the unkempt deck, spotted a crushed can and kicked it the length of the gangway. It skittered along the rusted metal, clanging and banging as it traveled down the way they had come.

The guard woke up, startled to see he wasn't alone. He stood, grabbed a metal pipe, and waved it in the direction of Nathan and Cole. "What are you doing here?" he said. "You ain't supposed to be here."

Nathan hefted the bottle. "We're lookin' for a place to drink. We were at Moochies but he threw us out. He said my buddy couldn't bet on the dog races in his place."

The guard considered this. "Moochie don't like bettin'. He threw me out last week because I was bettin' on the dogs."

Cole passed the guard the bottle. "Look, we don't want any trouble. We just figured nobody would be around." He gestured at the freighter outside. "That bucket hasn't moved in weeks."

The guard nodded as he gulped down a long swallow. "The dock boss has this heap tied up because of some pay issue." He burped. "I'm here to make sure no one takes her." He pointed out the window. "Just look at it. Who the hell would want it?"

The guard turned back to see Cole holding a gun on him. Nathan stepped forward. "We would, friend. Now we need you to be cooperative. If you are, you can go home with a little money in your pocket. If you're not, you probably won't go home at all."

The guard stammered. "What's going on?"

"Not that it concerns you but the *Martha Tooey's* owner doesn't see things the dock master's way and wants his ship back," Nathan explained. "We're going to take it and you're going to sit here while we do it."

"I'll lose my job! Mickey will—"

"Mickey? He's the dock master, right?" Nathan asked.

The guard nodded.

Nathan pulled out a wad of credit markers and held it out to the man. "Tell Mickey you quit. Take it and follow us."

The guard looked at the markers. They were Nathan gestured again. "What's your name?"

"Frank."

"Frank, look at this money." He counted off the markers. "What's that pay you?"

"About three month's salary," he answered.

This place really is a dump, Nathan thought. "Take the money, Frank."

The man considered his options and then reached out and snatched the wad from Nathan's hand. Nathan gestured to the airlock. "Is there anyone else on board?"

The guard shook his head. "I'm the only one. There were a couple other guys but Mickey caught 'em selling the freighter's fuel on the black market. Since then I'm the only one."

"And your relief?" Cole asked.

"I'm on for another four hours. Jimmy won't be around 'til then," he explained.

That matched what Nathan and Cole knew from their surveillance over the last few days. "Okay, then," Nathan said. "Open her up."

They entered the freighter and made their way up to the bridge. It was a mess.

"What the hell happened in here?" Nathan asked as he kicked dirty clothes out of his way.

The guard shrugged his shoulders. "Them other guys that were sellin' the fuel? They were livin' up here."

Nathan removed a key from his pocket and inserted it into the master control panel. Lights came on around the ship. Gauges and monitors on the bridge glowed to life and he checked one after the other.

"How are we doing?" Cole asked. He was sitting in the elevated pilot's chair but still had his gun in his hand.

"Good enough," Nathan said as he tapped a gauge. "The batteries are okay but the fuel's a little lower than I'd like. We've got a little less than one full bunker out of four. This guy's friends must have made a fortune selling as much as they did."

"They did all right," Frank said.

"What was your cut?" Cole asked.

"Enough."

Cole nodded and looked at Nathan. "Do we have enough to get under way?"

Nathan did some quick calculations in his head. "I'd like a little more but it will do." He entered some commands into a computer and a deep throbbing sound filled the bridge. "Looks like we found the one thing on this planet that works like it's supposed to."

"Can I go?" Frank asked.

Nathan didn't look away from the gauges. "Not yet. Just be cool. It will take about five minutes for the plasma to generate and another five to reach drive pressure. You can go as soon as we're ready to launch."

Nathan turned back to the controls and settled into the pilot's chair. The gauges were coming up nicely and the board was green. He checked the cameras for the cargo holds and saw they were still full. Perfect. He was getting the ship *and* her load.

"Is this what you guys do? You're pirates?" The guard asked.

Nathan looked at Cole with a raised eyebrow and then turned to the guard. "Do you see an eye patch? Is there a parrot on my shoulder? We aren't pirates," he said. "There's a payment dispute about the load. The customer doesn't want to pay for it now that it's delivered so he bribed the dock master to hold the ship. The customer thinks the owner of the ship will give in just to get the ship back. That guy, Mickey, had the crew taken off and locked the ship in the dock. We're here to repossess it."

"You're repo men?"

Cole smiled. "The best there are."

Nathan turned back to the control panel. He pulled a small lever and the ship lurched sideways. "Uh-oh."

"What's up?" Cole asked.

"The docking clamps didn't release like they should have. Frank, what's up with the docking clamps?"

"They're controlled from the dock master's office. That's how Mickey likes it."

Cole gestured out the window. "We've got company, boss. There's a pod coming over the bow."

Nathan turned and saw a bright yellow work pod speeding across the hull toward the elevated bridge of the freighter. It was a small thing, big enough to carry one man and some tools. It had two mechanical arms attached at the rear with various attachments secured to its mid-section. Nathan leaned over to the switch on the wall and shut the interior lights off. "Well this is heading south in a hurry," he said. "Cole, get Duncan on the radio. We're going to need him and Marla sooner than we thought."

Cole relayed the message while Nathan and Frank watched the pod approach. "That's going to be Mickey," Frank said as he moved away from the wheelhouse window. "He can't see me here. If he does he'll have me arrested."

"Be cool, Frank." Nathan said. "Just duck out into the corridor. He won't see you there." The guard turned to leave and Nathan grabbed his arm. "Don't go too far, I don't want you changing your mind and coming back with a bunch of friends. Stay in the doorway where I can see you."

"Duncan and Marla are on the way," Cole said. "They'll be here in a few minutes. What's this guy up to?" He pointed at the work pod floating toward them.

"I don't know. Furthermore, once Duncan and Marla get us disconnected from the dock I won't care."

"Does he have any guns on that thing?" Cole asked.

Nathan squinted out the window. "Nah. It looks like your standard work pod. They use them for welding and hull repairs. Stuff like that."

"Mickey's crazy," Frank said from the doorway. "You don't know what he'll do to keep his cut of this ship."

Nathan turned to him and realized the guard was not only hiding in the shadows of the doorway but he was kneeling down as well. "We just need to keep him confused for a few minutes. Once my ship gets here Mickey will get the message."

"He's crazy, I'm tellin' you," Frank said. Nathan ignored him.

The yellow work pod settled in front of the bridge, slowly sliding right to left as the pilot peered in. Nathan and Cole hunkered down behind the pilot's chair and a map table. Nathan could see the pod had dirt streaks and burn marks on it. Like everything else in this dump, it wasn't maintained well. Suddenly a spotlight flooded the bridge with bluish-white light.

"Ah!" Frank shrieked, sounding like a teenager caught sneaking in after curfew. Nathan glanced back to see him scurry out of sight into the corridor. Cole snorted.

The light moved around the room as the work pod slipped around a corner. Nathan and Cole moved ahead of it, keeping the pilot's chair and map table between them and the light.

"He knows we're here," Cole said. "He just wants to see who it is before he decides to call the law."

"The law's pretty easy to buy off here," Nathan said. "I gave them two thousand to go on break an hour ago. We got about a half hour before they show up."

Cole looked incredulous in the reflected work light. "When did you have time to bribe the cops?"

"Last night," Nathan answered. "You were down at Moochies trying to hook up with that burly lady welder."

"I don't see any reason to mock my date's profession." Cole responded.

"It's not her profession I'm mocking. Tell me, did you get away without bruises?"

Cole slid around the map table to escape the moving light. "She was a powerful woman. Let's leave it at that."

Suddenly, the hatch slammed closed. Nathan looked toward the doorway as the wheel began to spin. He leaped from his hiding place and grabbed the wheel but it sealed as his hand reached it. The light from the pod outside blazed in and illuminated him. "Open this door, Frank!"

No one answered.

He threw his weight against the wheel. Nothing. "Damn, it's locked," he said.

"Locked from the outside?" Cole asked.

Nathan pulled on the wheel again. "He's got it tied off, the deadbolt is on the inside with us. I can feel it giving a little but…" He pulled again. "No, it's not going to give." He pounded on the door. "That greasy punk. If I ever see him again I'll airlock him."

Cole stepped from behind the table. "This is what you get for being a nice guy. Instead of bribing him you should have let me knock him out." He glanced at the service pod hovering outside. "Can this guy hurt us?"

Nathan looked the pod over as the spotlight swung back and forth between himself and Cole. "Not unless he rams us but that would hurt him too. Still, I'll see if there are any pressure suits in here. Why don't you check in with Marla and Duncan again?"

Nathan stepped to the storage locker in the rear and pulled the door open. It was clear that the same workers who had been selling fuel had stripped out whatever the locker held. A lone helmet with a cracked visor sat on a shelf. "Nothing here, Cole."

Cole held his mobi up to Nathan. "Marla says they can see us so they should be here any second. What do we need them to do?"

"This tub is only connected to the station at two docking pylons. If Marla gets in position over us, Duncan can break us free with the cannon."

Cole looked at him with wide eyes and muted the mobi. "You want Duncan to shoot us free? Is that the plan? Really?"

Nathan shrugged. "It's plan B. Plan A was for us to use the controls here on the bridge to release the freighter. That didn't work so now we have to resort to plan B."

"You're sure there's no plan C?" Cole asked.

"I'm sensing you don't have any faith in your crewmates."

"Look, I've tried to train him. You know I have. He's great with the computers and he redesigned the *Blue Moon Bandit* from the ground up, I know, but have you seen what happens when he gets near guns?"

"There's no other way, Cole."

The larger man opened his mouth again but was interrupted as the bright work light shut off. It flickered rapidly and the container ship's comm system chimed. Cole pointed to a red blinking light on the panel. "I think he wants to talk to us," he said.

Nathan nodded and stared out at the pod again. The work light flashed again. *Someone seems angry*, Nathan thought.. He walked to the comm console and pressed the button marked "SEND". "You've reached the wheelhouse of the *Martha Tooey*. How can I direct your call?"

"What are you doing on my ship?" The voice boomed from the speakers around the bridge. It didn't sound like a happy voice but Nathan knew that wasn't unusual for this stage of repossessions process.

Nathan smiled. "We're duly authorized repossession agents hired by the ship's owner to retrieve his property. In this case the container cargo vessel *Martha Tooey*."

"Can't have it. The ship's been seized due to non-payment of the loan on her. The owner didn't make his payments and the bank wants her back."

Nathan looked at Cole. "Why can't they try something original? Every time we go out on a job these guys always try the same line." Cole shook his head. Nathan hit the button again.

"The owner and the bank holding the note on the ship hired me. You have no grounds to hold her. Furthermore, I have a letter from the owner, co-signed by the bank, authorizing me to locate, board, and return this vessel to its homeport. Now release the clamps."

There was a moment of silence that confirmed what Nathan already knew; this guy was nothing more than a thief. The question was how far was he willing to go to get his cut of the freight?

"You aren't going anywhere," Mickey said. "I don't care what your letter says. I'm the dock master and I say when and if a ship leaves."

Cole angled one of the ship's long range cameras out into the yard and pointed at a monitor. "Nathan? I think this guy whistled for some help."

Nathan looked past the work pod and sighed. A mid-size freighter was moving into position in front of the *Martha Tooey*, no doubt called out by Mickey. He checked the drive pressure. It was just about where he needed it.

"Tell Marla to get the *Blue Moon Bandit* between us and that other freighter," Nathan ordered. "I'm betting they won't hit her."

Cole spoke into his mobi and Nathan shook his head. This guy had finally gotten his temper up. No way was some pissant dock manager coming between him and a six-figure retrieval. He saw his own ship do an elegant turn and slide in front of the larger freighter bearing down on them. He punched the button on the comm console.

"Look, Mickey, we're taking this ship. I suggest you move that work pod before you get run over."

This time the voice coming back was almost cheerful. "I don't think so. In a few seconds you won't have the room to move."

Nathan shook his head with exasperation. "Your road block is blocked, Mickey. I have friends too. If you turn around you'll see your big freighter blocked by my little freighter. Of course, my little freighter has a cannon. I don't believe yours does. That's a fact that I'm sure my crew is letting the pilot of your ship know of right now."

There was silence for almost a full minute. Cole confirmed that Marla and Duncan had already communicated with the freighter and that it was stopped. That was news Mickey was probably just learning. The speakers crackled again.

"You think you're smart?" the voice asked. "You think I'm letting you move this tub without putting up a fight? That's not how I do things." The signal snapped off and the spotlight went out. Suddenly a bluish flame splashed against the window. Nathan stepped forward to get a better look.

"Do you believe this? He's trying to burn a hole in the glass." Burning hot gas from a cutting torch flared from an extended arm on the maintenance pod. Nathan could see the demented grin on Mickey's face as he worked the torch back and forth over the thick glass.

Cole spoke quickly into his mobi. "Uh, Duncan, this guy is trying to vent us into space by burning a hole in the windshield." Cole nodded as a voice responded. "Yeah, I know it's not really glass. Mm-hmm, crystalline polymer designed to provide protection against solar flares. I understand but... do you think you could just fly over here and bump him out of the way before it gets really hard to breathe in here?"

Nathan held out a hand, "No, I don't want them to move. If they do that freighter will just get in our way." Nathan

shielded his eyes with a raised hand and stepped toward the
window. It was beginning to glow and minute cracks were
spreading outward from the point of the torch. He could see
Mickey was having trouble keeping it centered in one place
because the thrust generated by the cutting torch was moving
the maintenance pod around. Still, Nathan knew the window
was going to buckle before too long.

"Strap in," he said to Cole as he climbed into the pilot's
chair. "We're leaving."

Cole walked over to the window and waved a single finger
at the work pod. He fell into a chair and pulled the safety
harness tight. "Any time you want to go, Nathan."

"Hold on." Nathan pushed the thrusters to max and the
ship lurched but stayed stuck to the dock. A vibration built
up and the debris on the bridge floor started skittering around.
Empty silver beer cans rolled forward and then back as the
ship rocked. Nathan smiled and slapped the comm panel.

"It's now or never, Mickey. If you maintained the dock
clamps as badly as you did everything else in your yard, you
know they won't take this for long. I suggest you get out of the
way."

Nathan watched as a melted gob of transparent glass broke
away from the window and floated off into space. The work
pod cutting torch left a black burn as it skittered across the
window.

Cole tipped his head at the damage. "Time to go, Nathan.
The window's melting."

Nathan nodded. "I'm trying. Apparently they maintained
the docking clamps pretty well." He pushed another lever and
the ship rocked violently to port. Cole grabbed the arms of his
chair as the bow began to move left.

"I thought so," Nathan said. "I can apply some torque with
the steering thrusters." He grinned and hit the comm button
again. "Hey, Mickey, enjoy the rest of your time here on planet
dirtball. We're leaving!"

Nathan jerked the steering thrusters to starboard and the
big ship broke free. Cole held up his mobi and filmed their
get away as the pod banged off the wheelhouse and began
spinning. It looked like it was intact but Nathan was sure

Mickey felt the impact. He grinned and watched as the bow heaved over to the right and then they began moving forward. They went past their ship, the *Blue Moon Bandit*, and then past the freighter that had tried to block their way. Cole stopped recording and called Marla.

"She wants to know if you're ready to jump?" he asked Nathan as they accelerated away from the docks.

Nathan checked the gauges one final time and nodded. "Tell her we'll see her and Duncan at the rendezvous point."

Cole relayed the message just as space in front of him flashed bright white, then black. There was a familiar moment of disorientation as the freighter folded back into normal space. As far as light speed jumps went, it hadn't been too bad.

An hour later Nathan and Cole were free of the locked bridge and back aboard the *Blue Moon Bandit*. Nathan relaxed as he walked the decks of his home away from home. He flew a lot of ships on this job but the *Bandit* was the only one that felt right.

— « o » —

Nathan was in the galley sliding chopped vegetables from a cutting board into a tall pot of chili when Marla walked in. His co-pilot was tall and plain but not unattractive. Her brown flight suit hung loosely on her frame and turned her into a shapeless person. She didn't wear makeup and her long auburn hair was pulled back in a ponytail.

"The *Martha Tooey* is slaved to our control system," she said. "We can jump her back home and put her in orbit remotely but we'll have to board her again to dock her."

Nathan considered that. "How long do we have until the next warpgate?" Marla held up three fingers. "We're on course to get there in three hours unless you want to make a light speed jump."

Nathan shook his head as he tasted the chili from a spoon. "Yeah, light speed jumps are out of the question. Some morons back on planet dirtball were selling the fuel out of her bunkers but I figure we've got just enough left to get to the warpgate at sub-light speed and then cruise to Saji's place on fumes."

Marla dipped a piece of bread in the pot and tasted it. "You need more cayenne pepper."

Nathan shook his head. "No, I don't. Last time you made chili it kept everyone in the head for two days."

"But it's bland."

He smiled. "You just don't appreciate the flavor. You're one of those folks who think anything not visibly on fire doesn't have enough spice. You need to educate your palate."

"My palate's fine," she teased. "It's your old stomach that needs attention."

"My stomach's not that much older than you." He shut the burner off. "Dinner's ready."

"I'll tell the boys," Marla said with a smile.

Nathan smiled back. "They hate it went you call them that."

She walked out the door and called back over her shoulder, "I know."

Dinner was a festive affair. Repossessing vessels paid well but repossessing stolen vessels with their cargo intact paid even more. Nathan's crew would soon have fat wallets and time off to enjoy them. After dinner he sat back and enjoyed a hazelnut coffee and the easy confidence of a job done well.

The fourth member of the crew, Marla's husband Duncan, leaned forward in his chair and picked up a roll from the basket on the table. His long dreadlocks fell toward the table. He was the ship's chief of the boat and engineer; black, stocky, and a couple centimeters taller even than Marla, which made him a giant in Nathan's view.

Cole put his feet up on the unoccupied chair between himself and Duncan. "Do you and Kathy have plans when we get back to Go City?"

Nathan nodded. "She was a little out of sorts when I left so I was thinking a little vacation would be in order. Maybe some time alone will help us. This here today, gone tomorrow lifestyle of ours isn't really her thing."

"She knew this is what you did before she moved in, though," Cole said.

"Yeah, well, that doesn't mean much," Nathan answered. "I get the feeling that she thought things would be changing." He shrugged. "Maybe I'm not cut out for domesticated life. Maybe Celeste was right when she divorced me."

Cole set his cup down. "Nathan, I'm feeling too good for this right now."

"For what?"

"For another round of self-pity. You want to be maudlin about your ex-wife, do it by yourself."

"Have you heard from Celeste lately?" Duncan asked.

Nathan nodded. "She sent me a message about three months ago. She's first mate on an ore carrier for a mining consortium."

Duncan whistled. "She's not flying that luxury liner anymore?"

"No, better pay.

"I always knew she would do well," Duncan said.

Nathan set his drink down. "As long as she wasn't here, right?"

"That's not what I meant," the big man said. "And you know it."

"Yeah, I know but it's the truth. She had too much going for her to hang around here," Nathan said. "Obviously that big mining outfit recognizes talent when they see it." He waved his hand around. "Chasing repo jobs on this bucket was a waste of her time."

"It's been two years since she left you, Nathan," Cole said.

"I'm sorry. I just wondered if you'd heard from her," Duncan said. "She's still a friend."

Nathan looked at Duncan. "She's your friend, huh? You ever talk to her?"

Nathan could swear that he saw the engineer blush. Duncan leaned back from the table before answering. "Well, I send her notes, you know, just to keep in touch."

"He's allowed to keep in touch with friends, Nathan," Cole said. "It's not like he's being disloyal to you by talking to her."

"I know that, Cole. Old friends keep in touch." He turned a glare toward Duncan. "Of course, you would think that one old friend would bring it up if he heard from another."

Duncan grinned. "I don't bring it up because you get like this."

"Like what?" Nathan asked.

Marla walked into the cramped eating area from the cockpit. "We're on course for the warpgate, everyone. Our ETA is just under two hours." She sat down at the table. "What are we talking about?"

"Celeste," Duncan answered.

Marla stood back up. "You know, I better check the universal positioning settings again just to be sure. That gas giant we're coming up on has a hell of a magnetic field." She quickly ducked out of the compartment.

"See?" Duncan said motioning at the retreating co-pilot. "This is why no one brings her up. You get all moody and irritable. Everybody knows it."

"I don't get irritable," Nathan said. "And not everyone thinks I do."

"Yeah?" asked Cole. "When's the last time Fat Eddie asked about her?"

"Or Kenny the Mooch," added Duncan.

Nathan poured another drink and looked at them. "That's all you got? A bartender and the captain of a tugboat who's older than everyone at this table combined? It's not like either of them are my closest friends."

Cole and Duncan looked at each other and then turned their gaze toward Nathan. He looked at the two of them with irritation. "What?"

Cole cocked an eyebrow at Duncan and the big man shook his head and then nodded at Cole. The muscle-for-hire turned to Nathan. "I don't know how to put this delicately but our circle of friends has sort of…um"

"Shrunk," Duncan offered.

"Yeah," Cole said. "Shrunk is a good word. Our circle of friends has shrunk over the last couple years."

Nathan played with a glass saltshaker, spilling some on the tabletop. "It's not like we run with the best people, fellas. Petty criminals, corrupt customs officials, and alcoholics don't generally constitute good company. Besides, our line of work keeps us away from home for weeks at a time. It's difficult to maintain relationships in that kind of atmosphere."

"That's true," Duncan said.

"Very true," Cole agreed.

"Don't patronize me," Nathan warned.

"We're not," Cole said. "What you said is true. Our lifestyle is not conducive to relationships outside of work."

"That's what I'm saying," Nathan responded.

"When's the last time you heard from Celeste?" Nathan asked.

A pained look crossed Duncan's face. "It's not really important."

Nathan grew concerned. "When was it?"

Duncan exhaled heavily. "About two weeks ago."

"And?" Nathan asked.

"Her assignment is going well. The captain likes her and she's making a ton of money."

Nathan leaned forward and Duncan noticed he was biting his lower lip. "If you knew that, why did you ask me if I had heard from her?"

"Well, I just wanted to talk about it. Once I saw that you hadn't heard from her in a while and that you were going to get how you get I decided to drop it. Then you got how you get. And here we are."

Marla passed back through and stepped into the galley. She returned a moment later with a steaming travel mug of coffee. She tightened the lid down and looked at the three men around the table. "Are we done with the discussion or have we just reached the uncomfortable silence stage?"

"Does she ever mention me?" Nathan asked, ignoring Marla's question.

"Well sure," Duncan answered. "It's not like she hates you. I told her about that luxury yacht we nabbed last month. She got a kick out of that."

The mobi on Marla's hip started to buzz. She pulled it free of its holder and set her coffee down on the table.

"What is it?" Nathan asked.

She tapped the screen a couple times. "It's the motion sensor we set up on the *Martha Tooey*. Someone is moving around the wheelhouse."

Cole looked at Nathan. "There was a lot of garbage in there. It could be the beer cans rolling around."

Nathan shook his head. "Duncan cleaned that garbage up while you and I were doing our walkthrough of the crew's quarters."

Marla tapped the screen again. "I reset it and I'm still getting alarms. Are we going to check it out?"

Cole looked at Nathan. "We didn't see anyone."

Nathan shrugged. "There could have been someone hidden in the engineering spaces or even in the hold. We better get over there and check."

Cole stood up and thumbed the lock on the equipment locker against the wall. He pulled out two sawed-off shotguns and tossed one to Nathan. "Okay. Let's go."

Marla docked the *Blue Moon Bandit* with the *Martha Tooey*. Nathan and Cole boarded her for the second time that day, this time in a much worse mood. They made their way down a dark corridor toward the wheelhouse. Nathan took the lead, walking calmly but purposefully. He was leery of stowaways but determined that nothing was going to come between him and his payday.

Nathan and Cole slid quietly along the wall near the hatch. The door was closed. Nathan leaned in, his ear nearly touching the metal door. It was quiet, but he waited patiently. He was rewarded when he heard something bump inside. He stepped back, nodding at Cole.

Both men took a position against the far wall. Nathan held up his hand and raised three fingers, one after the other. When he reached three, he spun the wheel on the door and pulled hard. The door opened toward him and Cole peeked inside and then pulled his head back. He held up one finger to Nathan, indicating only one person was inside.

Nathan stepped to the door. "Whoever you are, come on out. No one will hurt you. This vessel has been repossessed and is being returned to its owner. We have no quarrel with you."

They heard a chair squeak from inside. A voiced asked; "Where are we going?"

Nathan thought the voice sounded young. "What's your name, son?"

Another squeak of the chair. "Richie Pearson."

Nathan stole a look inside. A young man about twenty years old was sitting in the pilot's chair. "Richie?"

The young man nodded. "Where are we going?"

"Go City," Nathan answered. "On Earth."

Richie nodded. "Okay."

— « o » —

Nathan, Cole, Duncan, and their new passenger sat around the table in the galley. The kid was on his second bowl of chili. They figured it had been a while since his last decent meal.

"What were you doing on the *Martha Tooey*?" Cole asked.

The new arrival pushed himself back from the table. "I'm a machinist mate on the *Martha*."

"Why weren't you put off and sent back with the rest of the crew?"

Richie swallowed some of his coffee. "I hid down near the coolant tanks. I didn't know what they were going to do with the crew, whether they were going to be let go or press ganged into service on some other ship. You hear stories of that happening, you know?" Nathan nodded. Everyone knew the stories. "Anyway, the guys that seized the *Martha* weren't real bright. They never looked around too much after the crew was taken off so I was able to stay hidden."

"But you got trapped by those guys selling the fuel?" Duncan offered.

Richie nodded. "Man, those two idiots wouldn't leave. They partied in the wheelhouse and crashed in the crew quarters. They didn't bother me too much because I could keep out of their way but they cleaned out the galley. After the first week there was nothing left. They couldn't have eaten it all so they must have sold it. These last few weeks I've been surviving on emergency ration packs from the life boats." He held up his bowl of chili and spooned more into his mouth. "This is definitely an improvement. It would be damn near perfect with a little more cayenne."

Nathan smiled. "We can take you as far as Go City. There's a union office there. They'll help get you home."

"I don't have much home to go to. I need a job. How about you guys? You need a machinist? I'm very good."

Nathan shook his head and stood up. "I've got all the crew I need. Duncan will get you settled into a bunk. You can sack out until we get back to Go City."

Richie dropped his spoon on the table and it clattered loudly at the mention of their destination. The young man picked it up and put his bowl in the sink.

"Is there any chance we'll be stopping at one of the orbital stations before we get back to Go City?" Richie said.

"No," Nathan said. "We go straight down." He noticed Richie had a furrowed brow and was chewing his lower lip. "Is anything wrong?"

Richie shook his head. "No, it's all good. I'm going to grab some sleep."

"Sure," Nathan said. "It will be a few more hours."

"Thanks."

As soon as Duncan and Richie disappeared down the corridor leading to the crew quarters Nathan turned to Cole.

"Is it just me or did he seem a little worried?"

"Oh yeah," Cole said, hefting a coffee mug to take a sip. "Something is most definitely up."

Chapter 2

Celeste Bezzle had the night duty as pilot of the *Charon*. The cargo vessel was making its way to Earth toward the end of a month long circuit among the human colonies of the Sol and Alpha Centauri systems. The ship collected the remains of deceased colonists who wanted to be buried on Earth. They may have left to explore or colonize but many people wanted to be entombed in the comforting ground of the mother world.

The 'body barge', as it was known throughout flight circles, was among the least glamorous jobs available to interstellar pilots. Celeste was capable of more than piloting stiffs on the slowest boat in space, but this was where she was. She considered her life, something she did often to pass the time on the night shift when things were quiet. She was pretty; a redhead still on the good side of forty with a figure that still got second glances when she wore something nicer than a flight suit. Duty on the *Charon* wasn't a resume builder. It was the kind of gig you took to pay bills; the sort of job that kept you from sleeping in an alley.

There were four other crew members aboard and a few hundred non-breathing passengers. At the moment the rest of the crew was asleep. Celeste kept the lights up in the pilothouse. Carting dead bodies between planets and stars was just as creepy as it sounded.

The ship was near a gas giant called Hubbard in the Alpha system. They were coming up on one of the planet's moons to a colony named Port Solitude. The dirty little colony was anything but a place of refuge. There were pirates here, Celeste knew, and she kept an eye on the sensors. Earth had exported its criminals to the stars as well as its explorers. The security forces kept an eye on things but they were spread thin and colonists always had some emergency demanding their attention. More than one cargo vessel had been boarded and stripped among the moons of Hubbard though the crews were usually left alone. The pirates wanted cargo and wouldn't hurt anyone unless someone resisted forcefully. Hurting crew members would bring heat down ten times faster than just grabbing booty.

Celeste sighed and rested a boot on the flight console. She'd had a good job just a year ago piloting a luxury liner for the Great Star line. The *Kimberly* was a large starliner that toured the Alpha system. Jump out from Earth, show the tourists a system with two suns, some brightly colored gas giants and let them get the thrill of being far from home. That job paid premium wages and let her go to the sunnier side of the colonies. There were casinos and clubs in different colonies and parties to go to. The body barge only made stops for sadness. The crew only visited gloomy faced families saying farewell to their loved ones.

Piloting the *Kimberly* had been a sweet job, especially for the pilots. Six-hour shifts, six days a week, and a little glad-handing with the passengers had been the sum total of her duties. The rest of her time had been spent partying, lying by the pool, and getting more sleep than she had ever known chasing down deadbeats with Nathan on the *Blue Moon Bandit*. Then Arnie Mulligan had ruined everything.

Mulligan was the captain of the *Kimberly* and a well-known womanizer. While stewards and wait staff were reprimanded for flirting with passengers, Arnie was known for carrying on affairs for the length of whole cruises. He had done so with singles who had taken a cruise with friends, divorcees looking for a little excitement, and even straying wives who let themselves get carried away while on vacation. Celeste could see why. Arnie was about fifty but he was in very good shape. He spent hours in the gym working out and had indulged in some cosmetic procedures, Celeste was sure. After one dinner at the captain's table they had been walking up to the wheelhouse to make a final check of things before turning in.

Arnie had been drinking and Celeste knew what was on his mind the minute he looked at her in the elevator.

"You look good tonight, honey."

"Cap, I think you should go to bed."

"Me too. I think you should go to bed. My bed."

Celeste didn't know whether she should be insulted more by his clumsy audacity or the lame pick up line. She decided on simply being insulted. She pressed the button for the next deck.

"You're drunk, Arnie. I'm going to get off here and we'll pretend nothing ever happened when we see each other tomorrow. Okay?"

He pressed the stop button. "Don't be like that, Celeste. You think I haven't noticed you?" His hand came up and stroked her arm. "You look pretty good in that uniform. We've all noticed."

Ugh. She could just imagine what he said to the rest of the male wheelhouse crew when she wasn't around. She pulled her arm away from him and reached for the door open button.

"Goodnight, Captain."

He moved between her and the door. His hands wrapped around her and groped her. She responded exactly as Cole Seger had taught her back when she was married to Nathan. She lifted her knee hard into his groin and delivered a quick right jab to his face. She might have kept her job if the doors had opened on a crowded corridor right then to spill Arnie Mulligan into a gaggle of passengers in all his pain-wracked glory. Witnesses would have worked to Celeste's advantage. Instead, he collapsed in the elevator and Celeste stepped out into an empty hall and continued to her cabin by way of the stairs. She reported off her shift the next morning and by two in the afternoon the fix was in.

She was terminated for attempted extortion. Mulligan admitted to making an improper advance on her but only so he could produce an email from Celeste wherein she said she would keep the whole incident under wraps for 25,000 credits. Celeste didn't know how her account had been hacked or who composed the message, but she was out of a job and blacklisted while Arnie received a letter of reprimand. The only job she could get after that was steering the body barge on its endless journey from pick up to cemetery. The job switch meant a sixty percent pay cut and a cabin that smelled like old socks.

The *Charon*'s proximity alarm went off and she leaned forward to check it out. This area was littered with asteroids and other debris caught up in Hubbard's gravity. On their trip through last month their hull had been penetrated by a micro-meteorite. No one in the cargo hold had complained but this trip through she was running slow, trying to give herself enough time to avoid anything in their path.

Celeste pulled up the controls for the rear cameras and scanned the area of space in question. Nothing. It had probably been an asteroid whipping by at 18,000 miles per hour on its way to burning up in Hubbard's atmosphere.

She reached into a plastic container and picked up a carrot stick. Munching, she reviewed the schedule. They would arrive at Port Solitude later in the day, docking at an orbital space station. The facility had sent an advanced shipping notice, letting the *Charon* know what they would be picking up. There was a consignment of mail, packages being sent back to Earth, and four bodies. Four more souls for the slow boat home.

After being fired by Great Star lines, she could have gone back to Nathan. Back to hunting down deadbeats and their forfeited boats; back to living on that flying locker room with Nathan, Duncan, and Cole. Chasing after people who owed and hid, who lied and obfuscated, who perpetually needed just one more month to come up with the payment. Flying around with dead people had seemed like a better idea at the time. Now she wasn't sure.

She found a celery stick next and bit into it. The captain of the *Charon*, Tom Geechy, had a nice little garden on one of the lower decks. He also grew tomatoes, lettuce, peppers, and onions so she could at least have a decent salad. That was about the only perk she had on the body barge; a damn salad.

An alarm sounded, high pitched and squealing, and then the lights went out. Celeste sat up straight and then floated out of her chair as the gravity cut out. She had the sense to grab both sides of the chair and pull herself down. She belted in and felt around under the flight control panel for the main breaker.

It should have been easy to find but like everything else on this bucket, it was difficult to work with. She remembered it being on the right but she had to reach so far that the seat restraint bit into her shoulder. She got the panel open and cycled the breaker. The lights should have come on but they didn't. She flipped it up and down again but the lights and control panel stayed dark. The emergency lamps finally clicked on, illuminating the wheelhouse with a weak yellowish light.

It would be ten minutes before anyone else realized something was wrong and made their way to her. The rest of the crew were probably floating around the ceiling of their cabins. By the time they fumbled their way down their walls and got into a pair of zero-g boots, the batteries in the emergency lights would probably be out.

"So it's up to me, of course," she said to no one.

She reached down to her boots and flicked a switch on each. Her feet got heavy and she released her seat restraint. The equipment locker at the rear of the wheelhouse was supposed to be well stocked for this kind of situation. It hadn't been when she was hired but she had taken care of that.

The locker door was a little stiff. She put one hand on the locker's frame and pulled hard on the handle. The door popped open with a squeal. The light from the emergency lamps hit the open locker door and cast a deep shadow inside. She felt around on the top shelf, pushing a pressure suit helmet out of the way and finally found what she wanted. The flashlight flooded the wheelhouse with bluish-white light. At least she could see properly.

She played the light over the locking mechanism and saw the pressure gauge built into the door was deep in the red instead of the atmosphere friendly green. That meant the corridor outside was open to vacuum.

She lifted the growler mobi mounted next to the door and spoke. "Attention *Charon* crew, this is Celeste in the wheelhouse. We appear to have lost power and may have a hull breach. Please give me your location and status."

The mobi was sound powered so it should have been unaffected by the loss of power. *Charon*'s crew should have reported to her as soon as the power and gravity switched off, but since they hadn't, she figured her earlier assessment of their status was correct. They were probably floating around their cabins trying to find their zero-g shoes. That was if the yo-yo's on this crew actually kept a pair in their quarters like they were supposed to. Those two deckhands Chuck and Jeff were just as likely to have traded them for booze at their last port of call.

No one answered her call on the growler mobi.

Something banged against the wheelhouse door. She took a step back and noticed the needle on the pressure gauge rising back into the green. The needle came to rest at the top of the gauge, showing a full atmosphere outside the wheelhouse door.

The lock rotated and door swung open. Celeste watched as two men entered wearing pressure suits she had never seen before. These two were not from the *Charon*. They removed their helmets.

One was tall, dirty blonde, and not bad looking. The other was shorter than his companion and bald. Shaved, she corrected, as she looked at the dark stubble on his head. The guy with the dirty blonde hair stepped in front of her.

"You're Celeste Bezzle?"

"I am. Who are you?"

"My name is Randy. Come with me."

She followed him into the corridor. The bald guy stayed in the wheelhouse, sitting down at the flight controls as she walked out. He led her down the corridor to the forward hatch. She could see it was open and connected to another vessel.

He motioned for her to walk through the hatch. Answers were not forthcoming.

The new ship was small, a shuttle for sure she thought. Randy directed her through an opening and she saw the crew of the *Charon* seated in the passenger compartment and restrained with plastic wire ties.

Captain Greechy nodded to her. "It appears we're being hijacked, Celeste. Best to do as the man asks."

"Please," Randy said, "Sit down." He gestured toward an unoccupied seat.

Celeste fell into the offered chair with no resistance. She bristled when Randy strapped her in. After examining the restraints, she saw they had been altered so she could not release them herself.

"I can't imagine what anyone wants with three hundred dead bodies," Captain Geechy said.

Randy stepped out of the passenger compartment but turned before he closed the door. "Captain, as long as you and your crewmates remain calm, no one will be harmed. We're not interested in you. It's your ship we're after."

Celeste sized him up. "I'm not going to believe anything a criminal has to say."

Randy looked at her and closed the door without answering.

"Did anyone try to stop them?" Celeste asked. "Did anyone get hurt?"

The captain shook his head. "They took us one by one," he said. "I assume they used an electromagnetic pulse to kill our power and boarded us. They worked too quickly to stop."

Celeste nodded. "They bled the atmosphere out of the corridors to lock us in our compartments."

"I guess we'll have to wait and see what happens," Captain Geechy said.

"Well, we should qualify for hazard pay," Celeste said. She settled into her seat and looked out the window. The next few days were going to be very interesting or very boring. Celeste wasn't sure she was happy about it either way.

Chapter 3

Nathan and his crew blew into the Sol star system and put the *Martha Tooey* in orbit around Earth. The *Martha Tooey*'s owner, Saji Vy, would have a replacement crew and tender ship take possession in a few hours. Nathan pointed the *Blue Moon Bandit* toward the surface and arced toward Go City, New Mexico.

Go City was the largest spaceport in North America, located in the desert of the American southwest. Built in New Mexico four hundred years earlier in the twenty-first century, Spaceport America launched the first private space flights. Momentum had taken off and by the middle of the century a city of fifty thousand people were living and working in the area and it was renamed Go City.

Space launches were not the only industry in Go City. It was the center of the spacecraft manufacturing industry in the western hemisphere. America had a second spaceport in Florida, the old Cape Canaveral on the "Space Coast", but Go City simply had more room to grow. That extra geography allowed for the manufacture of spacecraft components, the assembly of modular components, and all the restaurants, hotels, and retail outlets necessary to support those industries.

Americans had jumped on space travel as soon as private industry brought the cost down. At first, short orbital trips had been the provenance of the extremely wealthy. As technological advancements made it cheaper to get into space the cost of a trip was soon attainable by the upper middle class. By 2040 people could get to the Moon for a vacation and a steady stream of people were rocketing into the darkness of space for pleasure and business.

Milky Way Repossessions had its corporate office located in a Go City strip plaza. The firm's only office employee was seated at a reception desk when Nathan walked in. Dinah was his administrative assistant. He greeted her, tossed her a memory stick, and told her to process the *Martha Tooey* repossession. Bills needed to be paid and he wanted them paid quickly.

His small office was neat and sparsely furnished. He fell into a worn leather chair and checked for messages. Nothing. Usually the banks he dealt with had so many ships with loans in default he could pick and choose what he wanted. People must have gotten into the habit of paying their bills. He picked up the mobi on his desk and speed-dialed a contact at a bank. Nothing. He dialed five more numbers and came up empty each time. With a sigh he got up, grunted a goodbye to Dinah, who was on the mobi with her mom, and wandered in the general direction of home and Kathy.

— « o » —

Duncan led Richie and Marla below decks on the *Blue Moon Bandit*. This was where the heart of the machine beat. As far as Duncan was concerned everything that happened on this ship was reliant on him and the machinery in these lower decks. He knew every module, every component, and every bolt.

The party came to a complex piece of machinery mounted in a steel frame. The metal tubing making up the frame was cracked and had been welded several times. Duncan pointed at it.

"You're a machinist's mate, right?" he asked Richie.

"That's right," he said and looked over the frame. "And you aren't much of a fabricator, are you?"

Duncan nodded. "I'm good at designing things but sometimes the execution leaves a little to be desired. Can you fix it?"

Richie pulled on the mount and it wobbled. "Yeah, I think so. Let me guess, you go out for a couple weeks, come back and this mount is loose. You weld it, you add some steel to it and it holds for a little while but it always breaks free. Am I right?"

Duncan nodded.

"This end of the crawl drive exerts tremendous force on the mounting bracket," Richie said. "Mounting to these beams is okay but you need to step up to thicker steel or titanium channel in the same dimension, which is what I recommend."

"Titanium's a bitch to work with," Duncan said.

"Not if you have the right tools," Richie said. "I've done it before. You hire me on to fix this and you'll never have to mess with it again."

"Look, I don't know about a long term billet but I can definitely convince Nathan to bring you on for a short time. I need some help and I think having you on crew would be cheaper than having the work done in the yard."

"Is there anything we should know?" Marla asked. "You on anything? Any narcotics? You drink too much? You like stims or downers?"

"I'm clean. You can check down at the union hall," he said.

"All right," Duncan said. "Let's go up to my shop. You can let me know if you need anything we don't have."

An hour later they were wandering Go City; home to engine factories, part suppliers, and blue collar bars. Richie led them through narrow winding streets, in and out of mom and pop shops looking for tools and equipment. Duncan had a credit line for the *Bandit*, set up by Nathan, to do refit and repair work in port. He made arrangements for a small load of titanium to be shipped to their hangar and the three of them hit the street again.

"That should do it," Richie said. "We'll rip out that old mount and build the new one up from scratch. It shouldn't take more than a day."

"Good," Marla said. "Nathan won't keep the ship down for long."

"He promised a week," Duncan said.

"Yeah, but he'll get a hot job and we'll have to get airborne sooner than that."

Duncan slipped an arm around her waist. "I was hoping to get you all to myself for a few days in the apartment. Maybe play house, forget that we spend most of our time in a tin can."

She smiled. "I want it too, baby, but a whole week? When's the last time that happened?"

Duncan turned back to Richie and realized with a jolt that the kid was gone.

"Hey where…?"

There was a clatter from the mouth of an alley as someone knocked over a trash can. He and Marla shared a glance and hurried to the mouth of the alley to find a large man in a leather coat dragging Richie by the shirt collar between the buildings. The guy in the leather coat slammed Richie against a wall hard enough to bounce his head off it.

"Hey! What the hell are you doing?" Duncan asked. Duncan and Marla entered the alley Marla reaching for her mobi.

Leather Coat spun Richie around and went through his pockets, ignoring Duncan. "You screwed up, kid. Atomic Jack is pissed in a big way."

Richie turned around. "I have it, okay? It's all good."

"Then pay up."

"What I mean to say," Richie said, "is that I will have it. I just got hired on a new ship. I can make a payment soon."

"We heard this same claim not three months ago," Duncan heard a voice say through a speaker behind them. He turned around and felt his stomach drop. He pushed Marla behind him, backing away instinctively, moving them closer to Richie.

The owner of the voice advance on them with another man behind him. The leader was encased in some sort of pressure suit. It was silver, pockmarked, and streaked with grime. The helmet was angular, coming to a narrow flat spot above the head. Duncan had a hard time looking at the figure; his skin was pulled tight over his skull. An orange glow emanated from his jaw and cheekbones bright enough to be seen through his skin.

"Jack…" Richie said.

"Don't lie to me, Richie," Duncan heard the man say through the suit's speaker.

"Who is this, Richie?" Duncan said.

"It's Atomic Jack," the young man said. "I owe him some money." Richie turned to the man in the pressure suit. "Look, I told you the truth three months ago. I signed on the *Martha*

Tooey but the ship got locked into the dock on Barrigan Three and I didn't get back until this morning. I haven't even been paid yet."

"I know all about the *Tooey*, Richie. The rest of the crew came home weeks ago. Why didn't you come see me?"

"No, Jack, I just got back. I was hiding on the ship and it just got repo'd yesterday. Everyone else came back early because they got found by the guys who seized the ship."

"You owe fifty thousand, Richie."

"And I'm going to pay at the rate we worked out. Jack, it's not my fault the ship got seized."

"The juice has been running for three months, Richie. You owe sixty now."

"What? Jack, come on. I was living in the engine room. It's not like I wanted to be there. Besides, I'll be getting back pay. I'll be able to give you a big chunk."

The orange glow flared from behind his skin and eyes. "I hear nothing but excuses."

"Jack..."

"Maybe if I take my glove off you'll figure out a better story."

Duncan's eyes widened. He most definitely did not want to see this man take off his glove. He kept trying to back up but Marla was pushing against him. What did she expect him to do?

"Aw, Jack," Richie said. "I'll square this. You know I will. I've never not paid before."

"No one ever does, Richie," he said. "Because I never give them the chance." He started fussing with the glove assembly on his containment suit.

Marla poked Duncan. He grimaced and took a small step forward. "Maybe I can help."

Atomic Jack looked at him, his eyes glowed a sickening shade of radioactive orange. "I really don't see how." He slipped off his glove and his hand burst into flames. The guy didn't yell, or make out like he was in pain. He just grinned and showed a mouthful of orange teeth.

Duncan swallowed hard. "We just hired Richie as a machinist mate. He's not lying about that. And we really did find him on the *Martha Tooey* after we reclaimed her yesterday, so if he was a member of the crew he should have his pay for the trip plus back pay and hazard pay for the ship being seized illegally."

"It won't be enough to cover the sixty large he owes," Atomic Jack said, moving his hand closer to Richie's face.

"Something is better than nothing. He's on our crew. He'll be drawing good pay as long as he works hard."

"And what is it you do?" The orange gaze was focused on him now.

"Milky Way Repossessions. We recover vessels. You know, in foreclosure or if they're seized illegally."

"He bets on the dogs," Atomic Jack said. "And he loses. Big." He slapped Richie lightly across the cheek, leaving a smoking red handprint. Richie yelped and pushed back against the brick wall.

"What's going on here?" a voice asked from the mouth of the alley. Duncan looked up and saw Cole walking toward them.

Leather Coat stepped in front of him, blocking his path. "Take a walk," he said. "This doesn't concern you." The other thug stepped up beside his partner.

"Duncan? You guys okay? I thought we were meeting for a drink."

"Apparently Richie owes this guy some money," Duncan said. "I think he's planning on burning it out of him."

Atomic Jack waved his flaming hand at Cole. "Leave," he said. "Now."

"Is Richie on the crew, Duncan?"

"Yeah, Cole. He's on the crew."

Cole made a quick movement with his right hand and a metal rod snapped into the air beside his leg. The two bodyguards moved to block him. He flicked his wrist up and struck the one on the right in the head, ripping open a gash on his forehead. The second got as far as drawing his gun before Cole brought the rod down and slammed it into his wrist. It cracked with a sound like dry kindling and his gun skittered off into the alley. Cole advanced on Atomic Jack.

The burning man pulled his glove back on, snapping it to the pressure suit. "No problem here, friend. It's just business."

He turned back to Duncan who was holding a hand up to Cole. "Your man has ten days to collect his back pay and make a sizable payment or I'm going to come looking for him again. You understand?"

"You really think you're in a position to threaten anyone, Pumpkin?" Cole said.

"I do. If I have to come looking for him again, I'll bring more guys. A lot more."

"I'm looking forward to it."

Jack moved around him, eyeing him the whole time. "He owes, he pays. Those are the rules." His two goons got to their feet, rocking unsteadily. "He knows the rules."

They backed out to the street, leaving the four of them alone in the alley.

Duncan grabbed Richie. "Who was that?"

"Atomic Jack," Richie said.

"Yeah, you said that before. What's his story?"

"He was an engineer or something. Got caught in a reactor accident. If he doesn't stay in the suit he ignites on contact with air. His nerve endings are all burned off so he doesn't feel any pain and his suit has some kind of regeneration built in. It's actually what keeps him alive because of the radioactivity"

"That is just fascinating."

Marla slipped an arm around him. "Not now, sweetie."

Richie touched his face where he had been slapped. It was red. "Damn this hurts."

"And now he's what?" Duncan said. "A bookie?"

Richie shook his head. "An enforcer for Jimmy Bago."

"Even I know who Jimmy Bago is," Marla said. "You're into him for sixty thousand?"

"I like to bet the dogs and didn't do so well."

Duncan put a hand on his shoulder. "He's going to kill you if you don't pay up, you know that, right? Did you see the look in his eyes? He'll enjoy doing it."

"Yeah," Richie said. "I think I'd better get to work."

— « o » —

Nathan let himself into his apartment and immediately noticed that Kathy's stuff was gone. The jade vase she had set up on the small table by the window, the pictures of her mother and grandmother, and even the ugly blue tablecloth Nathan had never liked. His stuff, however, was right where he left it.

"Huh," he said.

He wandered into the small living room and looked around. The recliner was there but the sofa and tables were gone. The small wooden end table he rested his drinks on was beside the chair but the rest of it, all the things they had bought together and the things she had moved in and arranged were gone. The only thing decorating the walls was a gigantic entertainment screen, which he had bought before they started seeing each other.

The bedroom was the same but he checked it just to confirm what he already knew. Her closet was empty, her dresser, and lingerie chest gone. There was a note on the bed. She had taken the time to write him rather than recording a holo. He picked up the single piece of paper and saw that an entertainment disc lay underneath. He recognized it at once and understood exactly what had happened. He didn't even need to read the note but he did anyway.

"I can't compete with the past," her neat cursive writing said, "You want me to fill a hole in your life but it's too large. And I didn't make it. I'll carry my own weight but hers is too much. I'm getting on with my life. You should do the same."

He looked at the note, noticed it went on for another three paragraphs and dropped it on the bed without reading them.

"Thank God."

He wasn't good at getting people out of his life and Nathan hadn't been any happier with Kathy than she had been with him. At first it had been fun but lately the fun had been non-existent. He hoped she would be the one to make the decision to leave.

As long as she hadn't left anything behind.

He took a quick look around the apartment but didn't come across anything she owned. Other women had done that, left behind some random, insignificant item to give themselves a way back in if they changed their mind. That wasn't Kathy, though. He admired the way she made decisions. She had a way of thinking about a problem from all sides, picking a solution and sticking with it. She had smoked when they met and one day, out of the blue, had decided to quit. Just like that she was off the cancer sticks.

And now she was off him. The lock code would need to be changed but he could take care of it later. He went into the kitchen and poured himself a double bourbon, carried it back to the living room and collapsed in his chair.

It was like hitting the big reset button and returning his life to the way it had been eighteen months ago.

"Henry, any messages?"

The apartment's artificial intelligence came to life in the holographic form of a portly, middle-aged man. Kathy had convinced him to spring for the AI system because he worked so much and she was left home alone. Almost constant spaceflight had not been her thing. So he dropped a few thousand on a holographic info-entertainment system with an interactive AI. Henry was the perfect assistant and companion; knowledgeable, detail oriented, and accommodating. Kathy had loved him immediately because she could program him to be everything Nathan wasn't. Nathan regarded the AI as nothing more than one more gadget that needed to pay for itself.

"You have several hundred advertisements."

"Dump 'em. What else?"

"Nothing."

"No personal messages? From anyone?"

"No, sir."

His circle of friends was indeed shrinking. Nathan sat alone in his apartment with the quiet closing in on him. He was aware, quite suddenly, that with Kathy gone there weren't any people in his life outside of workmates. Something needed to change. He just needed to figure out what.

Chapter 4

Nathan made his way up Ternan Boulevard, past the strip malls and restaurants that catered to tourists, out to where the warehouses sat, feeding parts to the starship industry. Large automated trucks hustled parts from the squat gray and brown buildings to the assembly plants where thrusters, gauges, seats, and a thousand other components were made.

He pulled into the parking lot of a non-descript warehouse, dodged a truck pulling away from a dock, and parked his float bike outside the business office. The bike had been bought in better times, when money had flowed a little more freely. If he had to replace it any time soon he'd be calling a taxi to get where he had to go.

The sign out front read Amalgamated Logistics but they did more than shipping and receiving here. Nathan swallowed his pride, something he did every time he came here, and walked up to the front desk. The receptionist looked up. She was a live person, not one of the hologram greeters you got at the bigger outfits.

"Can I help you?"

"Yeah, I'm here to see Lucy."

"Your name?"

"Nathan Teller. She'll be expecting me."

The girl made a quick call and waved him through. He walked through a heavy door and heard a magnetic lock reengage after he passed. Lucy Bega believed in tight security.

The office was old and the décor hadn't been updated in the fifteen years Nathan had known Lucy. She had blonde hair littered with gray. She was sixty-ish, overweight, and partial to smoking some kind of smelly herb concoction. Today she wore a man's work shirt and faded jeans. A picture of her last husband adorned the wall to her right but Nathan knew the man had cut and run almost four years prior. Lucy was married to her work and it had taken three husbands to convince her of that.

She was on a call and waved him to a worn chair. He flopped into it and looked out the window behind her. The woman was worth at least seven figures and the view out her window consisted of loading docks. She finished her call.

"Good trip?" she said.

"We got the *Martha Tooey* back, cargo intact."

"Anybody hurt?"

"Not on our team."

"I suppose that's good enough. Did Saji's guys take possession?"

"We parked it in orbit yesterday. Payment should have come through."

"Let me check." Lucy said.

Lucy ran a factoring company. She loaned money up front to freight haulers and anyone else who ran a starship. For a percentage of their payment, she gave them money to buy fuel and provisions or make repairs so they could make their runs. The problem was, once you started borrowing the money you were perpetually in hock. Many times the run didn't pay well enough to leave a starship captain any money once they paid back the loan and the factoring company's fee. There was a long line of captains who had sat in this very office and practically begged Lucy to take a smaller percentage just so they could go out of business with some small amount of dignity.

"We're good," she said. "We invoiced Saji yesterday and payment was made this morning." The factoring company invoiced the customer and collected payment. That way no one could 'forget' to pay them back.

"Good. I'm glad we're square."

"You actually made a little on this run," she said, looking at the settlement sheet on her terminal. "There was a bonus for recovering the cargo intact and another for getting the *Martha Tooey* back less than two weeks after taking the assignment."

"It was a good score," he said. "I'm looking for more like it."

"That was a gift. You'll chase down a hundred deadbeats with personal yachts and small freight haulers before you see a big steak like that again."

"Maybe."

"Well, I've got to run to a meeting. Call me when you get another job and we'll hook you up. I'll shave a point or two off your next fee."

"Actually Lucy, I think it may be a while before you see me again. Recovering the *Martha Tooey* gets Milky Way Repossessions solvent again." Nathan was doing the math in his head. Every time the *Blue Moon Bandit* broke orbit it cost about twenty-five thousand in fuel, provisions, fees, and permits. He thought he was pretty close to that figure.

Lucy got up from her chair. "Honey, we both know you mean well and you do a hell of a job but money goes through your hands like shit through a goose."

Nathan followed her out of the office. "I'm serious, Lucy. Things are starting to look up."

She walked down the hall and without looking back said, "We'll see."

Nathan went the opposite direction and left through the reception area.

— « o » —

Duncan was sitting at a table in a conference room when Lucy walked in. The table was capable of accommodating the eight chairs spread around it but only the two of them were scheduled for this meeting. As nice as the table was the rest of the room was run down. Lucy didn't seem to care that the paint on the walls was a dull orange, that the carpet had seen better days or that the ceiling was unfinished. Duncan could tell Lucy didn't like spending money on amenities.

He looked out the only window in the room and watched as Nathan mounted his float bike and left the parking lot. Lucy sat down at the head of the table.

"I've got the statements here," she said. "We've had a good quarter. Fees are up and it looks like more freight haulers are feeling the rising cost of fuel. The solid hydrogen mines on Ceres had some trouble, which is really pushing up the cost of refined fuel. I've cut our rates to be more attractive and starship owners are taking advantage. I think we'll see this growth through the end of the year."

"Was that Nathan Teller I just saw leaving?" he said.

"Oh yeah, we were just settling up on your last run."

"I didn't realize he was financing with you."

"You mean with us, right?"

"I guess," Duncan said. "I mean, I didn't know he was financing the business at all. I thought we were self-sufficient."

"Look," she said, "you invest with me all right? You need to see quarterly reports, not details of who we're loaning money to. If you start getting involved with our customers, we'll be out of business in a month. You're too nice. You would listen to every sob story and loan at a loss. I'm the bad guy. I'm good at saying no and good at twisting arms when they need twisting. I'm also extremely good at making sure your money works hard for you. Leave it alone."

"It's just, it could be a conflict. Loaning money to my captain."

"Not if he doesn't know about it," she said. "Besides, he says Milky Way has enough to self-finance your next run. I don't see this as a big problem for you."

Duncan considered it. He had been investing with Lucy for a little over two years, which meant he had partially financed dozens of runs for Milky Way Repossessions. And no harm had been done as far as he could tell. In fact, Nathan made good money. Duncan couldn't understand why he would need financing. What was he doing with his money?

Lucy held up the quarterly report. "Are we still doing this? I have meetings with three other investors this morning."

"How long has Nathan been financing Milky Way with you?"

She thought about it. "About fifteen years on and off but pretty steadily over the last couple years."

The divorce, Duncan thought. He's been financing since shortly after Celeste left him. Was it the settlement? Was he paying her some outrageous alimony or was it something else?

"If it hasn't been a problem yet, it probably won't be. Let's get back to the reports."

Duncan listened as Lucy explained how their investment in her business was progressing but he couldn't help thinking about Nathan. The guy should have been doing very well for himself and here he was borrowing money, steadily, from a factoring company. Was Milky Way Repossessions as financially solid as he thought? If it wasn't, what did that mean for him and Marla and their future? Damn, they'd better not languish planet-side for long.

Chapter 5

Duncan rolled over and cursed himself for not pulling the curtains closed all the way last night. Bright New Mexico sunlight was streaming through a thin gap between the curtains like a laser beam, hitting him square in the face.

He stared at the clock. Almost two in the afternoon? The last thing he remembered was the party shutting down about three so he'd been out for about eleven hours. He checked the entertainment system to make sure they weren't still logged in. The last thing he wanted was for anyone still up in the voyeur room to be watching him sleep.

Marla was beside him, still snoring because she was out of range of the laser beam coming through the window. That was it. He was going to upgrade to the programmable shaded windows. He was doing well enough now that he could afford to make some improvements.

He rolled out of bed and pulled on a robe. A champagne bottle almost tripped him and he kicked it out of the way. He and Marla had celebrated last night. Their investments with Lucy Bega were paying off nicely. An expensive dinner at Raul's downtown had become drinks at The Red Rock and that had led to a loosening of inhibitions that got them into the voyeur room. Around midnight they turned on the full immersion entertainment system and joined a dozen other couples watching each other as they celebrated their own events around the globe. They'd done it a few times before and he was much less self-conscious about it than he had been the first time Marla had suggested watching other couples and allowing those couples to watch them. From what he could remember, last night had been the best time yet. There had been an energized young couple from Paris who had caught the attention of everyone else in the room. He didn't remember much else.

He showered, dressed, and made coffee. Marla sat down, disheveled and half awake. She poured a cup of coffee and stared out the window. Her hair was plastered to the left side of her head and standing straight up on the right.

"We're not as young as we used to be," she said.

"No."

"We're certainly too old to drink like that."

"I agree," Duncan said.

"You see, it seems like a good idea at the time…"

"Yes."

"But then you wake up feeling like this and you know at least half the day is ruined," she said.

"More than half the day," he said. "It's almost three."

She looked at the clock. "Oh, damn it."

"We don't get a lot of down time," he said. "I guess we're not used to carrying on like that."

"How did we get home?"

"Taxi," he said. "Not only couldn't we drive, I'm not sure where we left our ride."

"Did we go into a voyeur room again last night?"

"Oh yeah, we sure did," he said. "And it was your idea."

"The couple in Paris…"

"You seemed to take a fancy to them."

They sat in silence for a moment, collecting their thoughts. Duncan rubbed his forehead. Marla hung her head, because of a headache or in shame at what they had done in the voyeur room, he didn't know.

She poured another cup of coffee. "Nathan call?"

"No. It's been a week and as much as I like time off, it's probably time to get back to work."

She perked up at that. "Yeah, things are going well on the money front. We need it to keep coming in."

"I'll call him this morning. Did I tell you I saw him at Lucy's the other day?"

"No," she said. "What was he doing there?"

"Getting paid for the *Martha Tooey* job. Apparently Lucy is his factoring company."

"I didn't know Milky Way used a factoring company," she said. "With the money we've been socking away I assumed Nathan was doing even better."

"He should be," Duncan said. "Pay from a job usually breaks down as half for expenses, two shares for Nathan, and a share for you, me, and Cole. I just assumed he was saving and investing that extra share. He owns the *Blue Moon Bandit* outright so he doesn't even have a payment to make. I don't know what he's doing with his money."

"Did he see you there?"

"No."

"Good. I'm not sure how he would take us partially bankrolling our own jobs."

"Yeah, that's a little strange. I spoke with Lucy and she said Nathan is going to be self-financing the next job. He says he's caught up."

"We did get a lot for the *Martha Tooey*," she said.

"Uh huh, big ship, cargo intact, maybe that was enough for him to get back on his feet."

"Should we talk to him?"

"No," he said. "He wouldn't take this well."

"But we could help him."

"You've got to understand," he said. "He's prideful. If he thought for a minute we were offering charity…"

"Well, it wouldn't be like that," she said.

"Look, we can't treat him as another investment. There's no way to approach him without it seeming like an act of charity. And if he found out we were making money off the money he was borrowing from Lucy that would really piss him off."

"Money changes things," she said.

He raised his cup to take a sip. "Bet your ass."

Chapter 6

The pirates were holding Celeste and the rest of the *Charon* crew outside the colony of Port Solitude on a moon orbiting the gas giant Hubbard. The *Charon* was in orbit around the moon. She thought she could see it every few hours, a small glimmer of light quietly passing by the small portal of her room. Room? No, she thought. It was a cell.

Her captors demanded nothing. The men were held in adjoining rooms. As the only female crew member aboard the *Charon* she seemed to rate private accommodations. She stretched out on the bed and fumed.

Her captors were nice enough. They were mostly young men and women, dressed in pastel robes. The men shaved their heads completely or left long ponytails. The women all had long hair, usually drawn in a ponytail.

At first she asked what they wanted with them. After receiving nothing more than genteel smiles, she escalated to demanding answers. It did no good. She still received nothing more than polite, non-specific answers.

A knock on the door startled her. She sat up on the bed and straightened the blankets.

"Come in," she said.

The door opened and Captain Geechy came in. He was a small man, about as tall as Celeste and thin. His thin mustache was meant to give him an air of authority but it sat on his lip like a worm. She rose from the bed.

"They've given me a few minutes to fill you in," he said. "May I sit? The *Charon* is being held for ransom," he said.

Celeste's eyebrow went up. "The *Charon* is being held for ransom. The ship? Not us?"

"That's correct," Geechy said. "They've no interest in us, apparently. I was told we are being held to crew the *Charon* when it is eventually released. They feel the company will pay handsomely to recover the ship and its cargo."

"They feel the company will pay for the ship and dead bodies but they don't have any faith in them paying a ransom for the crew?"

"He didn't say that explicitly."

"But they aren't calling your wife or my parents and asking for ransom?"

He squirmed, this line of thinking clearly had not occurred to him. "No. They are only contacting the company. I suppose the ransom is a considerable amount of money. Certainly more than our families could pay."

"Well it would definitely be a boatload of bad press if SajiCo lost a starship full of deceased on its way back home. They'll have to face that or pay up. They'd better pay up." Celeste stood up and paced the room. "Did he tell you if the ransom demand had been sent yet?"

"Yes," he said. "Apparently the company has agreed to pay it."

She stopped and turned. "Good. Once the credits are transferred we can be on our way."

Captain Geechy stood up. "No, Celeste. We have to stay until the ransom is delivered."

"Delivered? You mean they're flying it in?"

Cash money was rarely used. Most transactions took place electronically. In fact, moving large amounts of cash created special problems, the least of which was having the stuff on hand to be stolen. This was crazy.

"All I know is that it won't be here for a few days. A courier is supposed to bring it from Earth."

"Who did you meet with?"

"He was rather young, no more than thirty I would say. A man named Dawson. Montario Dawson."

"Did he seem crazy?"

Captain Geechy seemed perplexed. "No. He was quite calm and businesslike, actually. Why do you ask?"

"I ask because his plan to get rich involves hijacking a starship full of dead people," she said. "That seems like the act of someone who isn't in their right mind. It concerns me that someone not in their right mind is holding me hostage."

"I see what you mean," he said. "Perhaps it has something to do with the cult."

Celeste's eyebrows knitted. "The cult?"

"It turns out we've been hijacked by the Children of the Apocalyptic Rainbow."

"The kids in the spaceports that collect donations and hand out flowers? The same ones who run several businesses that specialize in employing underprivileged youth and ex-convicts. Laundry, food services, cleaning and the like?"

"Yes. So it would seem."

"I've eaten in their cafeterias," Celeste said. "I've stayed in hotels where they clean the laundry. I thought they were usually very peaceful." *Although, that explained the smiling caretakers and the white robes...*

"Me too."

"What are they doing in the Alpha system hijacking starships?"

Captain Geechy shook his head. "I don't know."

Goddamn it, this was not what she signed up for. "We better get hazard pay."

Captain Geechy swallowed, "Um yes," he said. "We'll certainly be eligible for that. Being hostages and all."

Celeste found herself shifting in discomfort, "At least we've got that."

Chapter 7

The punching bag jumped as Cole landed a right jab. He followed it up with a left, another combination, and then backed off. He grabbed a water bottle and guzzled it. The gym was quiet at this time of night but he was feeling anxious. Nathan hadn't found them a job so there wasn't any work to be done. He'd been hitting the gym hard the last few days, working off extra energy and trying to keep in shape. The boredom was making him antsy.

When the Blue Moon Bandit was in port there wasn't a lot for him to do. He could help Duncan with the ship's systems if the engineer needed it but sometimes he just ended up in the way. Marla was more knowledgeable and a bigger help.

The closest thing he'd had to any action had been that business in the alley with the new guy, Duncan, and Marla. The fire guy had been interesting. Certainly not something you see every day. He wondered absently if the new guy had made his payment or got himself barbecued. He made a mental note to call Duncan and find out.

He showered, changed, and went out for something to eat. A diner down the street was twenty-four hours. He grabbed a booth, ordered a grilled steak salad and a beer, and looked the joint over. There was a couple in a back booth. They looked too young and clean to be out late. Otherwise, the place was empty.

The salad came and he dug in, trying to pretend the steak was real and not a synthetic protein mixture molded to look the part. Real meat was expensive and he was watching his money until the next job. The door to the diner opened and a blonde walked in.

She was wearing a leather jacket and tight jeans. Her hair was tousled like it had been blown in the wind. It just made her look better. She knew how to walk, crossing the floor to a booth before seeing him. He smiled and her path changed. She sat down across from him.

"Betty," he said.

"Cole."

"You're out late", he said. "And riding too."

"I'm hungry and I still like the bike. I see you're still eating healthy."

"Trying. Gotta stay in shape."

"Well, you're certainly doing that. Just come from the gym?"

"You know me so well."

"It was either there or the gun range," she said. "Lucky guess."

Platinum locks curled around her ears. He felt himself stirring like he always did around her. "Just getting off work at the pawn shop?"

She nodded. "Pulled a twelve hour shift today. That damn Sean takes his time hiring help. We lost a girl last month when she went to nursing school. I've been working overtime ever since."

A waitress came over and Betty ordered a cheeseburger and a beer.

"I don't know how you look so good eating crap like that," he said.

"Your mother teach you any manners?" she said. "You comment on what a girl eats? Worrying about the size of my ass isn't your problem anymore."

"Your ass looks fine."

"Damn straight it does."

"Forget I said anything," he said.

"I make a habit of doing that."

He held up his hands. "I give. Don't get all riled up. I was just making conversation."

"You could ask me about my day. Sometimes I have really good stories. You wouldn't believe what people pawn."

"Okay. How was work today?"

"It sucked. Nothing happened."

"I see…"

"But last week, ah, now I've got a good story from last week."

"Do tell."

Her beer came and she sipped it. "A guy comes in, looking to sell a kidney."

"You guys traffic in organs?" he said. "I didn't think you were licensed for that."

"We don't take them out, we just broker them. You know, set up the buyer with a seller."

"Okay. So what's the big deal?"

"Wasn't his kidney."

"What?"

"He had it in a cooler packed in ice," she said. "Like he was off to a picnic."

"He had someone else's kidney?"

"Oh yeah. We asked him who it belonged to and you know what he said?"

Cole shook his head.

"He said we shouldn't worry about it. All we needed to know was that it was a clean organ and that we shouldn't have any trouble moving it."

"I assume he was selling it and not pawning it."

"He wanted two grand for it."

"Sounds like a steal at that price."

"Oh, it was steal all right," she said. "I'd tripped the silent alarm when he opened the lid. Earth Protective Services came in as we were haggling, took one look in the cooler and asked him where he got the kidney."

"What did he say?"

"He told them it was none of their business and that they shouldn't worry about it."

"No, really?" EPS were not known for their patience or having a sense of humor.

"Yeah," she said. Her cheeseburger came and she took a big bite. "The EPS officers bent him over the counter, slapped a restraint bolt to the back of his neck, and walked him out by remote control."

"Did they ever figure out where the kidney came from?"

"His wife."

"No kidding?"

"No kidding," she said. "One of the Protective Services officers came back later and told us the guy and his wife had an argument about dinner and he killed her. Left her in the bathtub. He was broke and figured that parting her out was the only way he could raise enough cash to get a ticket off world. We were just his first stop. He had a whole list of places to visit and organs to sell."

"That's just crazy," he said.

"You ever see anything like that when you were a marshal?"

"Well, we mostly hunted down fugitives and that included murderers so yeah, I've seen some screwed up stuff.."

"Well in the pawn business you see all kinds of nutty stuff." She finished off her cheeseburger and offered him her fries.

"No," he said. "I still don't eat those."

"You going home?"

He nodded. "Yeah, it's late."

"You have to get up early?"

"No, Nathan hasn't found us a job for about a week."

"Things are bad?"

"I don't know. It could be that people have started paying their bills. I'd hate to think that people with private spacecraft have suddenly started living within their means. It would be bad for business."

"Look, I'm kind of glad I ran into you," she said. "We need some help down at the shop. I almost called you but I heard you were off-planet."

"I've been back for about a week now."

"Okay, well it's kind of short notice. I need a strong arm down at the shop tomorrow."

"For what?"

She looked around the diner again and leaned in close. "Sean has some special deal going down; a private sale to some big shot. He wanted me to get some extra security. I have a private company lined up but I would rather have someone I know. Do you still have your license and permits?"

"Sure," he said. "I have to keep them up to work with Nathan. What would I have to do?"

"The sale is at two in the afternoon tomorrow," she said. "Why don't you come by about one so we can get set up. The whole thing should be over by three."

"What's it pay?" he said.

"I can give you five hundred."

"Am I carrying a gun?" The answer was going to be yes, even if she said 'no'. He wasn't going into this kind of set up unarmed.

"Yes," she said. "You'll need a gun. Sean wants to put on a show of being well protected."

"Then I'll need a seven-fifty," he said.

"Why?"

"If you're asking me to wear a gun it means I might use it. I need a thousand for that but since we're old friends I'll take seven-fifty."

"I don't know..."

"Stop it. We both know what a couple of guards from a private agency would cost for four hours. Plus you're getting me instead of a couple rent-a-cops."

She considered it for a moment. "All right, seven-fifty."

"Who is the customer?"

"I really don't know," she said. "You know Sean. People pawn all kinds of things. If he thinks he can make a buck he'll sell to anyone, including people whose business isn't exactly on the up-and-up."

"Okay. Well, it doesn't matter. Sean is a businessman. He won't want trouble."

She swallowed the last of her beer and pointed outside. "You want a ride home? I'm leaving."

"On your bike?" he said.

"Yes."

"I don't know..."

She stood up. "You can walk if you want. Burn off that salad."

"All right. It's pretty late."

They walked out in to the night air. Even at this hour Go City traffic was busy. Shuttles from the starliners came and went at all hours of the day, ferrying people up to orbital stations so they could board the large starships or bringing them back from voyages to the colonies in the Sol system or Alpha.

They mounted the hover bike and Cole put his hands on her hips, giving her a squeeze. "Don't get too comfortable," she said. "I'm just giving you a ride home. I'm not coming up."

"Why not?"

She turned her head. "You didn't even pay for my cheeseburger."

She gunned the engine and they tore off down the street. Cole gripped her more tightly. Flying with Nathan was one thing but zipping along city streets half a meter off the ground at what felt like the speed of sound was quite another.

She got him to his building in five minutes flat. It would have been a twenty-minute train ride. He got off the bike and it bobbed with the release of his weight.

"You sure you don't want to come up?"

She smiled. "I'm sure."

"You used to like coming up."

"You remember that EPS officer from the story? The one who came back to tell us what happened?"

"Yeah."

"I go up to his place now."

He smiled. "You're a cop groupie."

"I am not. Dating you and him does not make me a cop groupie."

"I'm pretty sure it supports my position more than yours."

"You really know how to talk to women. Hard to believe you're still single." She flipped down the face shield on her helmet and sped off into traffic, weaving between a cab and a pod car. Cole watched her go and wondered, not for the first time, how the good ones kept getting away.

Chapter 8

Duncan swore as he busted a knuckle turning a wrench on a stubborn bolt. His large frame was wedged in the housing of the *Blue Moon Bandit*'s starboard side ram scoop housing. He was balanced on a hydraulic scissor lift that wobbled every time he pulled on the bolt he was trying to loosen. Richie was next to him, shining a light into the dark space. The New Mexico sun beat down on them as they leaned into the ram scoop housing making the small space even more uncomfortable.

"Are you sure Nathan heard a rattle from up here?" Richie asked as he maneuvered the trouble light.

"He said he did," Duncan said. The wrench lay inside the scoop as he caught his breath.

"In outer space he heard this rattle?"

"From inside the ship while we were in space," Duncan said. "This scoop has an inner liner that comes loose."

"So replace it."

Duncan glared at him. "The *Blue Moon Bandit* has a budget," he said. "A scoop liner isn't in it."

"Is Captain Teller tight?"

"No tighter than any other ship owner. You spend what you have to, to keep them flying, and not a penny more. I think we're done here. Why don't you look over the upper hull and see if everything looks alright."

Richie boosted himself up onto the faring and walked back over the starboard engine. He could feel the heat from the hull baking through his boots and pulled a pair of gloves on in case he had to touch the composite shell of the ship. The morning sun had been up for a few hours but Richie could tell it would be brutally hot soon.

The ship looked good. He recognized the type. It was a converted freighter, built to haul hazardous waste off planet. It was a tough design, built around an incredibly strong structure meant to contain radioactive waste in the event of a crash or collision.

The ship also had massive engines, capable of carrying it from Earth's surface straight into space. It was expensive to launch spacecraft from planetary surfaces so direct-to-orbit ships like the *Blue Moon Bandit* were rare. Most people and payloads were sent into orbit via magnetic catapults. He could see such a structure off in the distance. This ship didn't bother with such a process. The *Blue Moon Bandit* was all about brute force. Huge engines provided massive thrust to a compact, sturdy vehicle.

Richie looked the hull over, searching for defects, signs of abuse or disrepair. It wasn't perfect, he saw, but it wasn't worse than the few other ships on which he'd served. There were some pockmarks, probably caused by impacts from micro-meteorites. He climbed down a ladder near the stern and walked underneath toward the bow. The bottom hull had burn marks, some very dark, evidence of atmospheric re-entries done in a hurry. Apparently Captain Teller could be hard on his ship.

Duncan climbed down the ladder and joined him in the shade under the *Bandit's* belly. He wiped the sweat from his forehead and took a long pull on a water bottle. "Did you see anything up there?"

"Just some scoring and pitting. Nothing I'd worry about"

Duncan nodded and gestured toward Richie. "Can I ask you a question?"

"Sure," Richie said.

"Why are you purple?" Richie's skin was a deep purple. The engineer hadn't noticed earlier because he had been up on the ladder and in the faring of the ram scoop when Richie arrived to work. "You look like a skinny egg plant."

Richie ducked his head, "I'm hiding from a leg breaker for the mob."

Duncan looked at him wide-eyed. "You haven't paid Atomic Jack?"

"It's taking a little longer to get paid than I thought," he said.

"He gave you a deadline and you missed it? I can't believe that."

"I need three more days and my back pay will come through, I swear," Richie said. "I couldn't go to him and ask for more time. He would kill me."

"He's going to kill you no matter what," Duncan said. "Now when he does it you'll be purple."

"Lay off the purple stuff, okay? Kids are doing these new dye treatments, you know? In night clubs? They're orange one week, red the next. I figured he wouldn't look my way if he thought I was a kid."

"We have to speak with Nathan," Duncan said. He leaned back against a landing strut, stretching his back. "The whole crew is in this because we stood up for you in that alley. Until this joker is paid, we all have targets on our backs. Are you sure you didn't get paid and gamble on the dogs? Try to run it up and pay this guy off in one shot?" Duncan stared at him.

"No, I swear," he said, holding up his hands. "I just haven't been paid yet. Call the union hall. They're helping me get this straightened around."

Duncan slid down the strut and sat on the landing gear. "Kid, I vouched for you and for the last week you've been a huge help fixing all the busted things on this heap. But since your debt has become a problem for the crew I am going to call the union hall. I'm going to check your story. If it's true, we'll work something out. If it's not, I don't want to see you again."

"Go make the call, Duncan. I'll be right here when you get back." Richie took off his hard hat and sat on it in the New Mexico dust. He took out a candy bar and unwrapped the end.

Duncan turned as if to make good on his promise but he stopped and looked back. "Look, we don't get rich doing this," he said. "We do a damn sight better than okay and none of us is starving but it's going to take more than a few trips out for you to pay off this jackal."

"I understand," Richie said. He knew Duncan would make the call anyways but maybe he'd decided to give Richie the benefit of the doubt for now. He took a bite of his candy. "Is Captain Teller a good guy?"

"Nathan? Yeah, he's a good guy. Tough but fair."

"Cheap?" Richie said. "The captains I've served under were all pretty tight with a buck."

"Oh yeah, he's tighter with a dollar than anyone you'll ever meet. I understand why, though. He owns the ship but he has to fuel it, fix it, and improve it. He has taxes, bills, and payroll. So when he expects us to be creative and come up with unorthodox solutions, we know why. He wanted me to talk to you about the pay scale."

"Yeah? You spoke to him about me?"

"Of course," Duncan said. "You think I can just put a guy on his ship without him knowing about it? Anyway, the standard rule applies."

"Which is?"

"You crew out when we need you and you pull a half share for the first year. After that you bump up to a full share."

"How much does the ship take?"

"Usually half of the gross pay for the job," Duncan said. "Fuel is expensive, as are replacement parts and consumables like food. The crew splits what's left. Nathan gets two shares because he owns the ship. Marla, Cole, and I get a full share and you'll get a half share. The good news is that Nathan owns the ship outright so there isn't a loan payment to eat into our shares." He frowned as if something he'd just said didn't sit right. Richie wondered what it was; he didn't get the sense Duncan had lied to him.

"Do you do all right? We haven't had a job in the week I've been on the crew."

"We do get dry spells," Duncan said. "The longest was about three weeks but I wouldn't worry. Spacecraft are expensive to operate and somebody, somewhere, is always behind on their payments. Nathan will be calling soon with a job."

Chapter 9

Nathan wasn't having any luck finding a job. The morning had been spent getting in touch with his contacts at the banks (again) and loan companies (again) and no one had an outstanding loan with a deadbeat for a signatory. Now he was sitting in a coffee house meeting with Falco, a German software developer who specialized in immersive environments. He could create realistic situations using a combination of software and specialized hardware. Falco had spent the past year working on a project for Nathan. He sat down at Nathan's table fifteen minutes late for their appointment.

"Nathan," he said. "How are you my friend?" He was shorter than Nathan and a little stocky. Not fat or even chubby but thick in that way that showed he sat a lot. He had dirty blonde hair and was still young enough that his face was flecked with acne. His English was almost flawless.

"That depends on how close we are to completion, Falco."

The German sipped his coffee before answering. "Nathan, I explained this already. The more changes you ask for, the longer it will take to get to the finished product."

"I know," Nathan said. "It's just that I thought we would be done two months ago."

"We were. Then you asked for changes."

"It needs to be right before I say it's finished."

"I understand," Falco said. "And I believe we have reached the end of the process." He slid a portable computer drive across the table. "Version 3.5 has completed QA. Please take it and conduct final user testing."

Nathan picked up the small drive and rolled it over in his hand. "This is it, huh?"

"I hope so. I have other projects waiting."

"You are so in demand?"

"Nathan, this job has taken too long. It is one of the most detailed and complex environments I have ever seen. If this does not meet your expectations, you may be asking for too much."

Nathan smiled. "Falco, about ninety-five percent of my problems exist because I ask for too much. I'll be in touch with you about settling the bill after I test it."

He got up and left the coffee house and the German. The man was brilliant, Nathan thought, but he was also arrogant and condescending. Every conversation with him left Nathan feeling like he was working for Falco instead of the other way around. He had completed hours of work drawing up the specifications for the immersion environment and then spent hours explaining them to the German developer. He had listened to endless questions and endured countless improvement suggestions. He was fine with someone having a better idea; what irked him about Falco was that behind every suggestion was the tiresome attitude that Nathan should have got it right at first instead of wasting time.

The apartment's emptiness bugged him, he realized, when he walked in the door. He missed Kathy but only as someone to speak with, someone to go to dinner with. The passion they shared had run out long ago. He had considered calling her since discovering her departure but dreaded the conversation. His loneliness made him weak. In that state he could be enticed into anything, even reconciliation. It wouldn't be fair to her though, and he had no desire to be that selfish. What was on the portable drive was making him feel bad enough.

He plugged in Falco's drive to the apartment's entertainment system and the program configured itself. The system had cost more than ten thousand to build and install but it had been necessary to properly enjoy the environment prepared by Falco. He selected the executable file for the new software and in a minute the living room environment was replaced with a cabana on a Cuban beach. Nathan stood quietly, eyes closed, absorbing the artificial reality.

Waves lapped the beach outside the small cabana. He could smell the ocean and feel a rise in temperature as the afternoon sun warmed the area. This was Playa del Este on the north coast of the island. Nathan and Celeste had spent their honeymoon here twelve years ago.

He walked out of the cabana, ducking under the low door. The white sand beach was warm but not too hot. Nathan had been on beaches where the sand seemed as hot as molten glass. This sand was powdery and fine, soft to the touch. The sun was bright but the air was comfortable. It wasn't muggy or sticky at all. It was an absolutely perfect 80 degree day at the beach.

Nathan felt the wind on his chest and realized he was in his swim trunks and carrying two beers, courtesy of the simulation. People walked up and down the white sand, enjoying the day. He walked toward the water where a group of large umbrellas shaded sunbathers. His mouth was dry and his heart skipped a beat, speeding up as he neared a blue and yellow umbrella. He licked his lips and stepped around the umbrella to the chairs where Celeste sat.

She was as beautiful as he remembered. He drank her in, steadying his breath as she looked up at him smiling. She was in the same bright blue bikini she'd worn over a decade ago. It was sexy but not flashy, guaranteed to get appreciative second glances but not cause ogling. She reached for her beer.

"Thanks, honey," she said. "I was parched." Nathan watched as she took a long pull, her throat working as the cold beer drained from the bottle. He sat down in the chair next to her. He had no idea what to say.

The water was gorgeous. He watched, silently, as waves rolled in and drew back out to the Caribbean. He drank his own beer, trying to think of something clever to say. He smiled and kept quiet, afraid to spoil the perfect moment.

Celeste snuggled back in her chair, adjusted her sunglasses, and rolled her head to look at him. "So tonight for dinner, why don't we try that café around the corner?"

"La Cubano Hermosa? Sure," he said. "That sounds great."

"I thought we could go late, around nine or so," she said. "The hostess at the front desk of the hotel said it's not too touristy and the food is great. A real family joint where the mom does the cooking."

"Yeah, great," he said. "I'd like that."

He caught himself staring at her again and adjusted his sunglasses as he turned back to the water. The environment was so real. Impossibly real. He looked into the sky for a ripple or distortion, the sort of detail that usually pulled users out of an artificial environment. Nathan could not find any. Normally artificial environment users could spot flaws because they were rushed to market so quickly. The marketplace demanded new content and consumed it with a voracious appetite. Even poor developers could rush product to market if an idea was good enough. Nathan and Cole had frequented adult clubs where the environments rented by the minute and offered sub-par realities beset by flickering, warping, and tiling. Nothing was less appealing than having an adult entertainer stutter and shake her way through dirty talk. This environment was, as far as he could tell, absolutely flawless. Falco had delivered and all it cost was his life savings. He looked back at Celeste and saw her staring at him.

"Everything all right there, honey?" she said. "You were staring off into space."

"Yes," he said. "Absolutely. In fact, I was just thinking about how perfect this was."

She stood up and walked to his chair, snuggling in behind him. He sighed as she began massaging his shoulders. "That feels good," he said.

She squirted oil on his back and kept rubbing. He was amazed that the tactile interface could feel so real. "You know," he said. "This is wonderful."

"What is?"

"You, me, and this beach," he said. "I can't believe how happy I am here."

"Hey."

He turned and saw her smiling. "Things are going to be good for us." Her hands wrapped around his chest. "We have our own business. We can go where we like and do what we want. It's going to be wonderful."

The memories came crashing back. A few good years and then the sniping and fighting started. They had arguments about money and about the hours it took to run their own business. There were loud discussions about Celeste wanting more control over how the business ran and over his control issues. How he could never relax enough to enjoy the life they had built. The arguing never led to meaningful changes and eventually she had finally had enough and simply left. He turned back to her and stared into beautiful green eyes. There was too much happiness and excitement in them.

"All stop," he said.

The environment faded away. The beach, the beer, and the girl all evaporated and the apartment swam back into view. He stood up, walked over to the apartment's small balcony and opened the doors. The sounds of the city greeted him. Traffic buzzed by at street level. The cars hovered a few centimeters off the ground and made a sound like bees when they passed by on the street below. He sat down on an Adirondack chair and looked up in the sky. A shuttle was tearing through the blue, bound for one of the space stations. The people aboard were living their lives. They were off to new destinations in the colonies or even to places in the Alpha Centauri system. He was broke and living in the past. He put his head in his hands and wondered what he was doing.

Chapter 10

Cole woke up late the same day Nathan was meeting with Falco. It was noon before he rolled out of bed and he felt great. Sleep was important to him, just like eating right and exercising. Getting enough sleep was the problem. He could easily sleep ten to twelve hours if left alone and wake up feeling fantastic. When they had a job it could be difficult to get even six hours. Nathan could get driven, working the job with manic fervor until it was finished. Cole had learned to grab plenty of rest between jobs.

He ate, showered, and dressed for the job at Sean's pawnshop. He selected khakis, a blue button up work shirt, and comfortable boots made from a composite material. Under the shirt he wore a thin carbon fiber buckyvest. The micro composite layers would stop a bullet and they were infused with a kinetic energy absorbing gel to dissipate the force of the shot. Hopefully he wouldn't test it today.

A small knife went into his back pocket and a six shot semi-automatic went around his ankle. Finally, he strapped his big iron around his waist and put his private security badge on his belt. As long as he carried his license, he was legal to walk the street armed. Almost six hundred years after the last cowboy gunfighter had walked the streets of the New Mexico Territory, Cole Seger strode down the street with iron hanging from his hip.

The pawnshop was a twenty-five minute walk from his apartment and he enjoyed the afternoon sun. Traffic zipped past in the street. It was a mixture of hover transports, float bikes, and electric wheeled vehicles. People on the sidewalks moved briskly, bustling among shops and food vendors.

The pawnshop was an upscale joint. Cole knew most people thought of pawnshops as places where petty thieves could fence stolen goods but Sean's place had an air of respectability about it. In Cole's view, Sean had done several things right. The shop was in a good retail sector of the city and not in some rundown neighborhood. It was brightly lit, clean, and invited people in to take advantage of good deals.

He pushed the door open and stepped into the cool air of the shop. A security guard nodded to him from behind a glass display case. The showroom was packed with items for sale. The merchandise was displayed neatly; giving customers the feeling they were in a high end boutique rather than a shop where people came to hock their possessions when things got too rough.

Betty stepped into the showroom from the back office and smiled at him. She waved to him and he nodded in return. He took a good look as she walked around the counter. She was wearing a black dress that hugged her shape, making her alluring and professional simultaneously. Her hair and makeup looked like they had been professionally done. As the public face of the shop, Betty knew how to keep herself wrapped tight.

She took his hand, shaking it lightly. Gold bracelets dangled on her arm. "Thanks for coming in," she said, flashing a million watt smile. "We appreciate the help on short notice."

"No problem," he said. "Nathan's taking his sweet time getting us a gig so I was getting a little bored. Where do you want me?"

A look passed through her eyes, just a quick little hesitation that caught his attention. "We're going to do this in the back," she said. "Sean's client prefers privacy." She moved in close and lowered her voice. "Sean knows his tastes and when something comes in that might interest him, they arrange a private meet."

"If they've done business before, why does Sean want the extra security?"

Her eyes were clear this time when she answered. "He's dangerous and Sean doesn't trust him. This buyer can be intimidating. He likes to treat Sean as an inferior and lean on him for lower prices."

"Yeah?"

"Yes. Sean's got the better of him a few times and this guy can hold a grudge. Sometimes I wish Sean wouldn't deal with him but he buys high end pieces and has the cash to afford them."

"So you think he could be dangerous?"

She nodded. "Maybe. That's why you're here. Let me show the back."

The back storeroom was large, bigger than Cole would have guessed when looking at the building from the outside. It was full of metal racking, the shelves packed with merchandise turned in for cash or waiting for a spot on the sales floor. He could see a large office, in a back corner opposite the loading dock. He moved toward it.

"You'll be meeting over here?" he said.

She nodded. "Let me show you." She opened the door and directed him inside and to the right.

"Our private offices are over there," she said. "Mine is in front and Sean's is in the back. Behind this door," she said, "is a small gallery where we do private showings for rare or expensive items."

Cole examined the room. It was big enough for a dozen people to sit comfortably, had a small table that sat four and a display stand that could be configured to hold items of varying sizes. He got the idea that customers were meant to move around in here, not sit. Get up, examine the merchandise, and haggle without spending time sitting down.

"Do you want me visible or not?"

She looked at him and thought a minute before answering. "I don't know. I hadn't given it any thought."

"If I'm the only security back here I should be out in the open," he said. "You do your meet and greet, make small talk and bring them in here to see the merchandise. I'll be in the room already, standing in that corner." He gestured to the corner opposite the door. "They'll think the merchandise rates a private guard and they'll be less inclined to pull any shenanigans."

"I don't see a problem with that," she said. "Just be quiet, okay? Be seen and not heard."

"Betty, I'm a professional. You'll forget I'm here."

"It will all be cool," she said. "You're just insurance. I'm going to go check with Sean and see if he needs anything."

"Okay," Cole said. "I'll be here."

— « o » —

Cole heard them walking across the warehouse floor, Sean's muffled voice among the footsteps. He put on a pair of sunglasses so he could observe the situation without anyone seeing his eyes and took his place in the corner. The small conference table held the merchandise for sale. A black cloth covered it. Sean had a taste for the dramatic.

"...in here and if you could step this way," Sean said, "we can take a good look at the merchandise." The conference room door opened and Cole's heart skipped a beat. Sean led the crowd in and was followed by Atomic Jack and the two goons Cole had met in the alley. One of the bodyguards was still sporting a cast for the broken wrist Cole had given him. Betty brought up the rear and closed the conference room door. Cole felt like the walls were closing in.

Cole stood still, hands crossed in front of him, silently hoping that he wouldn't be recognized. He'd gotten a buzz cut since they'd seen him last and he was wearing different clothes. No leather jacket, no engineer's boots, and he had his shades. Sean was addressing the group. Cole tried to make like a piece of furniture.

"It's one of the greatest collections I've ever seen," Sean said. "All the pieces are from the latter half of the twentieth century and early half of the twenty-first century. These items used to be as common as silverware but they weren't built to last. Hardly any of them exist anymore. A gentleman here in Go City passed away about a year ago, a collector, such as yourself, and his widow is having trouble paying the bills. She came to me and sold the collection just last week. You were my first call."

Jack was giving Sean a hard stare, trying to intimidate him early on, before negotiations even started. His sallow skin glowed a faint orange, slightly brighter here in the conference room than it had been on the street. The life support apparatus still chugged along, sucking in clean air and, he hoped, pumping out air that had been scrubbed clean of the radioactivity polluting Jack. Cole gave Sean credit. Staring into something akin to a jack o'lantern and negotiating price would intimidate anyone.

"Okay, I don't have a lot of time," Jack said, his mechanical voice completing the nightmare theme he was adopting. "Let's see what you've got."

Betty stepped around the table and helped Sean pull away the cloth. On the table lay dozens of gadgets. Some of them looked familiar but Cole didn't recognize most. They appeared to be plastic and quite old. Some looked like kitchen implements and some looked obscene.

"See anything that piques your interest?" Sean asked. He was a little too full of himself Cole thought. He could tell the pawnshop owner thought he had a real score here but Atomic Jack wasn't a man to be arrogant with. Cole had asked around about him after their encounter in the alley. Everything he heard was bad. As an enforcer he was second to none. If you owed a debt and Jack came looking for you, things were going to get bad quickly if you couldn't pay. Unfortunately what made him such a great enforcer, a bad attitude and a frightening appearance, also made him unfit for moving up in the outfit. He was never going to sit with the big boys and run anything. According to Cole's contacts he was stuck at street level. That made his attitude even worse.

"This is quite a find, Sean. You've done very well." He picked up an item that looked like a small white football. "Do you know what you have here?"

"I've done some research," Sean said. "Apparently that item is used to remove calluses and dead skin from the feet. You pull the top shell off and there is an implement like a cheese grater inside. You run that over the hard parts and it shaves them right off."

"That's right," Jack said. "It's truly disgusting but the manufacturer sold millions of them."

"This collection is varied," Betty said. "It is a good representation of the whole 'As Seen on TV' marketing phenomenon. You have the more common kitchen gadgets as well as the workshop items." She picked up a cardboard package that was still intact. "Apparently this material was an epoxy. You mix the green and white material together to fix broken pipes and the like."

Jack took it from her. Cole gave her points for not flinching when his worn gloves touched her hand. "I've seen this before," the mobster said. "But never in the original packaging."

He turned his dirty pressure suit toward Sean. "Are you selling individual lots or the collection as a whole?"

Sean straightened himself up. "I could make more selling individually but that's a lot of time and effort. Mostly Betty's time and effort," he said. "I'm inclined to move it all as a complete collection."

Cole kept moving his gaze from Atomic Jack to the bodyguards and back again. If they recognized him, if things went bad because that new guy on the crew, Richie, hadn't paid up yet, it was going to be a bloodbath in here. He breathed through his nose, willing himself to keep calm. If one of the bodyguards drew a gun, Cole was going to have to put all three of them down. The guy with two good arms would go first, followed by the gimp and then Atomic Jack. He was keeping it together but he could feel a bead of sweat rolling down the right side of his face, passing under the frame of his glasses.

Sean and Jack were haggling now, moving the price for this junk up and down, holding out for more, settling for less. He caught Betty staring at him. She looked a little bored with the deal making.

"Ten thousand is my low point," Sean said. "Anything below that price and it becomes more profitable for me to part it out on the G-net." The Galaxy Net was a computer network spanning known human civilization. If people were around, they were connected to the G-net.

"I can't pay more than nine thousand," Jack said.

Sean smiled. "I'm sorry we couldn't make a deal, Jack. I always enjoy doing business with you."

"You misunderstand me, Sean. I'm taking it at nine thousand and you'll be happy to get it."

Cole tensed up, straightening his posture a little, and watched the bodyguards intently from behind his shades. He really hoped he wasn't going to get into a gun fight over four century old kitchen gadgets.

Sean looked Jack in the eye. Betty looked at Sean with a raised eyebrow. Sean stared down at the merchandise, circled the table, and then came over to Jack. "Ten thousand. That's my final offer." Sean just put it out there, like he hadn't heard Jack's threat. Like the negotiation hadn't taken an ugly turn.

The mob enforcer in the pressure suit looked the collection over once more. He picked up a box containing three long stemmed glass globes, used for watering plants. The box was worn and split but it was there and the items inside weren't broken. He set it down, acting like he hadn't just threatened the pawnshop owner.

He offered a gloved hand to Sean. "Deal."

Sean took it without dropping his gaze from those horribly bright orange eyes. "Deal".

Betty and the bodyguards packed up the merchandise while Sean and Jack went into the office to complete the transaction. When they were done, they carried the stuff out to their vehicle. The one with the broken wrist came back in. He and Cole were the only ones in the conference room.

"I know you from somewhere, right?" the guy with the busted wrist said.

Cole took his sunglasses off. "Not today you don't. Not here."

The guy backed up. "You're from the alley," he said and raised his wrist. "You did this to me."

"Be cool. Whatever you have in mind right now? It isn't happening here."

"Yeah?"

"That's right," Cole said. "What's your name?"

"Kinty."

"Look, Kinty, you start anything and your boss doesn't get his toys."

"They're out there and we're in here."

Cole stared silently, letting Kinty decide how things were going to go.

"Of course," Kinty said, "the boss likes his little treasures. He'd probably be upset if he and Sean couldn't do business anymore"

"Probably," Cole said.

Kinty raised his broken wrist. "I still owe you for this."

"It's just business, pal. Don't take everything so personally."

Kinty looked out the window and Jack's other guy waved at him. "It looks like the boss is getting ready to leave. I'll see you around."

"Sure."

Atomic Jack and his crew left. Cole sat down in a conference room chair and chuckled. Betty came in.

"What's with you?" she said.

Cole laid it out for her. He told her about the new guy on the crew and the money he owed Atomic Jack. He told her about the run in they'd had in the alley. Her face went white.

"You idiot!" she snapped. "We could have had a shootout in here."

"I asked you who the customer was," Cole said. "You told me it was a guy who wanted privacy. You didn't say it was a radioactive gangster in a pressure suit!"

"Okay, okay, let's just thank our lucky stars nothing happened. I'll have to make sure you two don't cross paths. I can't have bullets flying in here."

He smiled. "So, dinner tonight?"

She just looked at him.

Chapter 11

"You sure it was him?" Atomic Jack said.

Kinty nodded. There was no doubt the guy who had broken his wrist was the security guard at the pawn shop. He'd kept his mouth shut so Jack could buy his antiques but now he was bringing it up. It had taken more than a week of bone knitting therapy to repair the break and he still had to wear a brace for a few more days. All because some guy couldn't pay up on his dog racing bets.

They were sitting in the back of Jack's bar, a place called the Wheelhouse. Kinty knew Jack used it to launder betting revenue. "He's overdue," Kinty said. He sipped his Tequila, his hand shaking a little as Jack glared at him.

The boss didn't drink anymore, Kinty knew. His suit fed him some kind of protein mixture intravenously. Being denied food, liquor, and female companionship made Jack one cranky boss. He turned back to Kinty and fixed those glowing orange eyes on him.

"He's hiding and that just pisses me off," Jack said. "You owe…"

"…You pay." Kinty finished.

Jack nodded inside his helmet. "You got it."

"I have contact information on the company that hired him, Milky Way whatever the hell. You want me to go find him?"

Jack grinned but it was an ugly grimace, full of dull orange teeth. "Go get him and bring him back here. It's time to make an example of him."

"You got it, boss." Kinty got up and pulled on a light leather jacket. He tucked a small gun into the waistband of his jeans.

"And Kinty?"

"Yeah, boss?"

"You don't have to be gentle."

Kinty grinned this time. "Yes, sir."

Chapter 12

Duncan walked into Nathan's apartment after knocking for the third time. Someone was clearly home. A heavy bass beat was coming through the door and he could hear voices inside. It was noon on Tuesday so it was the wrong time for a party. Maybe the captain was watching a movie.

He was so wrong.

Duncan stepped into a full-blown simulated environment. The experience was so disorienting it took him a minute to digest the fact that Nathan was thrashing around wildly in a hotel bed with his ex-wife, Celeste Bezzle. The engineer in Duncan was impressed with the programming that had gone into the realism of the environment. He tried to back out of the apartment, without being seen, but Nathan looked up at him, startled and wide eyed.

"Get out!" Nathan said.

"I'm trying!" Duncan moved his bulk back through the door, slammed it shut, and leaned against the doorframe.

He stood there for several minutes. The music stopped and he could hear movement in the apartment. The door finally opened.

"Get in here," Nathan said.

Duncan helped himself to a beer from the kitchen and sat down on the couch in the living room. He tried not to laugh but he couldn't help himself.

"Stop it," Nathan said. "It isn't funny."

"Oh, yes it is."

Nathan ran a hand through his hair. "I could have sworn I locked that door. You scared the hell out of me."

"Yeah, well, I know I'll never be the same," Duncan said. "Look, my hands are still shaking." He laughed and spilled a little beer from his outstretched hand.

"You're an asshole."

"I knew you were still carrying a torch for her," Duncan said. "But doing the whole virtual environment thing is a little crazy."

"Tell me about it."

Duncan looked around the apartment. "Where's Kathy?"

Nathan's eyebrows went up. "She's gone."

"Where?"

"When we got back from the *Martha Tooey* job, I found a note and her stuff gone."

Duncan got up and walked to the window, looked down on the street. "You know Nathan, you said she wasn't hip to this sort of life. You know, here today, gone tomorrow. She probably just wanted some stability."

Nathan smiled. "Duncan, you know what I like about you? You are an optimist. I think being with Marla has really helped you in that regard. You always look for the best in things, and people."

"I don't understand."

Nathan gave him a small laugh, not the funny kind. "I screwed up."

Duncan came away from the window. "What did you do?"

Nathan collapsed back on the couch. "While we were out on the *Tooey* job, a courier delivered a beta version of the environment you just saw. Kathy popped it in the system and saw what I'd been paying for."

"Whoa."

"Whoa, indeed."

"Have you spoken with her?"

"What do you think?" Nathan said. "I'm in no hurry to chase down an ex-girlfriend so I can explain why I'm making fantasy environments starring my ex-wife."

Duncan considered that for a moment. "I see your point but you guys were together for a while. Are you really going to leave things that way? Don't you feel the need to clean up the ending a little?"

"I'm a pilot, not a playwright," Nathan said. "She's the one who took off. If she wanted to talk, she could have hung around."

Duncan put his hands up. "Whatever you say."

"Don't be like that," Nathan said.

"I'm not being like anything."

They sat in silence. Duncan started thinking about the environment again but from a technical standpoint. It really was sophisticated, almost professional grade. How much would something like that cost?

"That environment looked good. Very good. Where can I get a copy? Without the Celeste character, of course. Marla really enjoys them."

"You can't buy it."

"Why not? What do you care what we do?"

"It's not for sale."

Duncan looked puzzled. "Why not?"

"It's a custom job."

"What?"

"I had it made."

Duncan let out a low whistle. "You had a custom environment created? Those cost, well, they cost quite a bit."

"I know. Believe me."

Duncan got up and crossed the room, shaking his head.

"What?"

"Nathan, how much did you spend on that environment?"

"Don't worry about it."

The engineer turned, trying to keep an accusing tone from his voice and only half succeeding. "Is this why Lucy's been fronting you money?"

"What do you know about that?" Nathan asked.

"Nathan, I invest with her. I saw you there the other day."

"I didn't know that," Nathan said. "Why didn't I know that?"

"Because what Marla and I do with our money is our business and not yours?"

Nathan sat down and leaned back in a chair. "No, you're right. I'm sorry. I shouldn't have said that."

Duncan sat back down on the couch. "It's okay. I felt pretty strange after seeing you walk out of there the other day."

"I bet."

"I have to ask. Is the reason we aren't working because you don't have the cash to put the *Blue Moon Bandit* in the air? Is this some sort of screwed up situation where we don't have fuel money?"

Nathan put his hands up. "Not at all. I really haven't been able to line anything up. There are no vessels to repo right now. Everyone seems to have developed the bad habit of paying their bills."

"You haven't been too busy to look have you?"

Nathan just looked at him with exasperation.

"It's just that it's been a while."

"I know. Oh, wait a minute. I got a message earlier that I never listened to."

"When?" Duncan said.

"About an hour ago. I was a little busy."

"We need to stop discussing this now," Duncan said. "I don't want to hear any more."

Nathan grabbed his mobi off the table and punched in his code. Duncan saw his eyes light up and then a smile spread across his face.

"What is it?" Duncan said. "Is it a job?"

Nathan set the mobi down on the table. "We're having drinks with Saji Vy tonight."

— « o » —

Nathan and Duncan arrived at Saji Vy's building just before eight o'clock that evening. Stretching three quarters of a kilometer into the desert sky, Vy Tower was the tallest structure in Go City that didn't launch a spacecraft. It was a glass and black chrome structure corkscrewing through three complete twists before reaching full height. The glass contained the newest solar cells that drank in sunlight and stored it for later use. The building had won awards, Nathan knew, for being not only energy self-sufficient but for producing enough electricity to power the other buildings on the city block it occupied. Nathan and Duncan entered the lobby, checked in at the desk and were directed to a private elevator.

They were whisked to the 209th floor as smoothly as if he were lifting off in the *Blue Moon Bandit*. The doors slid open on a tastefully decorated hallway. Two guards stood against the wall opposite the elevator wearing dark business suits. The guard on the right, the one with close-cropped brown hair, approached them. The other guard, a lanky black man, covered his partner and eyed Duncan. "Captain Teller, Mr. Jax?"

"That's us," Nathan said.

"Mr. Vy is this way, in the living room."

Nathan and Duncan followed the guard down the hall while his partner returned to his position by the elevator. Nathan observed three security scanners discreetly hidden in the corridor. They came to a heavy door at the end of the hall. The guard let them into the room and Nathan was taken aback by its sheer opulence.

He knew Saji Vy was rich. The man owned shipping companies, a fleet of luxury liners that traveled between solar systems, and had real estate holdings on who-knew-how-many planets. Nathan had visited wealthy people often in his career, sometimes to help them get their starships back and sometimes to repossess starships from them when times became hard. He thought he knew what to expect when visiting Saji Vy but the grandeur of this room was far outside Nathan's scope of imagination.

This is the living room? Nathan thought as he took it in. He was sure his entire apartment could fit just in this room. The floors were black marble tile, but inlaid in each was a circular pattern of mother-of-pearl, and set within that was a diamond shape formed from black onyx. The interior walls were covered with a pale yellow silk accentuated with a mildly reflective looping design that captured the eye as Nathan turned his head. Victorian sofas and chairs covered in a burgundy fabric were grouped with dark Mahogany tables in a sitting area. Persian rugs sat beneath the furniture to protect the marble flooring. The centerpiece of the room was the exterior wall. It was a screen, floor to ceiling and wall to wall, that rotated through what appeared to be a series of live views from around the world. Nathan watched as a lush jungle faded away and a snowy mountain peak unfolded on the screen in highest definition he had ever experienced. A Lenticular cloud shaped like a jellyfish and the color of dull slate hung lazily above the mountaintop.

A man in the traditional coat and tails of a butler approached from a doorway to their left.

"Good evening, gentlemen," he said. "My name is Benton. Mr. Vy will be along shortly. May I get you something to drink?"

They followed the butler to the sitting area. Duncan had a gin and tonic while Nathan took bourbon on the rocks. They sat down on one of the sofas.

After a moment an older gentleman entered the room from same door Benton had used. Nathan and Duncan rose. He was shorter than Nathan expected, only five-seven or so. His hair was long and gray but pulled back in a neat ponytail. His skin was deeply tanned. He walked with a cane but, after observing a few steps, Nathan felt it was more of an affectation than a necessity. He smiled warmly and sat at the sofa opposite Duncan and Nathan. Benton handed him a glass of red wine and retreated to a corner of the room. All three of them sat.

"Thank you for coming, gentlemen. I'm Saji Vy." He leaned back on the sofa and took a sip of his drink.

"Thank you for inviting us, Mr. Vy.," Nathan said. "I'm Nathan Teller and this is Duncan Jax, an associate at Milky Way Repossessions."

"A pleasure to meet you both," Saji said.

"Sir, if you don't mind my asking why did you invite us here this evening?"

"Right to the point, eh? Well, first I wanted to thank you for returning the *Martha Tooey*," he said. "That vessel represents a considerable investment and I'm pleased I don't have to replace it."

"We were happy to do it," Duncan said. "Vessels of that size are very profitable for us."

"Indeed," Saji said. "I understand your agency is one of the best at recovering lost vessels of all types. Your reputation seems to be well deserved." He took a sip of his wine. "Tell me, Captain Teller, how would you like to help me with another matter?"

Nathan set his drink down on a coaster on the table. "Sir, what is the job? Why did you call us here? We usually deal with brokers. In fact, I've worked for your company before and always through brokers."

"This matter requires a certain amount of discretion."

"Not a problem," Nathan said.

"I own a vessel named *Charon*. It transports deceased colonists from their homes on distant planets and moons back to Earth," Saji said.

"Oh, you mean a body barge," Nathan said.

"Yes," Saji said. "I believe that is the colloquial name for it. Anyway, the *Charon* has been hijacked and is being held for a ransom."

"The hijackers have been in touch with you?"

Saji took a sip of his wine. "They have."

"You want us to deliver the ransom and retrieve your vessel?"

"In a manner of speaking," Saji said. "It's not as simple as dropping off a bag full of cash and picking up the ship."

"They've made it more complicated?" Duncan said.

"Indeed. The group holding the crew is called the Children of the Apocalyptic Rainbow."

Nathan nodded. "I've heard of them. These kids attacked a cargo vessel and overpowered the crew?" Nathan said. That was definitely strange.

"Apparently," Saji said.

"An inside job?" Duncan said.

"My thought as well but my human resources department assures me the crew is solid. We tend not to trust felons with important cargo."

Nathan smiled. "Mr. Vy, do you really consider deceased colonists important cargo?"

"Very," Saji said. A look of exasperation crossed his face. "The *Charon* performs a valuable service. There are hundreds of bodies on board and they are due to arrive on Earth soon. We cannot afford an interruption of service. I will not have grieving family members waiting at spaceports and speaking with the media about their missing loved ones. The bad press will reach far beyond the transportation service and stain other areas of my business. SajiCo took possession of those bodies and they must be delivered."

"Anyway, back to Mr. Jax's question about the ransom; it is not money but rather a resource for accessing computer networks and working with them. The hijackers would like the services of this resource."

"To do what?" Nathan said.

"They wouldn't say," Saji said. "I assume it isn't anything legal. It appears they have hijacked my vessel in order to facilitate some further criminal enterprise. Truthfully, I'm not sure I care. I want my vessel and its cargo back, intact, as soon as possible."

"And the crew?"

Saji nodded. "If it wouldn't be too much trouble, yes."

Nathan considered the request for a moment. He sipped his bourbon and took a deep breath. "Mr. Vy, this really isn't the sort of thing we usually get involved with. We retrieve vessels from owners that don't pay their bills. I'm not crazy about the idea of putting my crew and ship at risk by interacting with a gang of criminals."

"I can appreciate that, Captain Teller," Saji said. "Believe me, the compensation is commensurate with the risk. I will pay you triple the rate you charged for retrieving the *Martha Tooey*."

Nathan paused. "A generous offer, to be sure, Mr Vy, but ..."

"And I will increase the rate paid on the *Martha Tooey* to include twice the percentage we are paying for the return of her cargo."

"Nathan, Marla and I are fine with this," Duncan said.

Nathan turned to him. "You know that for sure?"

"She's all about the money, Nathan. And you can speak to Cole but I think we both know that dangerous situations are kinda his thing."

"If I lose my ship, I lose the business, Duncan. It's not just about this one paycheck."

"Nathan, I have much at risk as well," Saji said. "I looked at several options before considering Milky Way Repossessions. After all, I have resources of my own that could be used for a job like this but I'm concerned about this group and their intentions. I want to reduce the risk of anything they do leading back to me. Using a third party like you to deliver the ransom allows me a certain amount of plausible deniability should they do something spectacularly stupid."

Nathan sat back, glass in hand. "I appreciate the honesty, sir, but if something goes wrong it's me and my crew who are left hanging in the breeze. You say you don't know what this group is getting up to with your asset and I say that's a very dangerous position to be in. If they want to start some holy war with a terrorist attack I can see why you wouldn't want to be associated with that. The thing is, I'm pretty sure I don't want to have anything to do with it either."

Saji was quiet for a moment before taking a breath. "I didn't want to tell you this, Nathan, until after you accepted the job because I didn't want to coerce you, but there is something else you need to know."

"What?"

"Your ex-wife, Celeste Bezzle, is part of the *Charon*'s crew. She is the first officer."

Duncan set his glass down on the side table with a heavy thump. "Aw, hell."

Nathan turned to him with anger in his eyes. "I thought you said she was first mate on an ore carrier?"

Duncan held his hands up. "I didn't realize she was on this body barge. There are a couple services. She didn't want you to know about the job," Duncan said. "She was embarrassed."

"She was?" Saji said. "Why?"

"I'm sorry, sir, but it's not the most prestigious gig," Duncan said.

Nathan stood up and paced in front of the wall screen. He saw there was a desert scene displaying now. It looked like the American Southwest with light brown sand and scrub brush. "What makes you think I'll run off to rescue my ex-wife?" Nathan said.

"You either will or you won't," Saji said. "I've been married a few times myself. I loved each of those women deeply or I wouldn't have bothered with the ceremonies. Each left me, but in every case it was my own fault. I keep in touch and I still see them. After enough time goes by the anger dulls and you begin to remember what attracted you in the first place." His lips curved in a small smile. "It may be a weakness of mine but there is nothing I wouldn't do for them, even now."

Nathan stared at him for a moment. "We'll take the job."

"Good."

"Wait," Duncan said.

Nathan turned to Duncan. "I thought you wanted us to take the job?"

"I did but for the pay," Duncan said. "Not so you could rescue your ex-wife. Carry that torch on your own time."

"A job is a job," Nathan said.

"Unless it becomes an obsession to rescue your ex. It's a good thing we heard the offer before you found out about Celeste or we would be doing it for free."

"I considered that," Saji said, "but I wanted to give you the option."

Nathan approached Mr. Vy with an outstretched hand. "We're at the south docks, pad 37. We can leave tomorrow afternoon around two."

"I'll arrange for a car to deliver the ransom," Saji said, shaking Nathan's hand.

Duncan got up and they thanked Saji for the drinks. They were quiet until they got to the street. Nathan flagged down a taxi and they gave it Duncan's address.

"So we're really doing this?" Duncan said.

"We are," Nathan said.

"For the money?"

"Mostly for the money.

"Because it sounds like it's for your ex-wife."

"Don't worry about it, Duncan."

"After what I saw at your apartment today? You must be joking."

"We need the work, Duncan. That's why I want this. Yes, I wouldn't mind seeing Celeste again. But come on, look at what he's offering. We would have to work three jobs for a payday like this."

"That's true."

"Besides, some of us aren't as well off as you."

"Are you kidding?" Duncan said. "As if there isn't enough pornography in the world you go out and spend your life savings making some for your own enjoyment. Do you have any idea how weird that is?"

Nathan shrugged. "It's a little out there, I'll admit."

"And that's what colors my perception of what you're

doing here. If we get out there in a bad place and you have to make a tough decision, you'll always pick what benefits her."

Nathan considered this for a moment. "I'll do what's best for all of us."

"We'll see."

He looked at Duncan. The big man regarded him, with suspicion he thought, but he didn't say anything. "You and Marla have plans tonight?"

"I think we're staying in. It's kind of late."

"Not too late for those rooms you guys visit on the G-Net though, right? Those rooms where you can watch or be watched?"

"Nathan, come on…"

"No, hey, I was just asking."

"No, see, what you're doing is trying to draw a correlation between that simulation you spent all your money on and what Marla and I do."

"Everyone has their own kink, Duncan. I just don't want you to think I'm some kind of weirdo."

"Hey man, to each their own. You want to get down with a light puppet, that's cool. I prefer the real thing."

"And an audience."

Duncan smiled. "Well, I am good at what I do."

Chapter 13

"Here's the list," Duncan said, handing a slim data pad to Richie. "Don't get cute and add anything to it. Just get what's on the list."

Richie nodded. He was still sporting that ridiculous purple skin tone. Duncan couldn't wait until Nathan saw that. He'd kept it secret just to see Nathan's reaction. He told Marla that he was giving even money that the kid would be fired on the spot. She wouldn't take those odds.

"What store does the ship have an account with?" Richie said.

"Big Bulk Mart on Livingston Avenue."

"Got it. I'll take the small skimmer."

"I'm trusting you with this. I'd go with you but I have to rebuild the plasma flow regulator again because apparently springing for a new one would break the bank. Don't screw up."

"You can trust me, man. I've bought groceries before."

Duncan watched the kid take the small skimmer and pull out of the south docks, heading north toward the store. He was satisfied with his work on the ship but he needed to be able to fill all kinds of roles to stay on the crew. Nathan ran lean so the pay would split in larger shares but that meant everyone had to chip in. If Richie had balked at picking up groceries Duncan would have cut him loose.

— « o » —

Richie found the store and parked the skimmer. It dropped softly to the ground and he got out, looking at the list Duncan had made up. He never saw the two enforcers slip up behind him but his muscles spasmed uncontrollably as he slumped into their arms.

— « o » —

Cold water splashed onto Richie's face and he was blinded by bright white light. He looked around but couldn't see anything past the lamp in front of him. Ropes bound him to a straight-backed metal chair. He struggled to pull free but his hands and feet were tied tight. For a moment he could hear nothing but water dripping to the concrete floor from his soaked clothing. Then a voice spoke from behind him.

"Where's my money, Richie?"

Oh crap, he thought. *This is the end.* Strangely he thought about the supply run he'd been on and how disappointed Duncan was going to be. His head jerked forward from a slap delivered to the back of his skull. The hand was in a heavy glove and Richie saw bright pinpricks of light fire off in his vision.

"Where's my money, Richie?" the voice repeated.

"I don't have it." That earned him another smack.

"What about your hazard pay and back pay? I thought we had a payment plan?"

"Oh man…"

Atomic Jack stepped into the light. "What happened, Richie? Why didn't you come see me?"

"Jack, I don't know. They haven't paid me yet. I'm still waiting."

"And ducking us, right? That's why you have purple skin?"

"I didn't want to come to you empty handed and I had nothing to give you."

"I have to tell you kid, this is the worst disguise ever. We've had all sorts of people run from us and hide but no one has ever colored themselves purple," Jack said. "Of course, I've turned a few people purple. Grape purple, jelly purple, and assorted shades in between. Another favorite color is black; burned bacon black."

Richie watched in horror as Jack pulled the glove off his left hand and low flames licked the air. He could smell something burning this close up. He hadn't smelled anything in the alley. Flames rippled across the thin skin of Jack's hand.

"Jack, I swear, as soon as my pay comes through you are my first stop."

Atomic Jack knelt down close to Richie's face. His pressure suit was grimy and smelled. This odor was different from the burning hand. It was more like filth, like Jack needed a good hosing off with a pressure washer. Richie got a good look inside the helmet and could see the rot and decay resulting from the radiation poisoning. It dawned on Richie that this man had absolutely nothing to lose.

"Richie, I loan money to people and they have to repay it. When people make bets that don't pan out, they have to pay up. If I let people walk all over me, well," he put a gloved hand on Richie's thigh and his leg twitched involuntarily, "it just wouldn't be good for business. I have to make an example so others don't think I'm soft." The gloved hand squeezed. Richie's whole body flinched this time.

"No one would think that, Jack. Everyone knows you're the man."

"Oh Richie, you don't understand. Those perceptions have to be reinforced constantly. If I let you walk, everyone with a sob story would expect the same treatment."

"Jack, we have a big job, very high paying. If you give me a week I'll be back on planet and paid from at least this job. I can't pay anything dead."

Jack's strange neon orange eyes drilled into him. "What's the job?"

Richie took a deep breath and the story spilled from him. He knew he shouldn't be talking but he was about to be burned alive. He would figure something out to tell Duncan later.

Jack's gloved hand tangled in Richie's hair, jerking his head back as he leaned in close. "If you're lying to me…"

"I wouldn't lie. I swear." Richie gasped, staring at the flaming hand that was dangerously close to his cheek.

"Well, we'll see won't we?" Jack let him go. "The body barge stolen, eh?" He straightened and pulled on his glove. He waved away the smoke lingering in the air and smiled, his teeth glowing dull orange. "That's the kind of story someone would pay to keep secret."

Richie swallowed. "You're going to blackmail Saji Vy?" Duncan was going to be pissed.

Jack ignored him. "Go back and get your provisions. Don't say a word to anyone about this. If you do I'll scatter you across the desert in pieces."

Richie nodded enthusiastically.

"You have ten days to put money in my hand. After that you're an example, I don't care what your excuses are."

Richie nodded again, even more enthusiastically. He knew he was getting the break of a lifetime.

Jack spoke to the men behind Richie. "Take his purple ass back to the parking lot. No marks on him."

"You got it, boss," Kinty said.

"I'll be in the office," Jack said. "I've got to think about this."

Chapter 14

Celeste had been sitting in her room for days, burning travel time waiting for something to happen. At least the kids in the robes were as nice as they were in the spaceports. One in particular, Linda, had begun chatting with her when she dropped off food or clean clothes. They had finally given her something else to wear besides her flight suit; a freshly laundered white robe that fit her comfortably. Breakfast had been pastries and coffee. The food here was good, much better than she would have eaten on the *Charon*. She also found herself eating more than she normally would have out of sheer boredom. It would be a miracle if she still fit in her flight suit when this whole thing was over.

There was a knock at the door.

"Come in," she said.

Celeste heard the jingle of keys and the door opened. She noticed two things; first, the guard who had been on her door since her arrival was nowhere in sight in the hallway and second, a man who looked to be in his early twenties entered instead of Linda. He was pudgy, no taller than her, and had brown hair. He carried a tray on which sat soup and a sandwich.

"Where's Linda?"

"She's busy with other duties. My name is Nicholas." He set the tray down on the small table. "Linda made you broccoli and cheese soup with a ham sandwich before she went, though. She said you liked the soup a couple of days ago so she made it again."

Celeste stood up and crossed the room to the small table. "How thoughtful, I'll have to tell her how nice that was."

"I'm sure she will be pleased to know her efforts were appreciated. We want your stay with us to be as comfortable as possible."

Celeste nodded. "About that, have you heard anything about when we might be leaving? Not that we don't enjoy our visit but I would like to get home."

"Our leader, Montario, hasn't said anything to me about that but have you considered staying with us? Did you get a chance to look over the literature Linda left with you?"

"You know, I did have an opportunity to read it but I don't think your lifestyle is one I would choose. You have wonderful ideas and worthy goals but I enjoy piloting starships. I like going from port to port, never knowing what the next day may bring. Your lifestyle is one of consistency and I think I would be a poor fit."

The man's eyes narrowed. "If that's what you think then I don't believe you understood our message. The consistency doctrine simply states that a well-planned life gives one strength to achieve goals. It's up to the individual to choose the path they follow. The green path is one of choice and is stronger than the red path of doctrine." He picked up the small tablet containing the religious text of the group. "Perhaps you and I could do a private study session right now and I could answer some of your questions."

Celeste shook her head. "I didn't say I had any questions. I'm just not interested in joining."

Nicholas took a step toward her. "How can you make a decision like that when you don't understand the Seven Paths to Enlightenment? I think it's clear that you either didn't read the literature or misunderstood it. I think you should allow me to review it with you."

"You're persistent aren't you?"

Nicholas took another step closer to Celeste and she became uncomfortable. He either didn't realize he was invading her personal space or he was trying to be intimidating. She didn't back down, though.

"Well, thanks for dinner, Nicholas," she said. "You can go now."

He reached out and put a hand on her shoulder and gripped it tightly. "I really think you should consider my offer. I'm being very kind and you don't seem to appreciate it."

Celeste looked at his hand on her shoulder, thought of Arnie Mulligan aboard the *Kimberly* and said, "You must be joking."

In one smooth movement she gripped the collar of Nicholas' robe, yanked him forward and brought her knee up into his groin, repeating what had worked so well with the last man who had laid hands on her without permission. The young man grunted and gasped for air, falling to his knees. Celeste looked at the open door and made the decision to get out of her room. She followed up her initial attack with a hammer blow to the side of his head and he slumped to the floor. That was something else Cole had taught her. Celeste checked to see if he was unconscious. Satisfied, she grabbed the young man's keys and exited the room.

The hallway was empty, just as she thought. The kids were slacking off and not bothering to guard their captives as closely as they had when they first arrived.

She snuck up the hallway past other closed doors. She supposed Captain Geechy and the other Charon crewmembers were here somewhere but she didn't know where. The corridor ended and she could go left or right. The showers she had been allowed to use were to the left with more residential quarters. She turned right and walked confidently. Her flowing white robes matched what the others wore; so long as no one looked at her too closely she should be all right.

The corridor emptied out into a common area, much like one found in a dorm. Several cultists were enjoying a meal and others were reading. Celeste counted five of them, all reading the same text she had in her room. It was titled 'The Seven Paths to Enlightenment', and it explained how each of the seven colors of the rainbow led a follower to peace. Of course, the text ended with some sort of apocalypse so the message was to live as good a life as possible until the end. Celeste didn't understand why anyone needed to give up all their worldly possessions to learn that lesson.

She walked through the common area and down another corridor. She had to give the kids credit. The whole place was spotless. They took cleanliness to extreme lengths. Even the light fixtures were clear of dust. She took another right and strode purposefully to the end of the hall. A guard stood outside the room there. She bit her lip and assumed she had found her destination. He held up a hand as she approached.

The guard smiled with perfect teeth that only come with good dental care. Somewhere along the way this kid had been raised properly and with good money. She suppressed an urge to deck him.

"Montario sent for me," she said.

The guard's brow furrowed. "That is most unusual sister. I understood Linda would be communing with Master Montario later tonight."

"Oh, well, she is ill. I volunteered to assume her duties."

He beamed at her thoughtfulness. "Oh, good sister, how generous of you. Truly you have embraced the purple path of charity. I celebrate your good work."

Celeste smiled. "Oh, you are very kind." And an idiot.

He knocked twice on the door, smiling as he did so and announced to Montario that his communion partner had arrived. She heard him say to come in.

Celeste walked through the door and took a quick look around. It was a suite rather than a single room. She spied a tray of fruit and took a paring knife from an apple, slipping it up her sleeve.

"In here, love," a voice called from the bedroom. Celeste walked into the room and leapt upon the figure in the bed.

"What the hell?" he said.

She pinned him and before he could shift his weight to throw her off she pulled the paring knife and held it to his throat. Eyes wide he put his hands up toward the headboard. Now that he was subdued she got a good look around. The bed itself was a canopy job made of mahogany. The dark wood was carved with an ornate design. The sheets were silk and not the synthetic stuff you found in most retailers. A tall wardrobe and a dressing table matched the bed. Posh digs for a farming moon.

Celeste adjusted herself on the bed and applied a little pressure to the blade, nicking him slightly but not enough to draw blood. "Enjoying yourself?" she said.

"What do you mean?"

"The food waiting for you in the other room is better than mine."

"Not much better."

"And what's this communion business?"

"You've got nothing to worry about, just keeping up appearances. The previous master was a bit of a letch."

"You called me 'love' when I walked in."

"Again, just keeping up appearances."

She got off him and dropped the knife on the polished mahogany nightstand.

"You've had me in that cell for almost a week," she said. "While you're here living in the lap of luxury. What's going on?"

He stood up, straightening his own white robe, tying it with a red sash. "Baby, come on. Don't be mad. I'm just sticking to the plan."

Celeste looked him over. He was about six feet tall with brown hair and blue eyes. Falling for him had been easy. She swung her legs off the bed and confronted him; thumping a finger into his chest.

"I'm sitting in that room bored out of my mind while these ridiculous children keep me locked up."

He backed away. "You knew this was going to be difficult."

"You could make it easier," she said.

"What do you want from me, Celeste? This is the only way to get what we want. If the cult members see you wandering around while the other crew members are locked up what kind of message would that send? We can't have them suspicious."

"I know but being locked up is driving me crazy. Come on, baby, can't you cut us a little slack?"

"If I do, an opportunity is going to present itself to escape. This isn't a prison and these kids aren't guards. You and your crew could outwit them in five minutes flat. It's not like you can bring them in on this."

She pouted a little, just a little, and sighed. "No, we can't."

He took her by the hands. "Look, I got a message from Saji Vy's people. A ship is leaving soon and will be here in a few days."

Her eyes brightened. "They're giving us what we want?"

"Sure are, babe. We'll be done with this thing in four or five days. Can you hang on that long?"

She sighed. "It's going to be tough."

"But you're a tough chick," he said smiling.

"Yeah, right."

His brow furrowed. "How did you get out of your room, anyway?"

Deep breath. "Oh, yeah, about that. I clobbered that guy named Nicholas."

He shook his head. "We can't hurt these people, as much as we'd like to."

"He was trying to force feed me a bunch of dogma and he put his hands on me. He was way too pushy so I taught him a lesson." She sighed. "Don't worry about it. He'll probably just try to convert me that much harder."

"That's true, but we still need to keep up appearances."

She looked up. "What do you mean?"

He stood up and walked to the doorway. "Trevor?" he said. "Can you come in here?"

The boy standing guard outside the suite came in. "Yes, Montario?"

He grabbed her wrist and jerked her off the bed. "This woman was to remain in her quarters. Somehow she got out."

His eyes grew wide with surprise. "I'm so sorry, sir. I don't know how this happened."

"It's all right, son. Just take her back."

"I will! At once!" He grabbed Celeste with a strong hand and started to lead her away.

"And check on the good brother who delivered her meal. He may be hurt."

"Yes, Montario."

"And Trevor? Be careful with her. She has not yet accepted our path."

"As you say."

Celeste shot Montario an angry look as she left.

— « o » —

After she left, Montario picked up an apple and took a bite. He had found Celeste a little over six months ago with the help of one of his operatives named Milo Gradzic. She was sitting at an outdoor café, nursing a glass of lemonade. Montario and Milo observed her from the corner of a building across the plaza. Milo swiped a finger across the face of his mobi and Montario's mobi beeped an acknowledgment.

"That's her file. She has all the qualifications you're looking for," Milo said.

"What about motivation?"

"She's got that in buckets," Milo said. "She was the pilot of a starliner named the *Kimberly* and was fired almost a year ago. I looked into the termination. She claims she was being sexually harassed by the captain and there was an altercation."

"Was she? Being harassed?" Montario asked.

"It could have gone either way but I think so. The captain has a reputation as liking the ladies and being pushy. I'd say she probably got the short end of the stick."

"So she's on the crew of the *Charon* now?"

"Yes, she's been the pilot for the past few months."

"What's her mood like?"

Milo chuckled. "The only way she could be more disgruntled would be if she set fire to the cruise liner offices. She is one very unhappy lady."

"Then she's just what we need, Milo. You've done well."

"So what's your approach? Do you have a plan for how to reel her in?"

Montario smiled. "I'm just going to walk over there and talk to her."

Milo's eyebrow rose up. "That's it? You're just going to talk to her?"

"And listen. I'm going to listen to her."

Montario crossed the plaza and walked up to her table. He was smooth, wearing a lightweight linen suit and dark glasses. He passed her, paused, and then turned back. He said something to her; she looked up, shaded her eyes with a hand and then smiled. After a few moments of chatting she invited him to sit down.

Now, six months later, his plan was coming together. Given her level of unhappiness to start, he guessed it wasn't a surprise she wasn't any happier now. Some women were just impossible to please.

Chapter 15

Nathan dropped out of the belly of the *Blue Moon Bandit*, wiped his face with a rag, and shoved it in the back pocket of his dark blue workpants. His white t-shirt was clinging to him where he had sweated through it in the New Mexico afternoon sun. The interior of the landing gear compartment was blazing hot but a bushing needed replacing in a strut. He'd noticed the ship sitting at a lower angle than it should have when he arrived and found the problem an hour ago. He kicked a ratchet toward the fire engine red toolbox and walked out from under the ship. A heavy-duty switch was hanging from a magnetic mount on the hull. He grabbed hold of it, pushed the 'up' button and the ship rose a few inches. He walked back under and grabbed hold of the jack stand that had been supporting the *Bandit's* weight. Another trip out to the hydraulic switch dragging the jack stand and he was ready to finish up. He punched the 'down' button and the heavy bulk of the transport lowered to the tarmac. He watched carefully as the landing strut took the big ship's weight. It settled in, comfortably taking the bulk and maintaining it at the right height. Satisfied, he picked up the ratchet and dropped it in the toolbox. He bent to pick up a socket when a long black car rolled up.

Nathan pulled out his mobi. "Duncan, our guests have arrived." The chief of the boat had been in the engine room with Richie running pre-launch diagnostics on the *Bandit's* systems since before Nathan arrived.

The driver stopped near the rear ramp of the ship, got out, and surveyed the area with a worried look. Landing pad 37 was in a crap-hole area, Nathan knew. In fact, the whole south docks was in a terrible part of town. His guests were probably used to shipping out on the tourist shuttles where they would be treated like visiting royalty, or the private landing pads on the north end where rich folks kept their private yachts for jaunts to Mars or the Jupiter system. The south docks were where working men and women kept service vehicles and junkers.

The driver opened the door and an Asian woman stepped out. She wore a short navy blue jacket over a blue blouse and a short navy blue skirt. She also wore black leggings and knee-high boots that gave her an extra couple inches. She snapped on a pair of shades and looked around. Nathan raised a hand in greeting. Her hand rose in return and she motioned for someone else to get out of the car. A tall, thin man exited the car and Nathan saw he had skin that was bleached so white the sun almost reflected off it. He was wrapped in a black leather outfit from head to toe. A jacket stretched up his neck like the world's most uncomfortable turtleneck and the pants were tight and tucked into a pair of mid-calf leather boots. Nathan wondered if they shopped for boots together. The man with alabaster skin folded his hands behind his back and walked toward the *Blue Moon Bandit*. Duncan and Marla met them at the base of the ramp.

Nathan chased down his last socket and buttoned up the red toolbox. He extended a handle from the back and rolled it around the back of the ship on built-in wheels, stowing it to the right of the entrance ramp. The ramp itself was between the left and right engine exhaust cowlings. The limo driver walked past him with a nod as he carried their bags into the ship. Nathan took a deep breath and wondered if it was too early for whiskey. He walked up the ramp and made his way to the galley where he found Duncan.

"What's going on?" Nathan said.

"Marla is showing them to their rooms."

"Their rooms?" Nathan turned to face his engineer with irritation on his face.

Marla walked back into the galley and attached common room with the new arrivals. Nathan extended a hand. "Hello. I'm Captain Teller."

She took his hand with a gentle squeeze and bowed slightly. "Hello. My name is Kimiyo Himura. I am a special assistant to Mr. Saji Vy."

Nathan held his hand out to the man in the leather outfit. He demurred and backed up a step without speaking.

"You will have to forgive Arulio," Kimiyo said. "He prefers to not have contact with strangers."

There was an uncomfortable silence for a moment. "So both you and Arulio are coming with us?"

"We are," Kimiyo said. "Arulio will be doing what is required to free the hostages and I take care of Arulio."

"When Saji said he had a resource that could access computer networks I was expecting some sort of device, not passengers."

"Hopefully we won't be an inconvenience, Captain Teller."

Nathan smiled and bit the inside of his lip. "I'm sure you won't be and please, call me Nathan. We're pretty informal around here. Are the accommodations acceptable?"

"They are just fine, Nathan," she said, almost stumbling over his first name. "Marla gave us a tour of your vessel."

"Well I'm sure that didn't take long," he said. "I'm afraid it's not a cruise liner."

"That's all right, Captain. Working for Saji Vy doesn't leave a lot of time for vacations. It's been quite some time since I was on a cruise ship."

"Well, the *Bandit* isn't exactly a scrap hauler either. Just don't expect us to keep you entertained."

"I have my work Captain. I'm sure I'll be busy enough."

Saji's assistant was cute, so as soon as Cole arrived he knew her time would be consumed with rejecting bad come on's and horrific flirting attempts.

Nathan nodded at her. "As for Arulio, we'll be traveling and working together for a bit. Some contact will be inevitable."

"We all know our jobs, Captain Teller," she said. "Arulio is very good at what he does. Computer networks dance and sing for him if he wishes. They also give up their secrets. In order for him to do the things he does, he has had extensive modifications performed. This has left him with a suppressed immune system."

"Hence the no touching, rule," Nathan said.

"He's a wetjack," Duncan said. "I've heard about them but I've never met one in person. And the outfit he's wearing,"

Duncan said. He looked at Arulio's attire more closely. The man with alabaster skin regarded him carefully but did not back away from Duncan's examination. "I thought this was simply leather," Duncan said. "But it's more than that, isn't it?"

"Yes," Kimiyo said, "but Mr. Vy prefers to keep details of Arulio's enhancements to himself. I'm sure you understand."

"Of course," Duncan said.

"Kimiyo, do you have any idea where we're going?" Nathan said.

She handed a data chip to Nathan. "Captain, this contains coordinates and contact information for the people holding the crew of the *Charon*. It's everything they've sent."

Nathan picked it up and tapped it on the table. "I see," He said, trying to hide his irritation at having unexpected guests. Marla was already staring at him like he'd grown a second head. "Well, I'll let you get settled in. We're scheduled for lift off in an hour. Marla, I'll need you in the cockpit for the pre-flight checklist." He handed her the data chip.

She nodded. "I'll be there in five."

— « o » —

Nathan headed to his quarters and stripped off the sweat drenched work clothes. He showered, shaved, and dressed in a comfortable jumpsuit with the Milky Way Repossessions logo stitched over the left breast pocket. He made his way to the cockpit where Marla was working through the pre-flight checklist.

"How we doing?" he said.

"Everything checks out," she said. "Duncan and Richie have really been putting in some hard work."

"What do you think of our guests?" Nathan said. "The bald guy didn't even talk, did you notice? He's pretty odd."

Marla looked at him sideways. "Are we being paid to care or are we being paid to deliver a ransom?"

"That's another thing. Since when are people ransom?"

"Other people's problems, Nathan. We've got a job to do so let's just do it."

"She seemed alright."

"She seemed very nice. They both did. And his name is Arulio. Don't slip up and call him baldy or anything."

"Yeah, okay," he said. He scanned his screens. "No more compensating for the twitchy number three thruster?"

"Nope. Duncan and Richie also claim to have fixed that rattle in the starboard cowling."

"Good," he said."That was driving me nuts."

"Never heard it myself."

"It was there. What about the crawl drive?"

She tapped off a few checklist items on her data pad. "Supposedly, it's done. Richie built a new extended mount out of titanium. This flight will be the test."

"You don't sound as confident with that one."

"As long as I've been on this boat that crawl drive has been a problem. I want to see it work before I express any confidence."

"Yeah, well, let's hope that's the least of our problems, shall we?"

Check list done, Nathan kicked the engines over and engaged the solid hydrogen fusion reactor, taking the *Bandit* off her batteries. As the plasma built to drive pressure he decided to take one last walk through and check on the passengers. Having them aboard threw off his rhythm. He looked in the common room first.

Kimiyo was sitting there, looking over a data pad. She looked up when she saw him in the doorway. "Are we ready to leave, Captain?"

"Just about. Like I said, you can call me Nathan. I'm just taking a last walk through so you have about five minutes. You can stay where you are and just use those seat restraints," he gestured to the side of the chair she was curled up in.

"Thank you, Nathan," she said.

Cole brushed past him as he turned to leave. "What's up, boss?"

"Just about ready for takeoff, Cole."

Kimiyo stood up. "I'll see to Arulio and then come back here. I imagine he can strap in somewhere in his cabin?"

Nathan nodded. "He can. There's a jump seat folded into one wall. Cole can show you where it is."

"We have guests?"

"We do. Kimiyo Himura, this is Cole Seger."

"I'm pleased to meet you," she said. "Come with me and I'll introduce you to Arulio."

He looked at Nathan. "Who?"

"Arulio is our other guest. He's Saji's wetjack. We're delivering him to the cult holding the body barge hostage."

"What the hell's a wetjack? It sounds like something you'd try to talk your girlfriend into doing."

Nathan smiled. "And with that, Kimiyo, I'll leave you in Cole's capable hands."

He worked his way back through the ship, checking the rear hatch and ending his tour in the engine room. Duncan and Richie were playing cards over a lubricant drum.

"All ready to go?" Duncan said.

"We are. It looks like you guys did some good work. I guess we'll see if we fall out of the sky or not."

"No," Duncan said. "Not today."

Nathan looked Richie over and his eyes narrowed. "What happened to you? Why are you purple?"

Duncan held his cards up and snickered behind them. Nathan looked at him. "You knew about this?"

He nodded his head, laughing. "Oh, yeah."

The young man cleared his throat. "Uh…I was just trying out something new, you know to hide from the loan shark."

"Do you think he's an idiot? I have to be honest; I think you're seriously underestimating him if this is your plan."

"Maybe…"

You look ridiculous," Nathan said.

"You see a lot of it in the clubs downtown."

"I imagine it's all the rage among the unemployed and those who owe money to the Syndicate."

"That will be cleared up as soon as we get paid for this job," Richie said.

Nathan shook his head and let out a heavy sigh. "I called the union hall this morning. Your application for back pay is being processed now. By the time we return you should have the money in your account."

"Thanks."

"What was the hold up?" Duncan asked.

"The kid's got an ex-girlfriend over there."

"Melinda?" Richie said.

"I guess. Anyway, she was holding up your application. Once I got through to a supervisor I was able to clear things up."

"I'll be darned," Richie said. "I thought Melinda would help things along. That's why I called her."

"Did things end well between you two?" Nathan said.

"Not really but I didn't think they were that bad."

"What happened?" Duncan said.

"I owed her some money, you know, from gambling on the dog races."

"Shocking that she would hold a grudge," Nathan said.

"Well, you know how women are," Richie said.

Duncan was laughing. "I think I do, I'm not so sure you know how women are."

"Anyway," Nathan said, "we're ready for lift off. Strap in, pray that you two have done good work and we'll get a move on."

Nathan made his way back to the cockpit and settled in. He checked the status board for all the ship's hatches. "I show green across the board and drive plasma pressure is up."

"Same here," Marla said. "I've also got seven restraint's showing green. The tower has granted us clearance to depart."

"All right," Nathan said. "Let's fly."

He put power to the thrusters with two large levers and pulled back on the yoke. The *Blue Moon Bandit* rose smoothly and quickly into the New Mexico sky. The blue sky soon gave way to the blackness of space. They shot through the shuttle lanes, whipped by a space station with large cruise liners docked, and headed out toward the Moon.

Marla continued checking the ship's status and fed information to Nathan. "All systems go for jump to the Neptune warpgate," she said.

"Too bad the Moon's on the other side of Earth right now," he said. "I always get a kick out of seeing it."

"It's historical, first step out into the galaxy," Marla said. "Hard to miss the significance."

"Sure there's that but I like the lights from the casinos at Mare Vegas. I can't believe how far out you can see them. Are we lined up for the jump?"

"Right on course."

He amped up the reactor output to charge the FTL jump initiator. "Did you double check our position? I downloaded the latest positioning software and I want to be sure we don't jump into the middle of Triton. Neptune's got one decent moon, I don't want us to barrel into it going faster than light."

"I double checked, Nathan. We're good."

Marla knew her job and Nathan was confident in her abilities but it never hurt to ask twice. He checked the jump initiator. "We're charged and ready to go."

Marla tapped a button on the comm system. "Hold on folks. We're going superluminal."

Nathan tapped a command into the flight computer and the stars outside the cockpit stretched out toward infinity and then went black. It would be like this for the next hour until they got to the Neptune warpgate. If everything went according to plan, they would be ahead of schedule.

— « o » —

Cole grabbed a longneck out of the fridge and slumped into a seat in the galley. He put his boots up on a chair and fidgeted with a handheld game. Light speed jumps always made him skittish, affecting his balance for moments afterward. Having a beer usually helped.

Kimiyo came in a minute later. She didn't speak but made a cup of tea, spiked with something from a flask, and sat down at the table opposite Cole. She relaxed smoothly into the booth along the wall, placed a boot on the chair in front of her and lit a cigarette.

"You smoke?" Cole said.

"Yes, does it bother you?" She said. "I can put it out."

"No, it's okay. Is it real tobacco?"

She nodded and offered him the pack. He waved her off.

"I quit five years ago," he said. "Where do you get it from?"

"It's lunar," she said. "There's a farm near Terra Caloris. It has a crater about half a kilometer wide with a deep shadow. The farmer who runs the hydroponics fields says the tobacco is good because of the water they mine from the crater's shadow. He says it is close to a billion years old because a comet crashed there. It gives the tobacco plant a unique flavor."

Cole nodded and sipped his beer. He didn't have anything to say about moon water and tobacco.

"You like to fly?" she said.

He shrugged his shoulders. "It's part of the job. Not my favorite thing."

"I could tell."

"You like to fly?"

"I do. Working for Saji means a lot of travel. The light speed jumps make me uncomfortable, though. There's that split second where you feel...odd."

"Nothing. You feel nothing."

"Yes, you feel like there's a void. Like *you're* a void. It's like where you were is empty, just for a moment. You feel like you might not come back and as soon as you acknowledge that thought? You come back."

"That's it exactly, like vertigo to the nth degree."

She took a long drag on her cigarette and exhaled slowly. Cole drank her in.

"So what do you do for Captain Teller?" she said.

"I keep a lid on things."

"Meaning?"

He shrugged. "When we repo ships, people tend to be upset with us. I'm a calming influence in a stressful situation."

"I think I understand."

"What about you and the albino dude? You guys an item?"

"No. I'm his minder," she said, taking another drag. "He can be helpless at times."

"Like what?"

"You understand that he interfaces directly with computers, with his mind?"

"Sure."

"Everywhere he goes, every system he passes floods him with information. At times he's so immersed in the background noise that he'd walk out into traffic if someone wasn't there to stop him."

"So that's your job? Keep him from getting so distracted he kills himself?"

"Among other things, yes."

"Still, it must be something to have all that information flowing into you."

Kimiyo shook her head. "He drifts in and out of reality. I wouldn't want to be so out of touch. It's not my way to turn myself over to things I can't fully control."

Cole nodded. "I understand. That's why I drink during light speed jumps. No control over the situation."

She raised her glass of tea in agreement.

Chapter 16

The *Blue Moon Bandit* popped back into normal space near the orbit of Neptune. Nathan saw the big blue planet right where it should be and double-checked his visuals against the universal positioning system. They were right on course for the warpgate.

"Marla, can you get us in the slot for the warpgate transition?" Nathan said. "I'm going to check on things."

Nathan got up, wandered back into the galley, and poured himself a cup of coffee. He saw Cole chatting with Kimiyo and raised a mug in their direction. Hopefully that wasn't leading to drama. A quick trip down a short flight of stairs and he was in the crew quarters. He knocked on a door and heard Arulio tell him to come in.

The wetjack was sitting up on his bunk, his head tilted to one side. Nathan raised his hand. "I thought I would check in, Arulio. We've cleared the first super-luminal jump and we'll be transiting the warpgate in a few moments."

"Thank you, captain. I'm quite all right."

"Okay, then. If you need anything, just let me know."

"Absolutely. Your ship is really quite unique."

Nathan stopped halfway out the door. "How so?"

"The operating system is stifled. Your AI isn't turned on. I've never flown in a vessel that didn't use an artificial intelligence."

"Oh," Nathan said. "Well, The AI is there, we just don't have the avatar turned on. Marla and I don't need a third person in the cockpit. But even without the avatar you can't fly faster than light or transit a warpgate without some computer help."

"It's so stifled," Arulio said. He stared at the far wall and lost eye contact with Nathan.

"Right," Nathan said. "I'll be heading back now."

The pale-skinned man on the bed had lost interest or was ignoring him so Nathan closed the door and headed back.

He settled into his seat in the cockpit. "This is going to be a strange job, Marla."

— « o » —

They blew into the Alpha system with a bright white flash from the warpgate. Nathan punched in the coordinates provided for the meet with the group holding the *Charon* and her crew hostage. Marla took them super-luminal and an hour later they were in orbit around a terrestrial world called Olympia. It was the most populated world in the Alpha system, having been terraformed more than two hundred years before. Olympia was the first planet in the Alpha system to be settled and updated for the occupation of humans. It had previously been a planet that had shared more in common with Venus than Earth. Its thick atmosphere had been extremely hot and full of choking carbon dioxide, but the same methods that allowed Venus to be occupied in the Sol system had changed Olympia into a paradise. Bright blue and white from space, it reminded Nathan of Earth.

It took an hour to clear customs at the orbital space station and then they were cruising down toward Clearland City. It was on the east coast of the largest continent on Olympia. As they flew over the city, Nathan could see factories, warehouses, and smokestacks. Kimiyo snuck into the cockpit and scoped out the city below.

"It is strange for a planet known as 'Paradise' to appear so dirty," she said.

Nathan shrugged his shoulders. "Building things means making a mess. There are industrial sites on Earth that still look like this."

"Still, I hope we aren't here for long."

"According to Saji's information we should meet with the contact for the Children of the Apocalyptic Rainbow somewhere around here. We'll contact them after we land."

"Thank you, Nathan."

"Go buckle in. We'll be landing soon."

"I will do so after checking on Arulio," she said.

Nathan dropped the *Blue Moon Bandit* onto a landing pad on the east side of the city. The area did look run down, he admitted to himself.

Marla was running through the post-flight checklist. He went to see the crew. They were in the galley sitting around the table. Nathan faced everyone and leaned back against the counter. "Okay," he said, "we've arrived on Olympia. This is where we're supposed to meet the contact for the group that is holding the body barge and its crew. That person is supposed to make sure we've brought what we're supposed to and provide us with the final delivery location. The meeting is tomorrow night, if I've managed to keep the time changes correct across two worlds and two solar systems."

"So what do we do now?" Richie asked.

"Well, it's dinner time so I think we should step out for a bite to eat," Nathan said.

"Cool," Richie said.

"Not so fast, my lavender friend. My understanding is that Arulio has trouble in social situations so he won't be joining us. The adults are going out. You'll be staying here as his babysitter."

Richie pointed to Kimiyo. "I thought she was his caretaker?"

"She is but she didn't dye herself purple," Nathan said. "I'd like to keep a low profile tonight and your skin pigmentation doesn't lend itself to that."

"Come on, lots of people do this. I won't stand out that much."

"We're not in Go City back home on Earth," Nathan said. "Help yourself to anything in the fridge. Everyone else, go get dressed for a night out."

Marla made a call and arranged for a car to pick up the five of them.

— « o » —

A van showed up with no driver. Nathan wasn't fond of auto-driven vehicles but the *Blue Moon Bandit* didn't have room to haul a car around. They piled in. Nathan sat in the front, Duncan and Marla took the second row seat, and Cole and Kimiyo piled in the third.

"Any idea where to go?" Nathan said. "I've never been to this part of Olympia."

"Is dinner on Saji?" Cole asked.

Kimiyo nodded. "It would be Mr. Vy's pleasure to buy you dinner. He insisted I pay for any meals and incidentals."

"Steak," Cole said.

"Real steak," Duncan said. "No synthetic protein."

"Guys, don't take advantage of Kimiyo's hospitality," Marla said.

"Come on, Marla. Don't be such a stick in the mud," Cole said.

"No, maybe she has a point," Duncan said. "And you don't get to call her a stick in the mud. Only I get to do that."

"Honestly, you two can be like children," Nathan said. "Let's knock it off."

"It is not a problem," Kimiyo said. "Please, select whatever you would like."

Nathan relayed instructions to the van to find a restaurant. It presented a list on the console screen. Nathan picked the nicest looking and the van started off. It drove them across town and let them out in front of a joint that didn't look as nice as its description in the car.

They stood on the sidewalk looking the place over. "This is why I don't like the automated cars," Nathan said. "This place probably pays to be at the top of the suggestion list. You can't throttle the driver for giving you bad advice."

"Come on," Cole said. "It won't be that bad. It's hard to screw up a steak."

"No it's not," Nathan said. "Believe me; you can ruin a good piece of meat with hardly any effort. Kathy did it more than once."

They went in and were seated in a large booth toward the back by a stern looking woman who looked at them like they might rob the place. They squeezed into the booth.

The waitress came and took their drink orders. She was a cute little blonde and Nathan watched Cole as she wrote down their orders. Normally he would be chatting her up but Nathan noticed Cole was on his best behavior.

"They have real steak," Duncan said, looking at the menu. "I'm getting a Porterhouse. Rare."

"See, Nathan," Cole said. "I told you this would be a nice place."

"How old is this planet?" Kimiyo said.

"Two hundred years since it was terraformed, if that's what you mean," Duncan said.

"I've heard they have never had a war here," Kimiyo said.

"How could that be?" Marla said.

Their drinks arrived. Everyone took a moment to sample their cocktails.

"Give it time," Nathan said. "The people who live here haven't had time to learn how to hate each other yet."

"Way to be optimistic," Duncan said.

"No, he's right," Cole said.

"You understand?" Nathan said.

Cole nodded. "I'm picking up what you're putting down."

"They got, what, a hundred million people on the whole planet?" Nathan said. "They're spread out on three continents and got another three that barely have settlements. Wait until they all decide they want to live on the same plot of land or need the resources someone finds under someone else's house. Then you'll see some fireworks." He raised his mug.

"That is a cynical outlook, isn't it?" Kimiyo said.

"Oil," Cole said.

"Farm land," Nathan said.

"Water," Marla said.

"You too?" Duncan said.

She took a bite from a celery stalk and smiled.

"This is a whole new solar system," Duncan said. "Brand new planets, relatively speaking. The people out here left all that nonsense behind them. In two centuries of settling this system it hasn't seen a war. Nathan, in your time flying a gunship for Earth Protective Services, did you ever make it to the Alpha system?"

"Sure. We helped police the settlements."

"Anything serious?"

"Any action you mean?"

Duncan nodded.

"No, nothing here."

"But in the Sol system?" Cole said.

"Yeah," Nathan said. "I saw some action there. It proves my point. People may move to new places but they're still people. They lie, steal, and kill each other. That's society and that's war."

Duncan leaned forward. "I'm just saying, this is a new place so maybe we get another chance. Not just a planet but dozens of them with everyone focused on making their home the best it can be. In all of human history we've never had an opportunity to grow without the danger of invasion, without putting an obscene amount of resources toward defending ourselves *from* ourselves. That doesn't happen here."

"Yet," Nathan said. "Back in the home system we went out into the dark, ripped worlds apart, smashed ice to make oxygen and made our homes on planets and moons that would have poisoned us. That action I saw that you mentioned earlier? That was a dispute on Mars over water. People lived in peace for a hundred years and then when they got thirsty? They picked up rifles and got down to it."

"And you think we've learned nothing since then?"

"I'm just saying, it's who we are. It's what we do, eventually."

The food arrived and they dug in. The steaks were real and thick.

"Dude, we're here delivering a ransom to free up a starship full of dead bodies," Cole said. "I think Nathan's got a point."

"He may have a point," Duncan said.

Nathan looked over at Cole. He and Kimiyo were splitting a bottle of red wine. It was something local, not imported from Earth. They must grow good grapes here, Nathan thought, watching as glass after glass was emptied.

"So what's the deal here?" Marla said. "What's going on tomorrow?"

"Should be an easy swap," Nathan said. "We meet their guy at some casino. They wanted a public place you know. Anyway we meet him, he checks out, makes sure Arulio is for real and then gives us another place to meet them."

"Off world?"

"I assume," Nathan said. "Olympia is too settled to try whatever it is they want to do. They'll want some crappy little moon where the law is spread thin. So, we'll wait for Arulio to do his thing, the *Charon* crew gets released and we go home. An amazing pay day follows and we do much celebrating."

"Just like that?" Cole said.

"With any luck," Nathan said.

They finished dinner and sat back with more drinks. Marla looked at Nathan.

"Hey boss."

"Yeah?"

She smiled uncontrollably. "What's it like knockin' boots with a light puppet?"

Nathan looked at Duncan. "Seriously?"

"It was too good to keep to myself."

"Are you going to tell Celeste about your little fantasy when you see her?" Marla said.

Nathan felt himself flush in the dim light of the restaurant. "Come on..."

"Did you bring a copy so you could show her?" Cole said.

"You are all horrible people. I don't know why I employ any of you." He waved to the waitress for the check. "No, Cole, I did not bring a copy to show Celeste. Making that immersive environment may have been a mistake."

"And expensive," Duncan said.

"Duncan, you are once again proving you can't hold liquor or secrets."

The engineer tipped a glass in his direction.

"But he gets to hold me," Marla said.

"I'm going to be sick."

The check came and Kimiyo took care of it. They walked out onto the street where the air had turned chilly. Nathan glanced at the sky out of habit, always a pilot, and saw it was a clear night. The stars in the sky looked very different from those on Earth.

"Cole," he said, "are you going to take a run by the meet location?"

"Heading over there now."

"I'll come too," Kimiyo said.

"That's all right. I can take care of it."

She shook her head. "Thank you but Mr. Vy made it clear this was my responsibility. Please, I would like to see the location before we meet tomorrow."

Cole looked at her. "You sure?"

"I can take care of myself."

"I don't doubt it."

A van pulled to the curb. Nathan, Duncan, and Marla piled in. Cole and Kimiyo walked off down the block. Duncan gave the van's computer the address for the *Blue Moon Bandit's* landing pad. Nathan watched Cole and Kimiyo until they were out of sight.

"Nervous about tomorrow?" Duncan said.

Nathan considered the question. "It's going to be odd, that's for sure. You?"

Duncan hugged Marla tight. "Nah, I'm good."

— « o » —

The van rolled up to the landing pad and let them out. Nathan paid for it and got a receipt for the expenses. Duncan keyed his code into the rear landing ramp of the *Blue Moon Bandit* and he and Marla walked into the ship. Nathan followed them a minute later.

Duncan and Marla walked to their quarters while Nathan walked toward the front of the ship to check things over. He got as far as the galley and stopped. Richie was tied to a chair, unconscious and shirtless, with burnt hand prints all over his purple skin.

"Duncan! Get up here, and bring a first aid kit!" He moved to a wall locker, thumbed the lock, and grabbed a shotgun. He grabbed a handful of shells and started jacking them in while looking toward the front of the ship. He didn't see anything moving near the cockpit and he slid the door shut separating the compartments. Duncan and Marla came running up. She was carrying the first aid kit.

"What happened?" Duncan said. His face showed shock. They were in a dangerous business but the danger usually didn't follow them to their home.

"I don't know," Nathan said. "I just found him like this. Did you see anyone down near the crew quarters?"

"We didn't see anything," Duncan said.

Marla was attaching a diagnostic probe to Richie's forehead. Without a doctor on board they had to rely on a medical computer built into the kit and the *Bandit*'s mainframe.

Nathan pulled another shotgun from the wall locker, loaded it, and threw it to Duncan, who almost dropped it. He hefted the gun awkwardly.

"Nathan, you know how I am with these."

"Well Marla's busy so it's just you and me until Cole gets back. We'll sweep the ship bow to stern. Shoot first and ask questions later."

"All right but you may want to stay behind me."

Nathan pulled open the door to the cockpit and they swept through it. The compartment wasn't very large so they were back in the galley a moment later. Nathan looked at Richie.

"How is he, Marla?"

"These burns are serious and he's got a head injury. Whoever was here worked him over hard."

Nathan went back to the wall locker and grabbed a pistol. He slipped a magazine in and chambered a round before handing it to Marla. "Keep an eye open. If anyone comes in here but us, assume they did this."

She took the gun and laid it on the table beside her because her dress didn't have pockets. She took scissors from the first aid kit and started cutting Richie loose. Nathan helped her lay him on the table. When they were done, he picked up his shotgun and joined Duncan at the other entrance to the galley.

"Okay, you stay here with him while we check the ship." He tapped a few keys on a wall-mounted keypad. "The intercom is open. If you need us, just holler."

She nodded and went back to Richie, following the instructions of the medical program. Nathan and Duncan moved into the corridor and pulled the door shut behind them.

"Did you see the way she took that gun?" Nathan said. "She didn't whine nearly as much as you did."

Duncan smiled but kept his gaze straight ahead. "I'm here to keep your junky boat in the air. Cole is supposed to shoot people."

"My boat isn't junky."

"Well, I do good work so maybe you just don't notice."

They walked the length of the ship, going through crew quarters, storage holds, the small medical bay, the reactor room, and the engine room. Duncan locked the rear hatch as they passed it and then they circled back to the galley. They knocked on the door and Marla let them in. Nathan noticed how she looked behind them before bringing her gun hand out from behind her back. She had good instincts.

"How's our purple mechanic?"

"I sprayed the burns with antiseptic and numbed them. The head thing wasn't too bad but the doc program had me give him an injection of nanites. They'll swarm the goose egg and relieve the swelling by mimicking anti-coagulants. I was also allowed to give a stimulant so he should be around any minute."

"Good work. Maybe you're being wasted as a pilot."

Richie groaned and Nathan stepped up to keep him from rolling off the table

"Easy, kid. Can you tell us what happened?"

Richie opened his eyes and raised himself up on his elbows. "Oh man…"

"Who was it?"

Richie looked up. "Nathan, I'm sorry. I couldn't stop them."

"Was it that loan shark from back in Go City? I can see your burns are hand shaped."

Richie nodded. "Yeah, it was Atomic Jack and his goons. It was him that burned me."

"What did he want?" Duncan asked.

"He said he wanted the ransom we were carrying for the body barge. They thought we were carrying money or something like that. I held out as long as I could. I didn't want to tell them about Arulio but…" His voice trailed off and he looked down at his chest.

"Dammit, Nathan," Duncan said. "I didn't see him during our sweep. I was looking for people that aren't supposed to be here and forgot to check on the ones who are." He hustled down the corridor to check the wetjack's quarters.

Nathan silently cursed himself for doing the same thing. "It's my fault, Duncan. I'm not used to having guests on board."

"He's gone," Duncan said as he returned.

"How could he have known, Nathan?" Marla said. "No one but us knew what was going on. Saji and his people don't want the publicity."

"Somebody talked," Nathan said.

All three of them turned to look at Richie. He hung his head.

"What did you do?" Nathan said. He was steely eyed now and feeling more upset by the moment.

"Captain, you have to understand. That orange faced freak is crazy. He was going to burn me. I didn't think telling him what we were doing would do any harm. I mean, how could I know he would do something like this? I thought I was just putting him off again, you know, until we got home."

"When did you talk to them?"

"Duncan sent me to provision for this trip. When I was at the store they grabbed me and took me to some bar they own. They were going to do me right there so I had to convince them that I had money coming in. They didn't want to hear about my back pay anymore."

"So you told them about this deal?" Nathan said, the anger rising in his voice. He turned to Duncan. "I thought you were watching him?"

Duncan held up his hands. "I was but I can't do everything at once. I can't provision the ship and rebuild parts for the third time. This is what happens when we run lean and cheap."

"Well, we can't all be rich, can we?"

"I guess it depends on what you spend your money on, Captain."

They stared at each other for a moment and then Marla stepped between them.

"Richie," she said, "when did this happen? How long ago were they here?"

"An hour or so after you left. I was sitting on the back ramp getting some fresh air and they just walked right up. I didn't even have time to pull up the ramp or call for help."

"What happened then?"

"They brought me in here, tied me up, and started asking me questions. When I couldn't produce any cash they started slapping me around."

"Where was Arulio?" Marla asked.

"He never came out of his room."

"Then what?"

Richie got off the table and sat down in a chair, leaning back. Marla handed him a bottle of water from the fridge.

"Look Nathan, I know you're angry but I held out as long as I could. That Jack guy is a sadist. He gets off on hurting people and you know he's wanted to hurt me for a long time so... he did." His voice choked up. "One of his goons ripped my shirt off and they took off while he worked me over. I assume they were looking for the ransom money but to tell you the truth I wasn't aware of anything but his hands. He took turns taking his gloves off and burning me with each one." He stopped and looked at Nathan who just stared back.

"And then?"

"It must hurt him to take the gloves off. He would have one out for a while and then switch off. His hands are actually burning when he takes them off, with flames and everything. After I don't know how long I just gave up and told him about Arulio. I'm sorry but we all have limits and having my nipples twisted while they're burning is apparently mine.

"So he had his boys go get Arulio out of his quarters. By then I was so pissed that he hadn't done anything to help, hadn't come to see what was going on or even called for help as far as I knew that I didn't care if they took him. I mean, I was screaming as loud as I could and he just stayed in his room.

"Anyway, his boys went to get Arulio and he just kept on burning me, like he didn't want to waste the opportunity. When they finally got back here with Arulio one of them wrote a note and left it on the fridge and the other one smacked me in the head. The next thing I knew Marla was waking me up."

Nathan turned to the fridge and grabbed the note held there by a magnet. Something else different he hadn't noticed. It had the address of a meeting place, a time and a figure. He read it to the group.

"The meet is in the late morning at some bar. They want a hundred-thousand." He looked at Richie. "That's way more than you owe. Probably gas money for coming to collect."

"Well, we certainly don't have that," Duncan said.

"Why should we pay?" Marla said. "Let's just put this guy down for good and get on with our business. I'm tired of putting up with his crap."

"That's who we are now?" Duncan said. "We kill people?"

"You'd probably feel differently, hon, if that was me sitting there covered in burns."

"Probably," Duncan allowed, "but it isn't. The guy covered in burns is the guy who bet the dogs and lost." He turned to Richie. "I'm sympathetic, bro, but you brought this down on us. Now we're talking about killing someone. Is that who we are?" He looked at Nathan when he asked.

Nathan shifted around and straightened up. "He was in our home, Duncan. We had a deal with him to get Richie square and he walked into our home and crapped all over us. What was his rule? 'You owe, you pay', right? Well I have rules too. No one comes on my boat and messes with my crew."

Cole and Kimiyo came laughing up the corridor just then. When they saw everyone in the galley Cole raised an eyebrow. "What's all this?"

They filled him in, Nathan showed him the note and the discussion picked up where it had left off.

"I'm going to have to report this to Saji Vy," Kimiyo said. "Arulio is a very expensive resource. The fact that he is in criminal hands is unacceptable."

"Does he know things he could reveal about Saji Vy?" Nathan said.

"He does but Arulio's mindware is encrypted. Even he doesn't know the access codes. He can't access anything proprietary but that won't stop them from trying to get information out of him."

"You can't tell Saji," Cole said. "You'll lose your job."

"That's true. He was my responsibility."

"Can you get the money?" Nathan said.

She nodded affirmatively. "Yes, but there is no way to gloss over that as an incidental expense. We would have to explain. Do you have it?"

"I can draw a loan from Lucy but not fast enough to get this done."

"Time's the issue, isn't it?" Cole said, sitting down wearily. "We have a hostage to pay ransom for in the morning so we can use him as ransom when we meet other kidnappers in the afternoon."

"Remember when we used to just repo starships?" Duncan said. "Those were good days. People would fall behind on their bills and we would go collect their yacht or freighter or whatever. Now we have strategy sessions for ransom drops and debate what we should do with loan sharks who can self-immolate."

"Perhaps we could just go to the meet and explain that kidnapping Arulio is not a good idea," Kimiyo said. "Stealing from Saji Vy is a terrible mistake. He holds a grudge and he can be ruthless."

"He won't listen," Cole said. "Atomic Jack thinks he's holding all the cards but his greed is blinding him to the fact that we may not have the money he wants."

"Criminals aren't known for their brains," Nathan said. "Isn't that what you always tell me?"

"Yeah. Penal rehab facilities are full of guys who think they're smarter than everyone else."

"So why don't we just call Protective Services?" Marla said. "Have them go to the meet and get Arulio back."

Nathan shook his head. "We could but that blows the deal for the *Charon*. Saji was very clear that he didn't want any negative publicity concerning the body barge. That point was made explicitly."

"He's like that," Kimiyo said. "You would be surprised at some of the things he has covered up." She stood up pulled a can of tea from the fridge and took a sip. "Nathan, I know you're the captain and you want to handle this your own way, but Arulio is my responsibility and I'm Saji's representative. We're going to play it my way."

"I appreciate what you're saying Kimiyo but Atomic Jack is our problem," he said.

"And I appreciate that," she said curling into a chair. "But now he's become my problem. It's under control."

"I really don't see how."

"Nathan, I have a couple hours work ahead of me. Why don't you all get some sleep and I'll fill you in before we leave."

Cole sat beside her. "Do you need some help? This isn't the first kidnapping I've been involved with."

"Thank you. I think that's a good idea," she said. "A little marshal's knowledge could come in handy."

"Ex-marshal."

"But still."

"We should probably work in my quarters," he said. "It will be quieter there."

Silence fell in the compartment as everyone looked at Cole. Nathan saw Marla shake her head.

"Or we could work here," he said.

The galley cleared out. Duncan looked at Nathan. "That's it?"

"Apparently."

"Okay, let's get Richie down to the medical bay."

— « o » —

Celeste lay back in cool sheets, her heart racing as Montario moved in the bathroom. Scoundrel he may be but Celeste thoroughly enjoyed her time with him out of her 'cell'. She stared at the brilliant red silk canopy above his bed. Being the head clown of this circus had its perks. Her room had a metal ceiling painted a dull off-white color. Those were the kinds of things you noticed when you spent days on end locked up. She sat up and sipped cool water from a glass on the stand beside the bed.

The plan was behind schedule by a couple of days already. Saji had taken longer than expected to get their ransom together. The initial meeting was later today, their time. As Montario exited the bathroom, doubt crept into her thoughts again.

He walked out of the bathroom with a towel wrapped around his waist. Celeste looked him over, admiring his strong shoulders. She considered that her current predicament could have been brought about because her judgment was clouded. He turned and must have seen the dour look on her face.

"Something wrong, babe? You don't look happy."

"Do you worry that we've made this overly complicated?"

"How do you mean?"

She sighed. "Couldn't we have been happy with just ransoming the body barge? Saji Vy would have paid a small fortune to get it returned."

He smiled and sat down on the edge of the bed. "Babe, I don't want a small fortune. I want a large fortune." He gestured, holding his hands apart. "A big one. Stacks of coin piled up as high as I can see."

"But this could have been a good, quick score," she said. "We grab the ship with me working inside and then walk with the money. No one would think twice if I quit after a hijacking."

He sat down and took her hand. He gave her that smile that she knew got him into more than a few beds. "Celeste, you have to trust the plan. Saji would have paid a hundred grand at most to get the body barge back. Anything more than that and I think he would have just accepted the bad press and sent in the marines. After that we would have had to look over our shoulders forever because he is not a man who forgets or forgives. I told you, crossing him is an extremely dangerous proposition."

"And yet that's exactly what we're doing," she said.

"This isn't crossing him, exactly."

Celeste looked at him with a raised eyebrow.

He held up his hands defensively. "At most this is an inconvenience to him. He'll get his ship and cargo back unharmed and it won't cost him a dime. Remember, inconveniencing Saji is one thing. Taking money out of his pocket is quite another. I don't think anyone has ever been hurt because they inconvenienced him."

"You don't think?" she said.

"Yeah I do," he said with a smile. "I knew a guy once, when I worked in a warehouse, who grabbed some freight off a receiving dock, right? This was back in Go City at a warehouse Saji owned. Anyway, it was part of a shipment of starship waste recyclers. Not a sexy score by any measure but the kind that will make paying the bills easier, you follow?"

She nodded.

"Well , Saji has quite an organization. Eyes and ears everywhere, keeping a look out. This friend of mine got as far as home with his take and there was a knock at the door."

"Saji?"

He shook his head. "In person? No, not for a couple pallets of waste recyclers. It was just a couple of guys from the warehouse. They sat my guy down and explained the facts of life to him. Give back the recyclers and nothing worse than losing his job would happen. If he didn't or couldn't, like if he'd sold them? They explained he was just going to disappear."

"Had he sold them?"

"Not yet, so he did the wise thing and showed them to a storage unit where he'd stashed them. He offered to cut them in on the sale but all that got him was a broken nose."

Celeste sat up straight in the bed. "That's what you've based this plan on?" Her eyes flashed with anger. "I thought you had better intelligence. This is all based on some story from when you worked in a warehouse?"

She jumped out of bed and started pulling on her clothes. "You're going to get us killed."

He sighed and stood up. "You're over reacting."

She turned and advanced on him, her green eyes narrowed. "I'm not."

He took her arm. "Come back to bed and let me explain. I promise you'll calm down once I explain further."

She shook his arm off. "You've seen the last of me in bed for a long time. I shouldn't have agreed to this. We're going to be killed."

"Celeste, cut the act," he said. "You wanted revenge on Saji. That's why you came in on this with me."

"But…"

"They used you! You were good at your job! You are a great pilot and they threw you away because some old bastard couldn't keep his hands off you. Driving a bus full of dead people is a ridiculous waste of your talent. Some seventy year old retiree should have that job but you got screwed because you wouldn't lay down for them."

She stared at the wall, seething.

"Well, this time it's you using him and his company to get what you deserve. It's just a scam. No one is getting hurt here. We're just taking money and we aren't even taking his. We're borrowing the services of his wetjack."

She looked up at him. "That's true."

"And the money? These kid's money? We're doing them a favor. I've never seen a bigger group of naïve people. They deserve to have their pockets picked just so they'll grow up a little. And let me tell you, every one of these kids has deep pockets. There's not one of them that doesn't have a trust fund feeding their "religion". You think I'm the first con man to take the reigns? It's a revolving door of grifters who get in, scam them for what they can grab before they get caught and then bolt. These kids will follow anyone who has ideas and confidence and I have both."

"You're not here for the quick scam, though."

"Oh no," he said. "I did my homework. I know what's here. There are fat stacks of cash just waiting to be picked up. I never want to work again."

She buttoned her top and backed away. "You told me you bought this scam from the previous guy, the other guy who pretended to be their leader."

"Right, my buddy Bobby. Getting in here cost me a lot of money but it looks like it's worth it. Hell, I don't even really understand why they call themselves the Children of the Apocalyptic Rainbow."

"Why didn't Bobby grab the cash? Surely there's some other way than what we're doing."

"It's in accounts at major banks. I told you, cracking that security encryption requires a wetjack."

"We could bribe someone."

He took her hands in his. "Celeste, you know as well as I do that bank employees are rewarded, handsomely, for turning in people who try to bribe them. They live for those bonuses. I have friends in prison because they tried scamming banks using inside people. It can't be done."

"What about anyone inside the religion?" she said.

He started to answer and hesitated.

"What is it?" she said.

He got off the bed. "Most of these kids are here because they're lost, right? They need a little direction. Be the best whatever they want to be, right? Well, there's this one guy who really wants to be all he can be. He buys into all of this hook, line, and sinker."

"What's this joker's name?"

"Caleb. Caleb Wooburn."

"He's hardcore, huh?"

"Oh yeah," he said. "Caleb's a little older than the kids you've seen. Most of them find their way into the group in their late teens or early twenties and get what they need after a few years."

"Like a sense of purpose or direction?"

"Exactly," he said. "Now, some folks come later in life but they have different problems, you know? Bad marriages, issues with their kids, or even job loss."

"A cure for the mid-life crisis?"

"Exactly."

She thought for a moment. "Does that last bit have anything to do with all the older people working these side businesses the cult runs? I've noticed that all the janitors, chamber maids, and food service workers wearing rainbow uniforms are older."

He seemed embarrassed. "Yeah, that's what we call our work therapy program."

"Work therapy?"

"We give the older folks jobs and tell them to focus their energies on the work."

"That's despicable," she said but laughed a little.

"They are great at what they do. We've got more requests for work than we can handle."

"That's not therapy. That's a revenue stream."

"The point is," he said, "people come into the group, get themselves straightened out, and then leave. At some point the young people realize they've given away quite a bit of their trust fund and wasted some good years taking drugs and having sex with strange people. They fade off and get on with their lives. The older people learn that they're capable of achieving whatever it is they want and get tired of tithing most of their paycheck to the group. They take off too but usually they're polite enough to give two weeks' notice."

"But this guy Caleb…"

"Yeah, Caleb is a special case. The guy I got this gig from? Bobby? He said Caleb's kind of a problem. Caleb is in his early forties and he's been here since he was in his early twenties.

Two decades of following the seven paths to enlightenment have scrambled his skull."

"He's like those guys that never graduate from college," Celeste said. "They just keep earning one degree after another."

"I'll take your word for it," Montario said. "I never made it to college. Anyway, Caleb can be kind of a problem. He considers himself to be the 'old man' around here.

He hits on all the new girls and bosses the older folks around. I try to keep him away from here on different assignments but it never seems to last."

"He's here now?"

"No, but he'll be back any time. I didn't want him around while we pulled this caper. He's so damn nosy he would never stop asking questions about why you guys are here."

"What did you do with him?"

"I sent him to the moon of Temple to help set up a new cleaning office at one of the spaceports. The trouble is, he's done this so many times it won't take him very long."

"Will the cover story fool him? That we're here because we had engine problems and you're helping to repair our ship?"

"Maybe. He's suspicious of me as all hell. You have to remember, he's seen a string of leaders come through here. Seen them come and seen them go. He's been bugging me to allow him to take on more of a leadership role in the group."

"So he does have ambition?"

"Somewhat," Montario said. "I think he's finally figured out that the higher up you go in the food chain here the easier the ride. That's why he's been busting his hump setting up offices and managing things. It's been tricky because that's all stuff that needs done and I don't want to do it and neither does anyone else around here."

"Your laziness is going to bring this crashing down around us."

"I'm not that worried about him. I'll just find something else for him to do. You know, in a funny way, our little con will benefit Caleb."

"How's that?"

"When we leave? The last thing I plan on doing is leaving him in charge."

She smiled and said, "You're terrible." Then she got a little more serious. "So this is it?"

"This is it," he said. "We get our wetjack, bust into the accounts, and run for the hills. You'll never have to do anything you don't want to do again. We could fly off and explore to your heart's content or live in the lap of luxury in the resorts of Mare Vegas on Earth's moon. All you have to do is hold it together for a few more days."

"Just sit tight in my cell?"

"That's it, honey. I'll take care of everything."

She pulled on her boots and stepped to the door. "Montario?"

"Yeah, babe?"

"Don't get us killed."

Chapter 17

They took two rented cars to the diner where the meet was scheduled to take place. Kimiyo and Cole left first. She was intent on negotiating Arulio's release from Atomic Jack without jeopardizing their meeting later that afternoon with the Children of the Apocalyptic Rainbow or her job with Saji Vy.

Cole looked Kimiyo over. She was dressed smartly in a dark blue jacket and skirt, opting to go very corporate for her meeting with the gangsters holding Arulio. Her hair was up and she was sporting expensive sunglasses. That one look told him she was ready for negotiations. She had a small leather case on the seat beside her. It was real leather too, not the synthetic stuff so it had been imported to Earth.

"Is your case from Mars?" He said. Mars had a thriving agricultural trade. Terraforming had left the equator of the planet littered with farmland and ranches.

"Yes. It was gift from Mr. Vy. Do you like it?"

"It's very nice." He was trying to gauge her mood. They'd spent some time together last night planning and she had been enthusiastic but since then she had slept and had time to anticipate the meeting. That time could have given her cold feet.

He looked out the window. Olympia was surprisingly like Earth. Cole didn't know what he had expected but the business district they were driving through could have been plucked from any large city back on the homeworld. In fact, it looked run down for being built so recently, relatively speaking.

"You need to trust me."

He turned to her in surprise. "I do," he said.

"No, when we're there, sitting down at the table. You need to be cool."

"I'll be like ice. This is your show."

She eyed him for a moment. "I can tell you're the kind of man who likes to be blunt. You don't want to waste time talking if there's work to be done but this isn't like that. There will be talking at the table."

"There's talking in what I do, too," he said. "When I was a marshal we talked to criminals. We talked to them when they were committing crimes, we talked to them during hostage negotiations, and we talked to them after the fact just to find out why they did the dumb stuff they did. You don't need to worry. When I say I know how to sit still and listen, I do. I can listen to you chat up a couple of thugs."

She turned toward him. "You need to understand something. I work for Saji Vy."

"This fact has not escaped my notice."

"Saji is one of the richest men on Earth. Having an interest in so many enterprises has made him exceedingly wealthy."

Cole sensed there was more. "And?"

"Those dealings have left him with a deep sense of paranoia. Saji has had things done to people who crossed him or…whom he perceived as crossing him. Ugly things. These men we're meeting? They think they're tough. They run book, own strip clubs, dabble in petty theft, and probably sell dope, and they're comfortable in that world, thinking they own it. That arrogance? That feeling that they can just push people around and do anything they want? It has left them with one foot in the grave and they don't even know it.

"So when I tell you to let me manage the meeting I mean sit there and let me do it. Do that and an hour from now we'll be drinking a toast to my success and relaxing with Arulio back on Nathan's ship."

Cole nodded and sat back against the door. "It's all you, babe."

"Thank you."

The van pulled up to the diner and deposited them on the sidewalk. The diner was big; bigger than Cole thought it would be. It stretched down the block, more like a buffet place than a diner. If it was full of people, that could be a problem. Of course, the neighborhood looked like it was past its prime so maybe the crowd would be light. There weren't a lot of vehicles in the parking lot. A van sat in the back and a couple of small fusion two seaters were near the back door. They walked in and looked around.

Cole had nothing to worry about. He could see kitchen staff going through their paces but there were only a few customers at the counter. The lights were low and the shades were drawn against the morning sun. It looked like a lot of the dining room was closed off. There were booths and tables but few of them held customers. A waitress was pouring coffee for a customer at the counter and threw Cole a half smile. It wasn't a welcoming gesture.

A curtain rustled in the back. Cole spotted the guy with the broken wrist from back in Go City looking out at them. What was his name? Kinty. He was getting tired of seeing this guy's ugly face everywhere he went. The thug waved him over. He nudged Kimiyo. They walked back to him and he pointed them toward a secluded table. That other guy from the alley back in Go City, was sitting at the table drinking a cup of coffee. Cole was glad they weren't in a booth. He did not want to be confined in any way.

They sat down, Kinty and the other guy on the side facing the curtained doorway. Cole pulled a chair out for Kimiyo and sat beside her. The hairs on the back of his neck stood up. He hated having his back to the door.

"Hungry?" Kinty said.

Kimiyo shook her head. "Thank you but nothing for us."

"Suit yourself. They make great waffles here. I love me some waffles." The big man sliced a piece of waffle off his plate and forked it into his mouth. Cole could smell synthetic maple syrup. "We're alone back here. The waitresses know to leave us be unless we call them. Who are you?"

"My name is Kimiyo Himura. I represent Mr. Vy in this matter."

"I'm Kinty," he said and then pointed at his partner. "This is Bonto. We remember your friend from Go City."

"Glad to hear it," Cole said. He looked at Kinty. "Wrist all healed up?"

He held up his fork. "Just fine. Maybe later I'll show you."

"Maybe."

"Gentlemen, we should concentrate on why we are here," Kimiyo said. "Your other matters are not relevant to this situation. Is Arulio all right? I would like to see proof of life."

Bonto smiled. "Of course he's alive." He pulled out his mobi and clicked a button. "Live picture, sweetie. He's safe and sound." A small hologram displayed above the table. Arulio was sitting in a cramped space on a plastic crate. Cole thought it looked like a van. He could see windows behind Arulio and a reflection in the windows that might be Atomic Jack. Light gleamed off something like a glass dome, like the glass dome of a helmet. He saw Arulio shift uncomfortably.

"Gentlemen," Kimiyo said, "I request the return of the man currently in your custody."

"Can't have him, love," Kinty said. "There is the small matter of payment."

"We will not be paying a ransom," she said. "Arulio is an employee of Saji Vy, a registered human-network interface for SajiCo. You have no claim to him."

"She's doing all the talking, tough guy?" Kinty said, looking at Cole.

"She is."

"Look, missy, that guy," he said, pointing at Cole, "has someone on his crew who owes us money. Money he has not been able to produce. It's too bad you and your boy got mixed up in this but that happens when you keep rough company. You owe, you pay. That's just the way it is."

"You are taking advantage of a situation that has nothing to do with Arulio or myself to reconcile a matter with a member of Captain Teller's crew."

"No shit, sweetie. It's called leverage. That's what we do."

Cole's eyes slid toward Kimiyo. Her face was placid.

"I see."

"Look, your boy is safe. I need to be paid and we all get on with our lives."

Kimiyo gripped the small briefcase on her lap. Cole could sense her frustration. "Mr. Vy is a very powerful man and this situation..."

"Don't."

Kimiyo looked at Kinty. "Excuse me?"

He dropped his fork and it clattered on his plate. "Don't tell me about how powerful your boss is. My boss? He doesn't care. You live in your world, we live in ours. When those two worlds mix? Ours generally comes out on top. Now stop boring us and give us the money."

Kimiyo looked him over. "That attitude is not helpful."

"I don't really care." He picked up his fork and took another bite of his waffle. Bonto smiled and sipped his coffee.

Kimiyo reached into her bag and pulled out an antique silver cigarette case. She opened it and pulled out a cigarette. Kimiyo looked over the two men on the opposite side of the table. She tapped her cig twice on the silver case and lit it with a matching sterling silver lighter..

"I really wish you could have been more reasonable," she said. She took a long draw and leaned forward.

Kinty shrugged. "Maybe we're just not reasonable men."

"Maybe," Kimiyo said as she exhaled a cloud of smoke in their direction. Bonto let the smoke roll over him with an impassive look on his face. Then both men looked at each other.

Suddenly the two of them jerked, their hands going to their faces, which had bleached of color. They started to rise but both of them gripped the table and sat back down. Cole shoved away from the table, pulling his pistol and aiming at one, then the other. What the hell? He watched as both men blinked heavily and shook their heads. Neither of them reached for a weapon. Kinty grabbed for the water glass on the table and gulped it down.

"What...what was that?" he said. "What did you do?"

She turned to Cole. "Hold out your hands." He did so, shifting his pistol from one to the other as she sprayed his hands, torso, and face with a can. "Stay back and don't touch the table or them." He nodded.

"What did you do?" Bonto asked.

She held up the cigarette case. "Hemorrhagic fever in a clandestine delivery system. It works like a fast acting Ebola virus."

Both men began to breathe heavily. Cole took another step back and eyed the curtain in case they had friends outside.

"We've had shots..." Kinty said.

"No, I'm sorry, not for this," Kimiyo said. "This is new, right out of our labs. Mr. Kinty, you spoke of leverage earlier." She held up another canister. "This is my leverage. When Arulio is returned I will provide the antidote. One of you goes, one of you stays."

Cole saw them eyeing the canister with the antidote and motioned at them with his gun. "Stay cool, boys."

"You're lying," Bonto said.

"I'm sorry but I am not. Please understand how sorry I am about this."

"How long?" Kinty said.

She smiled at him. "You have about fifteen minutes."

"Jack will kill us," Kinty said.

"I already have," Kimiyo said.

Cole eyed them, waiting for them to do something stupid, but they just talked. After a moment, Kinty walked over to them.

"I'll go," he said.

Cole spoke up. "If anyone walks through that curtain except you and our man I'll kill them. You understand?"

Kinty nodded.

Cole pulled the curtain back and let him walk out, his gun steady on the other guy.

Cole took Kimiyo by an arm and moved her to the other side of the curtain entrance. "Stand over here, just in case he has friends outside and tells them where we are. Now, what were you thinking?"

"I'm managing a problem."

"By using fast acting Ebola virus?" Cole said. "Did they teach you that in business school?"

"Actually, they taught us the best way to resolve an issue was to use the resources at our disposal and to think independently. When you work for Saji Vy you just get different resources. What were you expecting?"

"I don't know," he said, "legal threats or some kind of red tape. I certainly didn't expect a designer virus."

"Perhaps we could discuss this later?"

Kimiyo moved back to the table. Cole looked at Bonto and saw he was holding a napkin up to his bleeding nose. "You don't look good. I hope your friend hurries."

— « o » —

Nathan and Duncan were across the street, facing the diner parking lot. They were huddled in the doorway of a building that looked like it had once been home to a real estate office. Now it was dirty and abandoned. It had a wonderful alcove, though. Nathan had used the Olympia G-net to scope the place out from the *Blue Moon Bandit* last night. A small rifle leaned against the door behind him, hidden by his body and the shadow of the recessed entranceway.

"Someone just walked out," Nathan said. "He's headed into the parking lot."

Duncan took a look. "That's one of the guys from the alley," Duncan said. "The one whose wrist Cole broke."

"Where's he headed?" Nathan said.

"Back of the lot. There's a van there," Duncan said, pointing it out. "He doesn't look good. He's kind of shuffling and coughing."

"He must not be taking his vitamins," Nathan said. "Yeah, look at him. He's going straight to that van."

— « o » —

Atomic Jack stared at Arulio with inquisitive, orange tinged eyes. The wetjack felt very self-conscious and tried to avoid his gaze by looking around the interior of the van but there wasn't much to look at. He was already feeling ill because he hadn't had his normal course of meds and nutritional supplements. When they had taken him these gangsters had failed to take his traveling bag, despite his protests.

"Your skin is so white," Jack said. "Is that a side effect of the conversion process?"

Arulio considered him. He was so strange in his bulky brown pressure suit. Its air pumps hissed loudly in the cramped confines of the van.

"Yes, the bleached appearance of my skin is indeed a side effect of my conversion. Your skin is very dark. This is an effect of your condition?"

Jack nodded inside the big glass helmet. "Yeah, my skin constantly regenerates when it's burned off."

"Does it hurt?"

"Burning? Like you can't believe," he said, shifting in his wide seat. "The regeneration isn't bad, though. It just itches like mad." He held up his gloved hands. "I can't scratch very well with these on."

"I would imagine not."

"I'm surprised someone would disfigure themselves willingly," Jack said. He gestured to himself. "I didn't have a choice in looking like this but you did."

Arulio paused again before answering. It was a habit that frequently annoyed those he conversed with, but he believed every answer required careful consideration.

"In life, we must frequently trade something precious for something we deem to be even more important. My physical appearance was the cost for my enhanced abilities. I weighed the choice carefully but it has been worth it, up to this point."

"Don't worry about your predicament," Jack said. "Your people got buckets of cash. They'll have you free in no time." He coughed slightly. A disturbing sight, Arulio noted, because his skin flared orange around his throat and jaw.

"This thing you can do," Jack said, "where you can intercept signals and data and things. It's satisfying?"

"Satisfying? At times it is euphoric."

"But the noise. Doesn't it become distracting?"

Arulio shook his head. He was uncomfortable talking to this criminal about such private things but felt like he had no choice.

"It's not noise. The signals, the data, they flow through me. I interpret what I want and ignore the rest."

Jack leaned forward in his suit. "You just filter it right out?"

"Parse it, actually."

"What if it's encrypted?"

Arulio started to tread carefully. "Some encryption is vulnerable, some is not. It depends."

"So if I got you close to a database that I need to crack, there's a good chance that you could get in, extract what I need?"

"My specialty is analysis, not breaking into networks or databases. It would be unethical to do what you are suggesting."

"Ethics don't play much of a part in what I do," Jack said. "Don't look shocked. I know what I am. I don't have any illusions of legitimacy. Stealing and extortion is how I make my living. With abilities like yours, though, I could run the table."

Arulio paused. Looking past Jack, out the back window of the van, he could see one of his men walking across the parking lot. It was the tall one called Kinty. He was holding a napkin against his nose.

"You have ethics."

Jack smiled. "I do?"

"Aboard the *Blue Moon Bandit*, when you were hurting Richie, you kept saying, 'you owe, you pay'. That is a rudimentary form of ethics."

Jack considered this. "I suppose so. Speaking of last night, why didn't you call Protective Services last night? You could have just got onto the net and whistled them up without us knowing."

Arulio was quiet for a moment. "I still could."

Jack shifted his position to lean in closer to Arulio. The wetjack was amazed how menacing the man could become with such subtle movements.

"I thought about calling for help but doing so would lead to questions about our journey. Those questions could put the hostages in danger so I refrained."

"Good choice," Jack said.

Someone banged on the side door of the van. "Open up, Jack. It's me," Kinty called.

Jack triggered the van's remote and the door opened. Arulio blinked against the sunlight. Kinty was bleeding from the nose and holding a wad of napkins against his face.

"They pay up?" Jack said.

Kinty shook his head. "Game's changed, Jack. I need to take him in."

Jack's scabbed brows furrowed. "What happened to you? What's going on?" Arulio watched Jack move through the door, his pressure suit banging awkwardly against the doorframe. "Tell me what's going on," he said.

Kinty's eyes were wide with fear. "Jack, my life depends on it."

"I don't care," Jack said while he looked him over. "Your eyes are bloodshot. Hell, they're bleeding."

"She poisoned me, Jack."

"Who? The girl?"

Kinty nodded. "Something like Ebola she said."

"Oh, bullshit. It doesn't work that fast."

Kinty opened his hand and held up the blood soaked napkins. "Look, Jack! I'm bleeding out here. She said it was something from one of their labs. I can feel the fever climbing up in me. My gut's on fire, Jack. Who knows what kind of stuff they make. She works for Saji Vy, for God's sake."

"And the deal is, trade the wetjack for what? An antidote? She gonna fix you up if you walk in there with that white skinned bastard? What do you think I'll do to you if we don't get paid?" He pushed Kinty against the van and leaned in until his glass dome touched his forehead. "I'll take care of this myself. Believe me. No way does that little girl get one over on us." He leaned back and let Kinty go. "Stay here and watch him. I'm going in there."

Kinty came up off the doorframe. "Can't let you do that, Jack." He grabbed Arulio and pulled him from the van. The wetjack stumbled because his hands were still tied.

"You don't have a choice, Kinty. I've never seen you like this before and I damn sure better never see you like this again."

They stood in the parking lot, eyeing each other. Arulio knew now would be the time to to back away from them but Kinty held him tight. The thug wiped his nose and fresh blood poured out, overwhelming the napkins. Kinty looked startled. He pinched his nose and yanked his gun loose from the holster under his jacket. Arulio stood impassively, reminded of a thousand violent videos he had seen on the net that played out similarly. Kinty raised the gun and pointed it at his boss. "Sorry, Jack."

The gun kicked, paused, and then kicked again. Jack turned his head in the great glass dome, a stunned look on his face. Then he exploded in fire as air rushed into the pressure suit. The oxygen in the air overwhelmed the carefully controlled environment and Atomic Jack burned. Kinty yanked Arulio back from the heat.

Jack stumbled and fell against the van, screaming as he went down. Arulio felt Kinty tug his arm.

"Let's get inside," he said.

— « o » —

"What the hell?" Nathan said.

"Looks like that capo just took out the kingpin," Duncan said. "Why would he do that?"

Nathan looked at Duncan. "Let's get them before the cops show up."

They hustled out of the alcove and crossed the street. Nathan kept the rifle tucked under his coat. He knew Duncan had a pistol in his hand hidden up his sleeve. They dashed into the diner a step after Arulio and the mob enforcer.

Nathan took a quick look around with a practiced eye. A waitress started toward them but Nathan waved her away and pulled out his rifle, keeping it pointed at the floor. "Hold on there, Kinty."

He turned and looked frightened, which was bad. Scared people made terrible decisions.

Kinty tightened his grip on the pistol he carried. Nathan raised his rifle. "Hold on there, don't..."

Kinty's arm flinched and Duncan fired at him from Nathan's right. The gun popped like a piece of blown bubblegum. The dart took Kinty in the throat and he fell to the floor twitching.

People in the diner jumped up from their seats. Nathan pointed the rifle in their general direction.

"All of you sit back down!" He said. "We'll be leaving shortly. Just relax and eat your eggs." The customers slowly lowered themselves to their seats.

Cole came out from behind the curtain with Kimiyo and the other enforcer from the alley. Bonto looked just as bad as Kinty. He was bleeding from his nose and eyes. Cole shoved him down to the floor beside Kinty.

"Did you shoot him?" Cole asked.

Nathan pointed at Duncan. "He did."

"Duncan shot someone? Really?"

"You don't have to sound that surprised," Duncan said.

"Well, we had this under control," Cole said. "You didn't have to shoot anyone." Kimiyo was on the ground, spraying something in the men's faces. She picked something out of Kinty's throat and held it up.

"What is this?"

"It's an info dart," Duncan said. "It does a hard data dump into the subject's subconscious, imparting short term knowledge in a massive dose. It's good for learning complicated subjects in a short time. The effect takes up a lot of brain processing power so the subject is usually unconscious during the data transfer." He pointed at Kinty. "He'll wake up with a very good working knowledge of Calculus."

Nathan nodded. "Well I was just going to shoot him with a regular bullet so your way is better."

Cole leaned down and spoke to Kimiyo. "Is that the antidote?"

She nodded. "Yes, it is. They will recover shortly with no side effects."

"Nathan," Cole said, "We should go."

"So let's go," Nathan said.

They walked out of the diner and Nathan pointed to a non-descript green van down the block and across the street. "That's us. While we were getting Arulio back I had Marla settle our bill and book us space at another ship yard. We still have to lay low for a few hours before our meeting with the Children of the Apocalyptic Rainbow."

Cole looked back into the parking lot where Atomic Jack lay with smoke rising from his suit. "My God. What did you guys do out here?" he said.

"Wasn't us," Nathan said, pausing to take a good look. The bookie's body was rolling around. Nathan couldn't believe that he might still be alive but he was moving nonetheless. That suit was really something. The van was on fire now and appeared to be melting into the pavement. "Kinty and Jack got into it and he popped him. Went up like a mushroom cloud." They walked quickly. "We should get out of here before Protective Services arrives."

"Got that right," Cole said.

The van pulled up to the *Blue Moon Bandit*'s landing pad and they piled out. Nathan tapped a code into the security panel and lowered the entrance ramp. "Everyone inside. I don't know if anyone back in that joint can identify us but there's no reason to take the chance. Hurry up." The crew hustled in. Kimiyo helped Arulio up the ramp. The wetjack moved slowly, irritating Nathan.

When they were aboard Nathan sealed the ramp and pushed a button on the ship's intercom. "Let's roll to the other site, Marla."

Nathan ran up the corridor. Everyone had gathered in the galley. "Buckle in," he said. "We're lifting off."

The engines whined as they started up. Nathan felt the ship lift off with a slight jerk and he gripped the table. He looked in the corner where Arulio sat with Kimiyo tending to him. "How are you doing, Arluio?"

"I am fine, Captain Teller. The bandits did not harm me."

"I have to take him back to his room for a full diagnostic test," Kimiyo said. They got up, Kimiyo leading Arulio by the arm, though he didn't seem to need the help. "Can you please let me know when you need to discuss the meet?"

"One hour," Nathan said. "We'll have a little briefing set up."

"We'll be there."

Chapter 18

Nathan watched as Marla steered the *Blue Moon Bandit* toward a landing pad at a nearby shipyard. The big, converted freighter did a pylon turn over a landing pad affording them a view of the area. Satisfied it was clear, she dropped the ship to the reinforced concrete pad. Its bulk settled softly on its landing gear.

Cole looked out a porthole from the operations deck located behind the cockpit. "Y'know, I thought the last place was bad but this looks like another few rungs down the ladder."

Nathan looked over his shoulder. "Our last parking spot was respectable enough but once things got loud," he looked at Cole, "we had to go." He straightened up. "This will do until we meet our contact in a few hours."

"You're blaming me for what happened at the diner?" Cole said.

"You were supposed to keep an eye on Kimiyo at the meeting. The next thing I know we're dealing with engineered viruses and a mob enforcer doing an imitation of a candle as he melts in a parking lot. Oh, and if anyone in that diner decides to talk or they manage to identify us from security camera images we'll probably have Olympia's Protective Services after us." His voice didn't rise, it rarely did. Sometimes that drove Cole crazy.

Cole threw up his hands and walked down the short corridor from the operations deck to the galley. "I'm not listening to this, Nathan."

Duncan's head lolled back in exasperation. "Come on, Nathan. None of this was Cole's fault."

Nathan turned to face the engineer. "No more than yours, right Duncan?"

"I was with you. How is it my fault?"

"You're the one who recommended we take Richie on the crew and he's the reason we had those guys chasing us in the first place."

Marla came out of the cockpit, a cross look on her face. "Don't you blame him, Nathan. You took Richie on the crew. You took this job and she's your ex-wife. All we've done is what you asked."

Nathan slammed his mug down on a workstation, spilling coffee over the rim. "This isn't about Celeste and don't pick sides Marla. Duncan can take care of himself. And so can Cole!"

"He's my husband. Who else's side would I be on?"

"It gets old is all," Nathan said. "It should have been a nice easy meet and now we'll be lucky if we're not in jail by the end of the night."

Cole walked back up the short passageway. "Nothing about this is easy. Nothing about what we ever do is easy. There are always complications. That's why we get jobs that pay well. We manage the complications."

Nathan lifted his mug. Outnumbered three to one on his own ship and another pair of troublemakers down below. It was undignified.

"Listen, maybe things have been a little more crazy than usual," he said.

"Maybe," Cole agreed.

"But the job is what the job is," Nathan said, finishing his thought. "We do it the same way we always do."

Cole looked at the coffee mug in Nathan's hand. "Maybe you need to stop drinking so much of that. You're really stressed out."

"Seriously," Marla said. "Do you realize how many pots a day you drink?"

Nathan eyed them. "It's the only thing that keeps me sane." He pointed at Cole. "You keep an eye on your new girlfriend. No more surprises. No more poisoning people, no more shooting anyone, and no more letting her run the show. You're in charge of her. I want her and her pet kept quiet and out of sight until they do what they need to do."

"You really think she likes me?" Cole said.

Nathan turned to Duncan, ignoring Cole's question. "You're the ship's engineer. Richie works for you. Get him up on his feet and keep him down in the engines. I want him working all the time. If he's got idle time he'll just find some way to screw things up. Put him on a leash if you have to."

"What about me?" Marla said.

"The usual, post-flight checklist, fuel status, you know," he said.

Nathan looked out the cockpit window at their surroundings. A wide, three-lane road ran in front of the landing pad. Across the road was a string of warehouses that had seen better days. A large one was directly across from their landing pad. It was made of steel and painted a dark blue with rust in places. It looked abandoned but he saw a group of men sitting on shipping containers, passing a bottle around. At least one of them appeared to be passed out on an upside-down plastic bin. Another one sitting on an industrial floor cleaner wore coveralls adorned with a rainbow logo.

"Keep the doors locked and the cameras up and running. We'll be lucky to get out of here without someone stripping off the hull plating for its recycling value."

— « o » —

A few minutes later, Cole was following Duncan down to the sickbay to check on Richie. "I hate when he's all riled up," Cole said. "A couple of things go wrong and we have to put up with him being cranky for the next couple days."

"Come on," Duncan said. "We're way outside our normal job description here. Cut him some slack."

Cole waved him off. "I know, I know. But his attitude has been crap since this whole thing started revolving around Celeste although he's still not as bad as he was right after the break up. Remember how bad that was?"

"As if I could forget."

"And now he hears her name again and bam! Instant jackass."

"Yeah, well, this whole thing will be over in a few days," Duncan said. "And then we'll get back to normal. Chasing deadbeats, sneaking around dark places."

"Yeah, let's check the kid."

They slid the door open to the small compartment. Richie was laying on one of two beds, flipping through movies on the ship's database. "Hey guys," he said. "You have some decent flicks, you know that? On the *Martha Tooey* I think everything was at least five years old."

Duncan jerked a thumb at Cole. "That would be him. He loves a good movie." He typed a command into the doc comp and started a series of diagnostics on Richie. A number of probes dropped from the mechanism over the bed. Richie stiffened as a blood pressure cuff tightened on his arm and a blood sample was extracted.

"How am I doing?"

"You'd be better off if your personal baggage didn't keep screwing things up," Cole said. Richie opened his mouth to protest and Cole put his hand up. Richie stopped immediately. "Your little gambling problem put all our lives at risk and left a guy shot and burning in a parking lot."

"Atomic Jack is dead?"

"Right now he's probably a pile of ashes being swept off the blacktop."

"Oh, thank God. Did you shoot him?"

"No, as much as I wanted to it was one of his guys."

"Which one?"

"Kinty. Anyway, I don't know if that solves your problem but when we get back to Go City you better figure it out. Nathan tells me he got your pay situation straightened around."

"Right, he did. I'll take care of things when we get back."

Cole nodded. "Good. I don't want to have this conversation again."

"'Course not."

"He checks out," Duncan said. "It's time for you to stop watching movies and get back to work."

"I'm still sore."

"Yeah, well, that's because someone burned off your nipple," Cole said. "You can have someone grow you a new one when we get home."

Richie turned to Duncan. "Can you give me something for the pain?"

Duncan scrolled down a list on the medical computer. "I think we have something here. You should know that stocking the medicine cabinet isn't a top priority for the cheapo who owns this ship." He thumbed the lock on the drug stores and rummaged inside the cabinet, brushing his dreadlocks out of the way. He selected a bottle and tossed it to Richie. "You're allowed two every six hours."

"You're already a gambler," Cole said. "Don't turn into an addict."

He swung down off the table. "I think I'll be able to handle it."

"I need you down in the port side engine room. We have a pump to change out."

"I thought maybe I could get some rest until the meet went down."

Cole smiled. "You thought wrong. You belong to Duncan now and it sounds like you have some work to do."

"Yeah, okay," he said. "I'll see you down there." The young man walked out of the sickbay and Duncan checked to make sure he was heading in the right direction.

"He's going to be a busy boy, isn't he?" Cole said.

"You have no idea."

— « o » —

Milo Gradzac sipped his whisky in the Heavy Dollar casino, eyeing the waitress working the booths in this section of the bar. She was a pretty little thing with blonde hair and a bright smile. If the meeting with the repo men went well tonight he thought he might be in the mood to celebrate. Given how nervous he was, though, he figured he might be celebrating alone.

The bar was inside the casino, just to the left of the main entrance doors. It was dim, with no windows to the outside. Milo thought that if someone sat in here long enough and drank enough a whole day could go by without noticing. He sat back in a corner booth, sinking into the worn leather. The bar was kind of retro, stealing decorating elements from a few different time periods and a few different worlds. The bar itself was some kind of imitation oak, or maybe not imitation. It would have cost a fortune on Earth thanks to deforestation over the last few centuries but Olympia was younger and had forest to spare. Chrome trim highlighted tables in some corners and dark walnut seemed to be the wood of choice in a section filled with booths across the way.

He grabbed a nut from the bowl on the table, munched it, and kept an eye on the door. This assignment was odd. He had never tested a wetjack. Milo had been the technology guru for the Children of the Apocalyptic Rainbow for three years. It was his job to keep the signal flowing which was better than sweeping hotel rooms or emptying garbage cans. Another nut snapped under his front teeth and he thought a little more.

He didn't particularly like the area around the casino because it was kind of rundown. The Heavy Dollar casino was in a converted warehouse district near the ocean. The area was being transformed, gentrified some might say. Along this strip, there were updated restaurants and clubs. A couple blocks in either direction, though, were streets and alleys that were done booming. Once the city had been built no one needed to ship and store freight as much as they used to. Milo had taken a taxi from the spaceport when he arrived and hadn't stepped outside since. He was pretty sure it would be possible to get mugged if he walked more than fifteen minutes up or down the street. Milo was used to playing it safe.

His left leg pumped nervously under the table, making it shake slightly and spreading little ripples in his glass of whisky. Why had Montario done this insane thing and more importantly, why had he agreed to help? He was in for ten percent of the take and only because three years of following the seven paths to enlightenment had done nothing to make him more confident. The Children of the Apocalyptic Rainbow had worked wonders on others but Milo was the same scrawny little guy with greasy skin and dark stringy hair that he had been when he joined.

The bar was moderately crowded, which was good enough for what they were doing tonight. If there were more people in here, there was more of a chance of being overheard. Any less and they would gain too much attention from the wait staff. His fingers tapped on the table.

The door opened and he saw a party of four enter the bar. A guy in a leather jacket, jeans, and dark glasses led them in, followed by a guy in a dark suit. They, in turn, were followed by a stunning Japanese woman in a leather jacket and skirt, and a tall, gangly freak with white skin sporting a leather suit better suited for some of the sex clubs down the road. That had to be the wetjack so this had to be the group he was meeting. He sat up straight and waved them over to his booth.

The guy in the suit led them over. "Are you Milo?"

"That's me. You're all from Saji Vy?"

"Right. I'm Nathan Teller. This is Cole, Kimiyo, and Arulio."

Milo pointed to the other side of the booth. "Have a seat." He looked around the bar quickly.

He watched as Kimiyo slid in the corner booth next to him, Arulio followed her, and then Nathan with Cole sliding in on the opposite end. Milo looked at each of the people in the booth and found them all staring at him.

"What do you need us to do?" Nathan asked.

"Um…"

"We've had a bad day, son. Don't keep us waiting."

Milo opened his mouth, suddenly dry, and started to respond when a waitress came over. They ordered drinks and resumed staring at Milo. He cleared his throat.

"Well, you've been invited here today to help us with a small problem."

"That's crap," Nathan said. "We're here to pay a ransom to you ridiculous people because you kidnapped a ship full of dead bodies. So let's get down to it."

"Mr. Teller, please don't think we've done this lightly. This is a tremendous opportunity for all of us," Milo said. "No one is in any danger and Mr. Vy's vessel and cargo will be returned immediately and in the same condition upon completion of our task." Milo was starting to sweat. He wiped his forehead with a cocktail napkin.

"And the *Charon*'s crew?" Nathan said. "I assume they will be returned in the same condition in which they were taken? Not all of the people on that ship were dead."

"Of course," Milo said. "The *Charon*'s crew is healthy and are being well treated."

"I want you to be sure about this, Milo. That ship was traveling through space and you people did something to stop it. I don't know what that was but I know it's damn hard to make a ship that's moving under its own power just stop so it can be boarded and hijacked. I'd like to know how you did that."

"I can't tell you that, Mr. Teller. All I can say is that we were able to stop and board the vessel without damaging it."

"Was it an inside job? Because that's generally how these things work, especially when a ship just stops moving all on its own."

Milo wiped his forehead again. "Mr. Teller, I know it may be hard for you to believe but we're a very capable group when we have to be. We didn't need help from the *Charon*'s crew to stop the vessel."

Nathan sipped his bourbon and considered it for a moment. "All right, Milo, what is it you want Arulio to do? What's the ransom for the ship's crew?"

Milo smiled, looking excited. "This will not be a problem for a wetjack of Arulio's capability."

"Excuse me, please, but how would you know what his capabilities are?" Kimiyo said. She raised an eyebrow in Milo's direction.

"Saji Vy has only a few wetjacks working for him. I knew that no matter which one was sent to assist us they would be up to the task but Arulio's accomplishments are legendary within the hacking community." Milo smiled as he said this. "In fact, may I just say what an honor it is to meet you sir?"

Kimiyo held up a hand and he looked at her. "Mr. Gradzic, I don't know what you've heard in your 'community' but Mr. Vy would not be pleased to hear about his business discussed openly."

Milo moved slightly away from her and glanced around the table. Four pairs of eyes glared back. "I didn't mean anything. I was just excited to meet Arulio."

"We got that from your gushing nerd love," Nathan said. "Now answer my question. What do you need Arulio for?"

Milo looked around again. He was relatively sure no one was paying attention to them. "There is a relatively large sum of money sitting in several accounts that we would like transferred to other accounts. We know where these accounts are, we have the numbers of the accounts, but we do not access to the accounts. We need the transfer to be accomplished quickly and without leaving a fingerprint."

"A bank job?" Nathan said. "You orchestrated all this to pull a bank job? Saji thought it might be some underhanded stuff like this."

Nathan pinched the bridge of his nose. "So where and when do we need to do this? Saji Vy wants it handled quickly, before the media becomes aware that several hundred dead bodies in his charge have been abducted. That only leaves us a few days before families start getting indignant and complaining."

"First things first. I need to send proof that he can accomplish the task."

Kimiyo set her Sake Martini down. "Please excuse me but I don't understand. A moment ago you were singing the praises of Arulio's reputation. Now you would like him to be tested? I'm afraid I don't understand."

"It's nothing that complicated." He shifted under the table and reached into his pocket. Cole held a steady gaze on him and slid his hand down likewise. Milo pulled a tablet from his pocket, noticed Cole staring at him and held it up. "Just a pocket tablet, man. No need to get jumpy."

"Keep your hands where I can see them," Cole said. "Don't reach into your pants again unless you tell me you're going to do it."

Milo nodded. "Right, sorry, I keep forgetting this isn't exactly on the up and up."

"That could be a problem, Milo." Nathan tipped his glass to the young man. "If you and your outfit treat this like anything other than what it is, you could get someone hurt."

Milo swallowed hard. "No worries, just a slip of the tongue." He looked at Cole and pointed to his shirt pocket. "I need to get something." Cole nodded permission. Milo pulled a card from the pocket and slid it across the table to Arulio's glass of ice water. The wetjack moved the glass and picked up the card.

"What is this?" Arulio said.

Milo pointed at the card. "That is a betting card used by the players in this casino. When you want to bet, you get one of these from the cashier and have it charged with whatever amount you want so you can wager. That card has exactly one Olympian dollar on it."

"Why?" Nathan said.

"You can't have a zero balance without one of the attendants hunting you down and asking to recharge it. I would like that card to be charged with ten thousand credits."

"From where?" Arulio said. "Is there a particular account from which you wish me to draw the funds?"

This time Milo tapped something on his tablet and held it up for Arulio to see. "This man has an account at 7th Commercial Bank of Olympia. Draw it from there."

"Is this somebody you have a grudge against, Milo?" Nathan said.

"No, I selected it at random from a list I was given."

"Are you sure? Because if this is some guy who stole an old girlfriend it could lead back to you and then to what we're doing. That would be bad."

"I'm sure, Mr. Teller. I can't reveal where the list came from but it's good information."

"He means one of the maids or janitors in one of the hotels gave it to him," Cole said.

"Not exactly," Milo said.

"Yes, Milo, that's exactly it," Nathan said. "I hope you guys planned your getaway better than you've planned everything up to this point."

"When does Arulio need to perform this task?" Kimiyo said.

"Now."

Cole laughed. "Right here? At this table? This is where you want to commit a few felonies?"

Milo nodded. "I need to know he's the real deal, so yeah, do it now, right here in front of me." He looked at all of them and picked up his drink. He was uncomfortable with the way Nathan was looking at him and finished it one gulp.

"It's all right," Arulio said in his soft voice. "I can do this. Just keep an eye out for anyone we wouldn't want to see."

Nathan looked at Cole. "Now I'm a lookout for a bank job."

Arulio picked up the casino card, turned it over, and ran his fingers across the back. He took a deep breath and closed his eyes. The wetjack sat silently for more than a minute before someone spoke.

Cole looked at Kimiyo. "Is he cool?"

"Yes," she said. "Arulio shuts off sensory input when he works. No sight or sound to distract him. He needs total concentration."

Cole pointed to Arulio's forehead. "He's sweating. That's okay?"

"The suit will compensate. It helps regulate his temperature. Arulio connects to networks and mines data with his mind. The stress of those endeavors can interfere with his body's ability to maintain a temperature within the prescribed safe range."

Arulio stiffened, released a deeply held breath, and his eyes opened. The wetjack turned to his right.

"The procedure is completed." He dropped the card on the table. Milo picked it up and noticed it was warm where his fingers had gripped it.

"That's it? I've seen wetjacks work before and they couldn't have done it that fast."

Arulio nodded. "The task is complete. You may check the balance on the card if you wish."

Milo held it between two fingers. "You broke into the customer card database here at the casino, the bank network, and the casino account network. You did all that in just a few moments? And transferred the funds?"

"If Arulio says the task is complete, you can trust him," Kimiyo said. "Perhaps you should verify the balance on the card."

Milo slid out of the booth and walked over to a slot machine just outside the entrance to the bar. He could feel four sets of eyes on his back. He slid the card into the machine and after a few seconds the balance displayed. He let out a low whistle

Milo sauntered back to the table with a grin on his face. He swung into the booth, sliding up to Kimiyo. "Worked like a charm, dear. Feel like partying tonight? I've got enough for a great dinner and some serious gambling."

Kimiyo looked at him and said, "I believe we would like to know where we can find the hostages and their ship. Can you please tell us that now?"

"No then, eh?" he said. "You're sure? No steaks? They raise fantastic beef here on Olympia. It's the real thing, not resequenced protein."

Kimiyo gave him a hard stare. He held up his hands.

"Okay, you have another small journey ahead of you." He slid a data chip across the table. "This holds the coordinates for your next port of call."

Nathan flicked it back across the table to Milo without picking it up. "We aren't going anywhere. Do you honestly think I'm going to fly all over this solar system so you can jerk us around with these ridiculous tests? This isn't a scavenger hunt, you know."

Milo pulled back as far as the booth would let him. "Mr. Teller..."

"Captain Teller," Nathan said.

"Right, Captain Teller, I'm not jerking you around. At least not on purpose. I was told to give you that chip if your wetjack passed the test. I'm just doing what I was told. Please, take the chip." He picked it up and held it out to Nathan.

Nathan took the chip. "What's your cut on this deal? You getting a good percentage?"

Milo nodded. "Ten percent of the take, which I understand will be substantial."

They got up out of the booth, lining up in front of it. "I hope it's worth it, Milo," Nathan said. "I don't like being pushed around like this and I have a long memory."

Milo shrugged. "Well, I hope it all works out. I'm exposed here too, Captain."

Nathan's group walked out. Cole turned back. "He really does have a long memory, Milo. Enjoy your night at the casino."

Milo gave them a minute to exit the casino and then looked around for the blonde waitress. Maybe he could still salvage the night.

Chapter 19

"Are you hungry?" Montario said as he and Celeste walked toward her room. "We can stop and grab something if you like. The cafeteria is right on our way."

"No," she said. "If you want something, though, go ahead."

They turned to walk in and Montario stopped. He saw Caleb Wooburn pouring himself a cup of coffee to go with the slice of pie he had sitting on the counter next to him. When he saw Montario across the room he waved. Montario returned it.

"Hold on," he said to Celeste. "That's Caleb. I should probably talk to him."

Celeste peeked around his shoulder. "He's the lifer you were telling me about?"

"Yes. He really shouldn't see us together. Why don't you go back to your room?"

She looked exasperated and he didn't blame her. "Alright," she said. "You know, after this is all over I don't think I'm going to step into a church of any kind for a long time."

"I don't blame you."

"Don't I need an escort? We're not supposed to be wandering around alone."

"That's not a problem. Your best friend is right there." Montario waved his hand to someone at the end of the hallway and Linda, the girl who had been serving Celeste meals hurried over.

"Linda, could you please escort Celeste back to her room? We've just finished a private study session."

The young woman smiled and said, "Of course." She turned to Celeste. "You can tell me all about what you've learned. I would be happy to answer any questions you have."

"Thank you so much," Celeste said.

Montario watched them go and entered the cafeteria grabbing his own cup of coffee and slice of pie. He made his way over to the table where Caleb sat.

"Mind if I sit down?"

Caleb gestured to a chair, "Please."

Montario sat down, reached for the sugar, and spooned in two helpings. "I hear the new office on Temple is doing well."

Caleb nodded. "Very well. There's a good group of people there. That new girl, Melissa? She'll make a great office manager. Pretty too. Whoo boy." He threw Montario a wink.

Montario took in Caleb with his greasy smile and wondered how he could be so successful working with people. "That's great. We had hopes for her. She's got the head for business, some schooling. I'm sure the office will do well."

"Oh yeah," Caleb said, leaning back. "Our reputation on Temple is growing. The office was flooded with requests. Give it six months and they'll have a hundred people employed. Our adherence to the principals is being rewarded."

"And allowing our good work to continue." Montario raised his cup. "You've done good work Caleb. Thank you." Caleb put his head down and Montario saw him flush. The odd son of a gun still liked praise.

"To see our good work spread, Montario, to see so many people come to us and find healing in the principals we espouse? Well, let me tell you, it makes me feel like there's no higher calling. Our work? It is fulfilling. It runs deep and wide through our lives and the lives of those we touch."

"Your faith in our teachings is strong, Caleb. We're lucky to have you."

This time Caleb raised his mug. He looked around the cafeteria and saw that it was empty. That was rare given the unusual hours kept by most of the believers at the base. He leaned in close to Montario.

"Hey, I wanted to ask you about that girl I saw you with. I heard we had some new folks here at home base."

"Oh her? I wouldn't exactly call her a girl. Celeste is well into her thirties. Their ship had some trouble."

"Still looks pretty good, though, huh?" Caleb said, giving his eyebrows a quick raise.

Montario grinned. "I suppose so. I've got Greg and some of his crew giving them a hand. I don't think it will take too long. You know how good that ol' boy is."

Montario watched as Caleb went after his pie like an animal, scooping several bites up in quick fashion. He chewed a bit and finally swallowed. It took some effort and most of his coffee to get it down.

"Yeah, Greg will get them up and running. What's the problem anyway?"

Montario's eyes narrowed. "With what?"

"Their ship. What happened to it?"

"Oh, that. I'm not sure. They may have taken a micrometeorite strike in the drive compartment. Something like that. Whatever it is, I'm sure Greg can suss it out."

"How many guests do we have here?"

"From the ship?"

"Yes."

"Oh, her and a few others. I think it's five altogether."

"Montario, why are you keeping these people locked in their rooms?"

He was taken aback for a moment. It was clear Caleb had been speaking to someone about the crew of the *Charon*. "Caleb, come on, they're not locked in their rooms. You just saw Celeste walking with me."

"Well, hell Montario, I wouldn't leave her locked up either. She's a looker. A real nice piece."

"It's not like that, Caleb. I asked them to stay in their rooms because they aren't like us, you know? They haul cargo. They spend a lot of time on their own, out there between planets and between stars. I didn't want them taking advantage of anyone here. We have quite a few attractive young women here and some of them can be very naïve." Montario raised his own cup. "But I don't need to tell you that, do I?"

"That we have attractive women here? No, Montario, I've noticed. Or were you inferring something else."

Montario smiled. "I believe I imply and you infer, Caleb."

Caleb grimaced. "Fine. Are you implying something?"

Montario held up his open hands. It was well known Caleb was a bit overly friendly with the new inductees. Montario knew he was currently seeing Linda and at least one other woman on the side.

"Look Caleb, when I took over from Bobby Forluck he told me about how you liked the new arrivals. He told me how you would review their files before they arrived, how you would bump into them as they got acclimated to the place and how you always seemed to find a pretty one to spend time with. It always struck him as vaguely creepy."

Caleb's eyes smoldered but he didn't raise his voice. "That's not exactly true."

"I think it is. And I think that's why you immediately assume my relationship with Celeste is sexual in nature rather than professional."

"She's been seen coming and going from your quarters, Montario. Don't play holier than thou with me. And let me tell you something about Bobby Forluck. He was well known for having attractive young women meditate with him. Don't kid yourself about him. There have been plenty others in the twenty years I've been here, at least half a dozen leaders. They all had good times here."

"I know all about Bobby Forluck," Montario said. "I have no illusions about him. I also don't have any illusions about what goes on here. I get that people like the openness of the lifestyle we have. It's attractive for some people. Just don't let it get in the way of doing your job."

Caleb shrugged. "Never have before."

"Good. I understand your next assignment begins in a week or so?"

"That's right. We have a new office opening on the largest southern continent on Olympia. It should be just as successful as the one we just opened."

Montario stood up. "Okay, then spend your time preparing for the new office. Let me know who you will be taking with you."

"Okay. Have a good night."

"You too." Montario walked toward the doorway, reconsidered and, scooped up a couple of sandwiches from the refrigerator before leaving the cafeteria. Celeste might be hungry regardless of what she said. He turned right in the corridor and headed toward her room.

— « O » —

Caleb watched him go and considered how different things had been for the last year, since Montario had become leader. He had come to them the same way each of the previous half dozen leaders had come. The current leader had a vision during meditation. In the vision, the universe provided the name of the next leader. Terms of service could last for months or years. The members of the group would search for the new leader and convince them to join the Children of the Apocalyptic Rainbow. In Caleb's experience, leaders never came from within. For some reason Caleb could not fathom, the universe only selected outsiders for the post of leader.

Montario was odd, though. In the last year, since Bobby Forluck had left and Montario had come on, the group had expanded quickly, growing faster than at any time Caleb could remember. In fact, he was constantly on assignment now. He hadn't been at Port Solitude for more than a few weeks at a time all year. Was Montario an aggressive leader or was something else going on?

They had accepted Montario as leader based on Bobby Forluck's word. His vision had lead them to Montario and, after a few week's cajoling, they had convinced the man to come here and be the new leader of the Children of the Apocalyptic Rainbow. They really knew nothing about him.

Caleb stared at Montario's coffee mug. He grabbed it, carefully, and walked over to a cabinet. He withdrew a plastic bag used for leftovers and dropped in the cup. He zipped it tight and walked back to his quarters. He had a friend on Olympia in Protective Services. Maybe he could tell him a little bit more about Montario after a DNA scan.

Chapter 20

"Does this happen a lot?" Richie asked. "You guys get left behind while everyone else goes out?" He walked into the galley where Duncan and Marla were sitting. The lights in the room were low and they were in the booth sharing dinner. Duncan looked up at him in annoyance.

"What's the matter, kid? Feeling left out?" He picked up a glass of wine and took a sip. The remains of steak, broccoli. and baked potatoes were on their plates.

Richie moved over to the fridge and pulled out a beer. "Come on, Duncan. Every time something important happens we get left on the ship." He twisted the top off the bottle and studied the label. He found it adequate and took a pull. "They go to meet with the guys holding my note and I'm not allowed to come. They go to meet with this guy about our job and we don't get to go. It's like they don't trust us."

Marla gave a little laugh. "Oh no, Richie, don't drag us into this. It's your ego that's bruised. Let me guess, you want to get in on the action, right?"

"It would be better than sitting around all the time."

"I gave you plenty of work to do," Duncan said. "Why aren't you doing it?"

"Don't worry, boss, I'm almost finished. I've got a diagnostic running on the crawl system and I checked our repair job on the drive housing. Everything is just as it should be." He took another swig of his beer. "And Marla, it's not so much action I want as fresh air or sunshine. I'm just stuck down in those engines. Believe me, I've had my fill of trouble with the kind of guys we can run into."

Marla began clearing the dishes from the table. "Look Richie, this is the job. We're the support team. We keep the engines running and stay ready to run if things get hot. Nathan and Cole do the deal. They're the face men."

"It's not about the adventure, kid," Duncan said. "It's about getting paid. We work for a living. We get a job, we go out, find a ship for a paying client and return it to them. Collecting that paycheck is why I get up in the morning. At some point Marla and I want to retire and we would like to do it before we're too old. So I keep the ship running and she drives it."

Richie scratched his head. "I know what you're saying, Duncan. I do."

"Nah, not yet you don't but you will," Duncan said. Marla stroked his dreadlocks as he spoke. "Look, we've been in some rough spots over the years. Getting threatened and having guns pulled on you is no fun. You probably know that by now, though."

"I do."

"So don't worry about spending so much time on the ship. This is a good gig. Marla and I figure we only have a few more years and we're done. We'll have enough money to buy a little place somewhere and enjoy sandy beaches."

"This job pays that well?"

"It does. Especially if you don't waste your pay. Remember though, the ship has to fly which means hours in the engines turning wrenches. This ship needs a lot of care, too. She's mostly solid but nothing here is standard. We've customized a lot."

"My man has reworked every system on this ship," Marla said, "and the *Blue Moon Bandit* will get up and go. The problem is that her structure can't always deal with it. The stress can bust her joints and break her back if Nathan and I don't handle her just right."

"I've seen ships like that before," Richie said. "Private yachts mostly, whose owners modify them for races or for outrunning pirates."

"You've served on those?"

"A couple. You learn to get off those crews before some cowboy tries to do circles around a comet and forgets to calculate the gravity quotient properly. I was also on a smuggler's ship once. Didn't know that until it was too late, though."

Duncan gestured for Richie to sit down. "What were they running?"

"Tax free liquor."

Duncan laughed. "You were running moonshine? Really?"

"Hold on, there. This was good hooch, I was told later on. Not the rotgut you get on some outer rim bars. We picked up a couple hundred barrels from Europa and took the long way to Enceladus. Jupiter to Saturn, you know? Should have been an easy trip. I thought we were hauling lubricants and etching acid to a mining colony. Anyway, we get jumped by a Protective Services cruiser. The captain almost crapped himself."

"I bet," Marla said. "Protective Services loves to bust smugglers."

"Oh yeah, they came right in on us. The captain panicked."

"Hit the thrusters? Tried to run?" Marla said.

"Yeah and he thought he would throw in some evasive maneuvers. He must have thought he was in a holovid, you know? He firewalled the throttle and started jinking all over the place. Up, down, zig zagging like crazy. The whole time Protective Services just hung back and waited for us to make up our mind about what we were going to do. I'm down in the engine room watching gauges red line and I can see this old junker isn't going to take much."

"What finally gave? Was it the maneuvering thruster relays?"

"No, way worse than that. All his gyrations popped the cargo hold doors. Twisted them right out of the frame, broke the seal and whoosh, everything in the hold blew into space." Richie had his hands spread wide above his head. "Hundreds of barrels, some machine parts we had for cover, and a bunch of supplies. The atmospheric venting blew us out of control."

"You got it under control though?"

"Oh, sure. The captain really was a decent pilot. Once he got the ship under control we got boarded and he was arrested."

"Not you though? That was good luck," Duncan said.

"None of the crew was arrested. The captain came clean. Pretty decent I thought."

"Yeah," Duncan said. "That could have been worse. I've served on some rough ships myself. Every decent pilot thinks they can be a captain."

"Not me," Marla said. "Once you're the captain you never get to fly. You have to run the ship, manage the crew, and find jobs. Real pilots like to fly."

"Okay, every other decent pilot wants to be a ship's captain. The point is there are a lot of ships flying around with captains that aren't as decent as they could be. Even Nathan has his moments."

Richie grinned. "Yeah?"

Duncan smiled. "Yeah, he can make some decisions that leave you guessing sometimes. One time, back when Celeste was his co-pilot, we took a job getting this wreck back for a private lender. No bank involved, you see, just some guy who came into the office."

"This was Celeste, his ex-wife?" Richie said.

"Right, she was the co-pilot before Marla," Duncan said. "Anyway, this guy walks into the office. Hard Six Harry was his name. He was kind of tall and lanky and about a million years old. He was a real cowboy, too.

"He had it all," Duncan said. "He was wearing a mustard yellow suit with a matching ten gallon hat and had the most remarkable bushy gray handlebar mustache drooping down that you've ever seen. The only thing missing was a gun belt and a six shooter.

"We were all sitting in the office," Duncan said, "because things were slow. We hadn't had a job in weeks. It was one of those little dry spells that pops up once in a while." He adjusted his seat and poured himself another glass of wine and topped off Marla's glass. "Anyway, he lays out a rap to Nathan about how he loaned money to a pilot to buy a ship and this woman stopped making payments. Harry hadn't heard from her in months and the ship was nowhere to be seen. Things were slow so Nathan takes the job."

"His name was Hard Six Harry? What's that mean?"

"We asked him that too but Cole already had an idea," Duncan said. "He gambles a lot. Hard Six Harry was a starship dealer, mostly used private stuff and he self-financed a lot of sales at exorbitant rates."

"Yeah, I've seen guys like him," Richie said.

"We asked him about his name and he tells us that back when he got started, he was short on cash. He claimed he walked into a casino and made a bet at the craps table. Do you play?"

Richie shook his head. "No."

"He bet that the shooter, the dice thrower, would throw a six by rolling two threes before he throws it the easy way, like a two and a four."

"Or a seven," Marla said.

"Oh yeah, or before the shooter rolls a seven."

"That sounds like a hard bet."

"It is," Duncan said. "Harry claims he won the bet and raked in a pile of credits, enough to keep him in business and let him expand. He said he'd been doing just fine ever since. He even ended up marrying a waitress from the casino's bar."

"So what's the problem?" Richie said. "It sounds like any other job from what I've heard."

"That's what we thought aside from Hard Six Harry being a little goofy. But his credits were good so we took the job. We ask around, do some legwork, and find out that the ship might be as close as Mars. We all saddle up and take a flight to the red planet."

"Did you find it?"

"Oh yeah, we found it, and called it in to Harry as per his instructions. It was a nice little two passenger long range shuttle. It was cherry too, just great for hopping around the solar system. You could probably get as far as Saturn before you had to refuel."

"Stay on topic, dear."

"Yes, Marla. Anyway, we put a hold on the ship with the dock master and the next morning we start the repossession process. We all go to the dock master, because this seemed like an easy one. We show him the paperwork from Hard Six Harry and prepare to take possession of the shuttle. While we're doing that, this blonde walks in, says she's leaving and wants to settle her bill for docking."

"Let me guess," Richie said. "It was her shuttle."

"Bingo," Duncan said. "At this point, Nathan had to inform her that we're there to take possession of the ship. Of course, a great deal of shouting and arguing ensued. The blonde claims the shuttle is hers free and clear and that there isn't any lien or note against it. She produces a bill of sale and title."

"Oh man," Richie said.

"Uh-huh. Things weren't looking good. The dock master is one of those guys that's been doing his job so long you'd think they built the dock around him. He asks for the letter of consent from the owner and a copy of the loan paperwork. Nathan's got the letter but not a copy of the loan paperwork."

"Oh boy," Richie said.

"Yeah," Duncan said. "Documentation is usually something Nathan is very strict about because it avoids problems like this. All that prep work ahead of time means less hassles later on. So anyway, Nathan's in a spot because he can't prove the lady skipped out on the loan. He was working a deal to call back to Go City and get the paperwork when Hard Six Harry bursts into the dock master's office."

"He flew in from Earth to get the ship?"

"No, man. Harry pulls a knife and starts screaming at the lady. He wants to know how she could leave him, didn't she know how much he loved her, and where did she think she was going anyway?"

"Damn. She was the cocktail waitress?"

"You bet. Her name was Goldie. We all stand up and try to back away from the man we're now thinking about calling Crazy Harry but the office is small. There's really nowhere to go and no way to get away from this sweating, screaming madman holding the knife. He keeps accusing his wife of cheating on him, she keeps telling him to leave and Nathan is doing this low, even voice thing that is supposed to calm Harry down but really, it's just pissing him off because he thinks Nathan is patronizing him."

"So what happened?"

"Hard Six Harry's finally had enough, you know? He says, 'why did you run off with Bill?'"

"Who?"

"Apparently Bill was Harry's mechanic. Anyway, Goldie, steps forward and says, 'Why did I leave? 'Cause your mean and I'm tired of your wrinkly old ass laying on me on Saturday nights.'"

"Jeez."

"That lit his fuse. Harry gets a wild look in his eye and starts swinging the knife. I'm thinking this is going to have a bad ending and then Cole steps up, grabs Harry's wrist, twists it until we hear it snap and then he takes the knife away from him. Harry collapses in pain and Goldie punches Cole. He was so surprised he backed up and Goldie dropped to the floor hugging Harry, holding his head to her chest and stroking his back."

"You're kidding," Richie said.

"I'm really not. We walked out of the office because domestic disputes are way outside our scope of work. We got back on the ship and flew home. The last we saw of Harry and Goldie they were sitting in that dock masters office hugging one another and professing their love."

"That's crazy."

"True but the point of the story is that if Nathan had followed procedure and got a copy of the loan papers we would have known Harry was a lunatic looking for his wife instead of his lost ship."

"Wow. I guess anyone can be a bad captain."

Duncan nodded. "This is what I'm saying."

They heard a noise and Duncan got up from the table. He checked a monitor on the wall and turned back to Richie and Marla. "They're back."

Nathan led his group into the galley and Cole and Kimiyo sat in chairs at one end of the table. Cole looked at the low lights and wine glasses and laughed. "Did we interrupt something, big guy? Maybe a little dinner for two on the *Blue Moon Bandit* in this lovely garden spot? Did you get the wine from those booze hounds enjoying the burn barrel on the next landing pad over?"

Kimiyo gave him an elbow to the ribs. "You're awful."

"Cut the crap," Nathan said. "We've got to look at this data chip and see where we're going next."

Duncan took the chip. "What's this?"

"The next stop on this scavenger hunt." He explained what happened at the casino. Duncan pulled out a small pocket computer and inserted the chip.

"Well, there's no games here. Just a set of coordinates and a date and time," Duncan said. He showed it to Marla. "Do you know where this is, honey?"

She started up an application on the device that would map the coordinates. It ran for a few seconds and presented a map and whatever additional information the database contained about the location.

"It's a small moon colony named Port Solitude," she said. "It looks like it orbits a gas giant named Hubbard. It's about a day away at cruising speed. Anyone ever hear of it?"

"I have," Cole said. "It's not the nicest place. Lots of criminal activity. When I was a marshal I was there a few times chasing fugitives down."

"Like what," Nathan said.

"Just name it. Piracy is real big there. Ships go missing all the time."

"That sounds just like what happened to the *Charon*."

"Yeah. It's also a place to hire unsavory characters to get other things done. If you need to put a crew together to pull a robbery, or some other job, you can find people there, if you know where to look."

"What's the colony's claim to fame?" Nathan said. "Mining, agriculture, industry, or something else?" He looked at the data on the small computer. "There's not much here in the database."

"It doesn't really have a claim to fame," Cole said. "The few times I was there it was pretty depressed. There was some mining, I think for bauxite, and some agriculture. I remember one guy we were looking for was working at a factory where they bottled pickles."

"Pickles?"

"Apparently the colony exports good pickles. I can't speak to how good they are, personally. I don't especially like them. They canned other vegetables for export too. Apparently you can grow stuff there. There's also a sizable port that attracts ships for export work. This stuff doesn't pay well so you get a lot of low life's working side deals. Protective Services tries to keep an eye on the place but the colony just doesn't have enough money for proper staffing."

"There's something else about this place," Duncan said. "Port Solitude is the home base for the Children of the Apocalyptic Rainbow." He was looking at the pocket computer and scrolling through the pages.

Nathan arched an eyebrow. "Yeah?"

Duncan nodded. "You bet. It looks like they've got a place right outside the main colony."

"Then maybe we're getting to the end of it."

"Nathan, are we leaving tonight or in the morning?" Marla waved her wine glass in the air. "I've been holding back in case we had to fly out."

"Just get us up and lock in the auto pilot. I think we could all use a good night's rest before tomorrow."

She nodded and squirmed out of the booth. Nathan followed her up to the cockpit. Duncan nudged Richie. "Let's get to the engine room. We can make sure everything holds together."

— « o » —

Cole and Kimiyo were alone in the galley. She looked at him. "You don't have a job to help with the launch?"

"Sometimes I help Duncan but he's got his very own assistant now so he won't need me." He opened a bottle and swigged some down. "How about you? Do you have to check on Arulio?"

"No, he's fine. He's in sleep mode and my pocket comp will alert me if any of his readings get wonky."

"That was some fracas at the diner. I like the way you handled yourself." He took her hand. "You had a good plan and executed it pretty well. Ruthlessly you might say."

"You weren't so bad yourself. I couldn't believe how fast you got the drop on those men." Her fingers stroked his hand lightly. It felt like a shock going through him.

"I didn't have much choice. We did make a pretty good team though."

"Yes, we did."

He kissed her, pinning her against the counter with his hand on the back of her head. She tried to pull him closer, grinding in. They broke apart as the engines started.

"My room," he said. "It's closer."

— « o » —

Outside, on the next landing pad over, the booze hounds took note as the *Blue Moon Bandit* prepared to lift off into the night sky. She hovered over the pad for a moment, as if getting her bearings. The four landing struts folded into their housings and the ship oriented itself to the correct heading. Then the big twin engines at her rear flared bright blue and white. She moved into the traffic pattern above them and disappeared a moment later.

"Hey Tom," one of them said to another. "Isn't that the ship that guy wanted you to watch?"

The one named Tom was propped against a crate, dozing. He opened one eye and looked across the pad. "Ayuh, that's the one. She just leave?"

"Just lifted off. You still have the mobi that guy give ya?"

"Ayuh, I'll send him word."

The old drunk texted a message and closed the mobi, slipping it back into the dirty coveralls he was wearing. The coveralls with the logo of the Children of the Apocalyptic Rainbow on the back.

"When that fella gives you the reward for doing that, you make sure I get my cut. You was dozin' but I was keeping an eye out."

Tom nodded. "Ayuh, Jimmy, you did a good job there. I'll make sure to remember you." His head drooped and he fell back asleep.

Chapter 21

An hour later, Montario's mobi beeped and he picked it up off the nightstand next to the bed. Celeste didn't move, though. She was a heavy sleeper. The message told him the *Blue Moon Bandit* had launched from its pad on Olympia. He called up his bank account and transferred a thousand credits to the account of the guy who sent the message. A week prior, Montario had Milo out at the landing pads handing out cheap G-net enabled mobis and explaining that there was a reward to watch out for a ship. A couple days ago, when they learned which ship would be carrying the wetjack, they'd sent messages to the mobis and sure enough they'd got an answer. One of the Rainbow members who had a drinking problem was hanging out at the same space-port where the ship had landed. That member had sent in a picture of the ship on the landing pad for confirmation and now it was gone. That made sense. Nathan and his crew had finished up with Milo just a few hours ago. Now came the hard part.

He started thinking about what was left to do and what could trip them up. Milo had confirmed the authenticity of the wetjack so Saji was playing the game straight so far. Milo had mentioned they should be careful though. The captain of the *Blue Moon Bandit* seemed to have a temper.

Caleb could also turn into a problem. Montario would have preferred him to be away from Port Solitude while the deal went down. The problem was he couldn't think of anything to keep him busy at the moment.

Celeste stirred and looked up at him. "What's up, baby?"

"Group business," he said, holding up the mobi. "It never ends."

"Really?" She snatched the mobi away from him and rolled out of bed. "Are they on their way? Did you get a message?"

He enjoyed the sight of her walking around the room without clothes. She scrolled through the messages and stopped walking.

"What the hell is this?"

He lit a cigarette and raised an eyebrow. "What?"

"This ship? This is the one bringing the wetjack?"

"Yup."

"The *Blue Moon Bandit*?"

"Uh-huh. Is something wrong?"

She threw the mobi at him. He caught it and looked at the picture. "Yeah, something's wrong," she said. "It's my ex-husband. The repo guy I told you about."

"He owns this ship?"

"Yes. Why is he the one bringing the wetjack here?"

Montario got up and pulled on a pair of exercise pants and a t-shirt. "I have no idea, honey. I sent the demands to Saji and told him where to meet Milo.

She pulled her clothes on and sat on the bed rolling up her socks. Playtime was over, Montario noted. "This is not good. Not good at all. We do not want them coming here."

Montario laced up a pair of running shoes. "Why not, babe? Everything is running to schedule so far."

"Why not?" she said. "I'll tell you why not. Nathan and his crew are smart. Outwitting people is what they do. Did I ever tell you about them?"

He looked at her."You told me he was a repo man. And you told me you didn't like the life."

"Right, well, he's very good at what he does. Very good."

"I'm still not seeing a reason to be concerned."

She came around the bed. "Nathan gets back all kinds of vessels. He finds people that don't want to be found, and he finds where they've hidden starships they don't want found. It doesn't matter where they are. As long as he is getting paid, he'll find the ship."

"Yeah, well, since we've already told him where we are I don't see that as a problem," Montario said.

"Don't be a dick about this," Celeste said. "Once he finds the person he plays on their weaknesses and personality until he can scope out where their ships are and then he cons his way onboard. He has never failed at finding and retrieving a ship. Ever."

Montario shrugged. "Look, he's a glorified taxi driver in this instance. He brings the wetjack here and the guy does what we ask him to do. There are no angles to play, no weaknesses to exploit. If Saji wants his ship back, and it appears he does, then everyone will play nice."

"Where's the ship, Montario?"

"It's up in orbit, Celeste. What was I supposed to do? Put it in the closet?"

"Right, just sitting up there in orbit. All by itself."

He sighed. "It's not by itself. There's a couple guys on it doing housekeeping stuff. I wanted to make sure there were no problems with it leaving once our business is conducted. I assume your ex will have an engineer look it over before we all agree the deal is done?"

"Of course."

"Well then no one will be sneaking onboard and making off with the ship. Besides, Saji wouldn't leave you and the rest of your crew here."

She laughed. "Are you serious? If Nathan can grab that ship and never put the wetjack in a position to do anything illegal or dangerous, he'll do it in a minute. I would be very, very surprised if Saji didn't order him to do just that. It's the least risk with the greatest reward."

"Saji would leave you here?"

"No. If he gets his ship back he'll call Protective Services and tell them we're being held here. You know what else? He'll do it the minute he has his ship back. You'll never see it coming."

Montario considered her argument. He was a grifter and a good one. He was good at figuring the angles. Hell, he'd been conning these kids and living the good life for more than a year now. Celeste was smart and clever. And just about as ruthless as anyone he had ever met. She might be on to something.

"Okay, let's assume what you're saying is a possibility. Would your ex, Nathan, really fly out of here with the *Charon* and leave you here? Remember, he doesn't know what we're capable of. He doesn't know what we would do to you if we don't get what we want."

She laughed. "After the way we parted? He'll want to give me as much grief as possible." She closed the distance between them with two soft steps. "Don't expect my presence here to give you any favor with him."

"Wow, babe. You make friends wherever you go." He stubbed his cigarette in an ashtray on the nightstand. "What was so bad about your break up?"

She shook her head. "It's nothing I want to talk about."

"So it was your fault, huh?"

She gave him a glare. "I said I didn't want to talk about it."

He held his hands up. "All, right, all right, I'll get a few more guys up on your ship. Maybe I'll send Caleb up there. Get him out of our hair."

"Good idea. That might give you a chance at getting our money."

"As long as you're here," he said, "can you tell me anything about this guy and his crew? Anything we can use to get up on them?" Montario looked her over. There was no reason to treat this development as a negative when it could so easily become an opportunity.

Celeste sat down on the bed and thought about it. "I don't know. Nathan doesn't smoke; he doesn't drink, at least not more than anyone else. He doesn't do any kind of drugs, even the ones that are legal."

"What about gambling?"

"Nathan? No way. All he does is sit in the pilot's seat of that ship and grind out the credits. If he gambled and lost, it would just piss him off. He'd obsess over how much work it would take to make it back."

"He sounds like the most boring person I've ever heard of. Why did you marry him?"

She shrugged. "I was young, he was older. He knows how to treat people, especially women. He listens, knows how to give a compliment. He has an excellent reputation as a pilot so when he tells you he noticed you or something you did, you light up a little bit."

"Yeah, but he sounds like a real tightwad."

She screwed her mouth up before she answered, thinking hard. "Not exactly. He's tight, don't get me wrong but when he cares about someone, he makes things happen. He wants his women to know how much he appreciates them. There were trips and gifts. He understood romance, you know?" She paused for a moment, remembering something. "He just really got set in his ways."

"You're not giving me a lot to work with here. I'm looking for an edge, some way to get over on this guy."

"What do you want me to say? There's not much there." She got up from the bed and moved to the door. "I'm going to go back to Captain Geechy and let him know that our 'ordeal' may be over soon."

"Try to act like this has been hard on you. Don't smile too much." He lay back on the bed and considered his partnership with Celeste. After a minute, he grabbed his mobi and called Caleb to make some preparations.

— « o » —

Nathan walked into the cockpit and slumped into the left-hand pilot's seat. Marla looked up at him, headphones wrapped around her head. They were the good kind, he noticed. Not the cheap ones or the crappy little buds some people favored. Marla took her music seriously and was grooving to something she liked, he could tell. She touched a button on her console and slipped the headphones off.

"How far out are we?" he asked.

"About two hours," she said. We're coming up on traffic approach so I just started cutting our speed."

"Good. How's it look?"

Marla touched one of the monitors in front of her and passed an image of the moon over to Nathan's console. It wasn't yet visible through the cockpit glass but the telescopes could pick it up. It was a strange looking place. The atmosphere was blue-green and striped with puffy white clouds. It certainly wasn't the majestic blue marble that Earth was from lunar orbit, but it was welcoming enough.

"How about traffic? Is the sky crowded?"

Marla nodded. "Not a lot of passenger traffic but there's dozens of freighters in the traffic pattern. Mostly around the three space stations they've got up in orbit. Cole said they export food, right?"

"Yup."

"Well, there you go. They'll be loading outbound transports for shipping to colonies and long range explorers who need to re-supply."

"I don't suppose traffic control is identifying the vessels in orbit?" Nathan smiled at her.

"Sorry, Nathan. They aren't going to make it that easy for us. Unless we happen to fly by the *Charon* and see it out the window I don't think we're going to spot it in orbit."

"What about reading the *Charon*'s transponder signal? Saji gave us the frequency and the code." Every starship had a transponder that broadcasted its identification. They were used for traffic control.

Marla nodded. "Now there's a better chance of that happening than just seeing it. We can listen for the transponder once we're in orbit. It's pretty much line of sight but we've been lucky before. I'll be listening."

"Good. Who are you listening to?" He pointed to her headphones.

"A new band Duncan and I heard in a club last week called Chrome Sunrise."

"They any good?"

"Not too bad. You may like them. I'll send a copy to your entertainment unit." She touched a monitor and slid a file from one folder to another with her finger.

"Thanks. I'm going to give the ship the once over before we land, make sure your husband and his sidekick have been keeping us running smooth."

Marla shook her head. "You know my man holds this bucket together. There's no reason to worry about him."

"Could we please not refer to my pride and joy as a 'bucket'?"

She looked over at him. "This is how you take care of your pride and joy?"

"Things are a little tight right now but this job should get us right again. Don't worry, she'll get the job done." He stood up. "Take it easy."

"You too. I'll let you know when we're scheduled for a landing location.

"Thanks."

Nathan wandered back through the *Blue Moon Bandit;* through the galley, the small common room, and back to the engine compartment. He found Duncan and Richie pulling something out of the port side engine. They didn't see him come in.

"Anything wrong, Duncan?"

The big man laid a wrench down and motioned for Richie to continue while he walked over to Nathan. "Nothing too serious, Nathan. While we're in Port Solitude I wouldn't mind getting a new lubricant pump. The bearings in this one are making some noise I don't like. We just re-packed the bearings in grease but I don't know how long that will buy us. It's a few hundred hours past its replacement schedule."

Nathan looked over at where Richie was working. "Can it wait until we get back home? It will be easier in our own hangar."

Duncan grimaced. "We really need an overhaul on this engine. We did the starboard one last year but we've been putting off this one. To tell you the truth, I hated to pull this pump out while we were under way but I didn't want it to fail when we're going through re-entry at Port Solitude."

"Sounds like you made the right call," Nathan said. "I just don't know what the situation on the ground will be like. You could pull this out because we were cruising on the starboard engine, right?"

Duncan nodded. "Right."

"Well, once we're on the ground I'd hate to have to try a lift off on one engine. I know it's rated for it but that's a hell of a lot of stress."

"First, you can take off with just the starboard engine," Duncan said. "I wouldn't let us fly in a ship that couldn't. Second, I think the pump will hold until we're home. I just prefer to do it as soon as possible but I understand other factors have to be considered and like you said, we don't know what is waiting for us down there."

"Thanks, Duncan. I promise we'll get home as soon as possible."

"Ah, one more thing, Nathan? Out here?"

Duncan moved the conversation into the corridor outside the cramped engine compartment.

"What's up?" Nathan said.

"I had to reconfigure the servers this morning. Our navigation software had an upgrade available and I installed it after I tested it."

"Great. So what's the problem?"

"I had to free up some space. The upgrade was pretty significant so it ate up a lot of server room." Duncan reached into his pocket and pulled out a portable computer drive. "This is everything I had to take off the entertainment drive, which was just about everything in your files."

"Aw, man, really?"

Duncan shrugged. "Sorry, but I've been warning you that we need to upgrade the servers. It takes a lot of software and processing power to run a starship, jump it past light speed, and navigate it. Entertainment has to come second."

"Why did you pull *my* stuff off the server?" Nathan looked at the drive. According to the label, it was fairly large.

Duncan smiled. "Well, your share of the entertainment server was larger than everyone else's. Combined. So it made sense to strip out your stuff and save it to one place." He pointed to the portable drive. "As soon as we get a new server I can get your stuff loaded back up."

Nathan ran a hand through his hair. "Yeah but I can't run these holovids off the drive. They need a server installation."

"I could loan you a book."

"Yeah, that'll be fun." Nathan looked back toward the engine compartment. "When we get back we're going to have to go over the maintenance log and the budget, make a plan."

"You said that a couple months ago."

"I know."

"We didn't do it, and now our spare parts pool is getting pretty shallow. I've been keeping us going but I honestly don't know if I can fix the next thing that breaks. I don't want to get stuck somewhere because we don't have a hose or fitting in ship's stores, you know?"

"I know and believe me, I do take this seriously, all kidding about me being cheap aside. We just haven't had the funds for what we need to do. I can see we've stretched what we have about as far as we could so as soon as we get paid from this job, we tighten things up."

"It may mean some downtime," Duncan said.

"It is what it is. At least we'll have an extra pair of hands helping us." Nathan nodded toward the engine compartment where Richie was still working.

"True," Duncan said. "He has a good set of hands so we should keep him on for a while. Anyway, we'll be done in about thirty minutes, plenty of time for us to land according to what Marla told us."

"Yeah, you're good."

The look on Duncan's face changed; he looked a little uncomfortable. "Hey, uh, things have been moving kind of quickly and I haven't had a chance to ask before now but how are you doing with the whole Celeste thing?"

"What do you mean?"

"I mean in a couple hours you're going to see her. Hopefully. Are you going to be okay with that?"

"Why wouldn't I be?"

Duncan tilted his head. "Seriously? Well, there's that whole holovid thing that just happened a few days ago…"

Nathan waved him off. "No, don't worry about that. It's okay. I've got it under control. I've actually been doing some thinking, kind of getting things together. You've got nothing to worry about."

Duncan held up his hands. "Oh, no, man, I wasn't worrying about me. I was just thinking about you. It's obvious you still have some feelings for her."

"No, it's okay, really, Duncan. I have it under control."

"How could that be? You were obsessed enough to make that holovid and almost bankrupt yourself doing it. Are you telling me feelings that intense have just vanished with a few days' consideration?"

Nathan stared at him. "Duncan, I have it under control. It won't be a problem." Duncan just stared at him, clearly disbelieving him.

"Have you seen Cole? I want to check with him and our guests."

"I'm pretty sure Arulio is in his room. He's probably in sleep mode or whatever he does when he's not hacking things." Duncan stopped there and didn't offer anything further.

"And Cole?" Nathan said.

"I think he's in his quarters with Kimiyo. I walked by his door a bit ago and it sounded like they were enjoying themselves."

Nathan rolled his eyes. "I'll start with Arulio then. Man, I hope Cole doesn't piss her off. I just want this job to go smoothly."

Duncan opened the door to the engine compartment. "Good luck with that."

Nathan wandered back to the crew quarters and stopped in the galley. He grabbed a can of juice and saw a can of Arulio's nutritional supplement in the fridge. He looked at the clock on the wall and guessed that Kimiyo had forgotten all about feeding the wetjack. He picked up the can and walked down the short corridor to Arulio's cabin. He didn't hear anything from Cole's as he passed by.

Must be enjoying the afterglow, he thought and rapped on Arulio's door.

"Please enter," came the response.

Nathan walked in and saw Arulio sitting on his bed, staring off into space through the small portal in the room. Nathan walked over and handed him the nutritional supplement before sitting in a chair in the corner.

"I thought it might be time for you to eat," Nathan said.

"Yes, it is. Thank you, Captain." Arulio opened the can and took a sip.

"Enjoying the view? You can't quite see it yet but we're approaching Port Solitude."

"I have been monitoring the activity on the flight deck. I am aware of our approach to Port Solitude."

Nathan nodded. "You mentioned earlier that the *Blue Moon Bandit* was a good ship."

Arulio turned to look at him. It was still a little unnerving to have those red eyes focused on directly at him. "This is a fine vessel. Despite Duncan Jax's concerns, all systems are fully functional and operating within suggested parameters. His maintenance schedule can wait until we return to Earth."

"How did you know about all that?" Nathan felt his stomach drop away like he was in a quickly rising elevator.

"The ship's intercom system was activated while you were speaking with Mr. Jax."

Nathan sipped his juice and then leaned forward. "The intercom in the corridor?"

"Correct."

"Who initiated the intercom? I didn't hear anything. It usually beeps when someone turns it on."

"The intercom configuration settings were updated two days ago to silence the audio alert that signals the activation of the intercom. This enables the intercom to activate without the second party realizing the intercom is activated."

Arulio tipped back his can and pulled a long drink.

"Arulio, do you know who updated the settings on the intercom?"

"I do."

"Was it the same person who listened in on my conversation with Duncan? Was it Richie?" The new guy may not have liked being left out of the conversation and decided to dip in on the sly.

"It was not Richie."

"Who was it?"

"I did it." He drained the last of his formula.

Nathan stood up and regarded the wetjack with a stare. "Why would you do that?"

Arulio stood up and handed the empty can back to Nathan who took it. The wetjack was silent for a moment, considering his response.

"Before we left Earth, Mr. Saji Vy made it clear that my safety during this exercise was paramount. More important than the *Charon*, the *Charon*'s crew, Ms. Kimiyo Himura, or the crew of the *Blue Moon Bandit*."

Nathan nodded slowly. "So that's why you've been snooping through the ship's network and listening in on our conversations. You've been keeping yourself safe."

Arulio gave a small nod. "In accordance with Mr. Vy's orders, of course."

"Of course," Nathan said. "And if I order you to return the intercom settings to their original configuration?"

"I would do so until I felt the need arise to change them back."

"Then please do so."

Arulio's eyes deadened for a moment. Nathan watched as he appeared to... go somewhere else? It was the same thing he'd seen in the casino on Olympia. Then life snapped back into those eyes.

"It is done, Captain."

The two men stood there, an awkward silence growing between them. Nathan couldn't tell if the wetjack was aware of how much a betrayal he was guilty of or if he even cared. What he was sure of was that this was no one to trust. Not a bit.

"I'll be going now, Arulio. I just wanted to make sure you ate and let you know that we were approaching Port Solitude. I imagine things will happen quickly once we reach our destination."

"I will be prepared, Captain. Thank you for bringing my meal."

"No problem." Nathan turned, opened the door, and stepped into the corridor. He saw Kimiyo coming toward him. She was wearing a t-shirt and sweats, carrying a can of Arulio's formula. He held up the empty can.

"I've already fed him."

"Thank you. How is he?" she asked.

Nathan took a deep breath through his nose before answering. "He's odd, Kimiyo. He's very odd. Did you know that he's been listening in on our conversations for the past two days?"

She smiled, a wicked little knowing smile. "Captain Teller, I assume that Arulio knows everything about me at all times. It's the only way to work around him and not go crazy. By the way, I should have told you to wipe your mobi's of anything private. He doesn't really have a lot of morals so odds are he's strip-mined them of anything interesting. What was he doing today?"

"He was listening in on the ship's intercoms. I asked him to stop but I don't think that's likely."

She shook her head. "No, I don't think so either. I'm very sorry. I know this is difficult but it's only for a few more days, if everything goes smoothly. Then we'll be off your ship and your life can get back to normal."

"It doesn't bother you that he knows so much about you? How do you live under that kind of scrutiny?"

She shrugged. "It's an honor to work so closely with Mr. Vy and I tell myself it's not forever."

"Better you than me. I was just letting everyone know, we're almost to Port Solitude."

"Thank you." She turned and walked back to the galley to drop off Arulio's can of nutritional supplement. Nathan went to his quarters.

An hour later Nathan was at the controls of the *Bandit* as it soared over Port Solitude toward a landing pad on the northern outskirts of the colony. He saw the settlement built by the Children of Apocalyptic Rainbow and did a slow circle over the place. It wasn't much. A few buildings, what looked like a small farmer's field and a few landing pads. Shuttles occupied two of the pads and Nathan was directed to the empty third one. He set the *Blue Moon Bandit* down with a gentle bump.

He left Marla to go through the post flight checklist and gathered the rest of the crew in the common room. Someone had put a pot of coffee on the table and he helped himself to a cup. It was the good stuff, grown on the southern slope of Mons Olympia on Mars. He took a seat at one of the three small tables in the room. Cole, Kimiyo, and Arulio sat at another, and Duncan and Richie sat at the third. Everyone was drinking coffee, eating donuts, and looked relatively rested. Nathan remained standing.

"Okay, we're here. First things first. Duncan, ship status? Engines okay?"

Duncan dumped some sweetener in his coffee. "It's all good, Nathan. Both engines are at 100% and ready when you need them. All other systems are nominal with no errors to report."

"Kimiyo? Your boy ready to meet with these folks?"

"Arulio is ready to do what is needed and I hope he can complete the task quickly."

"I think that goes for all of us. Okay, Cole, Kimiyo, Arulio we'll be going in. Duncan, Marla, and Richie, hang out here on the ship. Keep things ready to go. I have no idea how this will go down."

Richie leaned back in his chair. "Come on, boss, I'm getting tired of staying on the ship. Let me come in."

Nathan raised an eyebrow at him. "Do you have something to offer? I mean, other than purple skin?"

"I'm good with people."

"Stay on the ship. We'll see what opportunities present themselves." Nathan stood up straight. "All right folks. Let's go meet the lunatics."

Chapter 22

"So that's them?" Montario gestured to the *Blue Moon Bandit*. It was on a launch pad seventy-five meters from the building he and Celeste were standing in with an official Children of the Apocalyptic Rainbow welcoming committee. He and Celeste were nearest the big picture window that faced the landing pad. Far enough away that they could speak without being over heard.

"Yeah," she said. "That's my old ship. Still looks pretty good."

"Don't get too sentimental. We just need them to do their job and fly out of here."

"Don't worry, Nathan won't want to be here any longer than he has to. Are you sure they didn't look for the *Charon* in orbit when they came down?"

"I'm sure. We have a group member working in air traffic control and he reported they followed the correct path in with no deviation. Besides, *Charon* was on the other side of our little moon. There's just too much sky for them to search all of it in the little bit of time they were in orbit."

"Don't underestimate them," she said.

"So you've said. Just remember this isn't my first job either. We play it smooth and we walk away rich. You just make sure you play the part of the hostage. Nothing too dramatic, just a little worried."

"I've got it." She looked out at the sky. "We've got some weather coming in. I wish they would hurry up."

Montario looked up at the sky and saw dark gray storm clouds gathering. The wind was picking up outside, blowing leaves and grass across the landing pad. It wouldn't be long before the first fat drops started falling. Montario frowned, he hated getting wet. He checked the clock on the wall for the time. The *Blue Moon Bandit* had been down for ten minutes.

"What do you suppose is taking them so long?"

Celeste rolled her eyes. "Nathan is such a pain in the ass about procedure. He's probably doing a post flight systems check, talking to Cole about contingency plans, and making sure Duncan has the ship ready to lift off if they need to. I heard they hired a new co-pilot so she's probably getting instructions too. Honestly, he used to drive me crazy with all that. And the coffee... if he was on a job he wouldn't stop drinking the stuff. Always set in his ways."

"You said Cole is the dangerous one, right? The one who used to be a marshal?"

"Oh yeah, you want to be especially careful with him," Celeste said. "Even if he walks in here without a gun, you'll want to be careful with what you say and how you act."

"This is pretty straight forward, except for them not knowing about your being in on it." He nodded back to the welcoming committee. "And them not knowing anything about anything. Honestly, how can people this naïve function in modern society? Wouldn't you think something odd was occurring by now?"

"Montario, these kids are here because they can't hack being alone in modern society. That's why they hand over their cash to you and waste their time getting high and getting laid. This is all just an elaborate way for them to hide from responsibility."

"True enough." He looked outside. "Ah at last, the ramp is coming down."

— « o » —

Celeste looked out to the landing pad and watched the rear ramp of the *Blue Moon Bandit* lower to the tarmac.

Montario turned to the welcoming committee and raised a hand. "This is it everyone. Our special guests have arrived. Let's make them feel welcome." He had a giant smile full of white teeth and the crowd of young people moved with him through the door. Celeste followed alongside, not smiling at all because she was nervous. The kids were all handpicked and beautiful. Young, perky, and all of them had a smile to match Montario's.

The wind blew a few wisps of errant hair across her face and she pushed them back. She looked at the sky again. It was going to storm hard and it was going to do it soon. She glanced back at the landing ramp and saw Nathan staring at her. Her breath hitched in her throat and made a small noise. She looked at Montario. He hadn't noticed.

Nathan was at the base of the ramp followed by Cole who immediately walked off to the side and started looking around when he reached the tarmac. Cole looked the same as ever, blue jeans, a dark t-shirt, and a leather jacket. The same real leather jacket he'd picked up on Mars years ago when Celeste flew with Nathan. Behind him, a woman led a white skinned man off the ramp, moving more slowly than either Nathan or Cole. The woman was Asian and exceptionally professional looking in a navy blue pinstriped business suit with low heels. The white skinned man wore some leather looking get up that looked like it belonged in an S&M club.

Nathan was wearing dark denim pants, boots, and a charcoal colored button-down work shirt. She thought he looked good, certainly better than the last time she saw him. He walked over to where the welcoming committee was standing, followed by the others. His hair blew in the wind, but he didn't seem to notice. Celeste felt her pulse quicken and told herself it was because things were coming to a head.

Montario extended a hand to Nathan with a brilliant smile. "Captain Teller. Thank you for coming all this way." The kids moved around them, surrounding them and greeting them. Several of the young women put flowered wreaths around Cole's neck and the young men greeted Kimiyo. Only one young woman approached Arulio and he stood still and unsure as she placed a wreath around his neck.

Nathan shook his hand. "You didn't leave us much choice." He turned. "How are you doing, Celeste? Are you being well treated?"

She nodded, and her eyes darted toward Montario. "I'm fine. We're all fine in fact. Captain Geechy and the others are still in their rooms, but we've all been treated well. I take it you've brought what they want?"

Nathan jerked a thumb over his shoulder at Arulio. "He's right there."

"A man?" Celeste let surprise color her voice, "Why did you bring a man? Where is the money?"

"This is what he asked for, Celeste, so this is what Saji had us bring." He turned back to Montario. "This young woman is Kimiyo Himura, she works with Arulio. That gentleman over there is Cole Seger. He takes care of security." He paused for a moment to let Cole glower at Montario. He did a fine job of it. "I don't want to be here any longer than necessary. I need proof the rest of the *Charon* crew is alive and well. I also need proof the ship is travel ready and able to continue to Earth with its cargo intact."

Montario smiled. It was that slick smile that Celeste knew he used when he was going to try and get his way. "Well Captain Teller, may I call you Nathan?" Nathan nodded. "Nathan, we have a timetable for what we need done and I'm sure it won't interfere with any of your demands. If you would all just follow me inside, I'll show you to Captain Thomas Geechy and the rest of his crew."

Nathan turned to Kimiyo. "Take Arulio back inside the *Blue Moon Bandit* and tell Duncan to secure the door behind you. We'll call when we need you."

Montario looked puzzled. "I'm sorry, Nathan, but why are you sending the wetjack back into your ship? We need him inside."

Nathan took a step toward Montario. The cult leader took an involuntary step back. "Look, here's the way it is. First, the wetjack has a name. It's Arulio. He's a person, not a mainframe. Second, you need to do what I asked and then you can have access to Arulio. That's the deal."

Montario's face flickered for a half second and then the smile reappeared. He raised his hands, palms up at Nathan. "No problem, my friend. No problem at all. I just wanted to let him know what he would be doing while you checked on the other hostages. You know, speed the process along. I know that Saji Vy wants his ship moving as soon as possible." He narrowed his eyes. "If you need to delay things a little longer until you are satisfied, that's fine." He smiled again.

Nathan rolled his eyes. "It will take as long as it takes. If that makes Saji angry, I'll let him know who to blame. Now are we going to talk out here and get rained on or are you going to do what I asked?"

The kids with the flower wreaths stopped what they were doing and stood silently as their leader was pulled up short. Montario raised his arms wide. "Everyone, let's show our new friends inside. We have much to do and not much time, I'm afraid. This way please." He beckoned to Nathan and Cole. They stayed still until Kimiyo and Arulio walked back up the ramp and secured it behind them. A peal of thunder banged over the landing pad and they turned to follow Montario and his entourage. The skies opened up as soon as they walked into the building.

— « o » —

Nathan turned and looked out on the pad. The rain hammered down hard, roaring against the windows so loudly that Nathan was taken aback by its ferocity. He turned to Montario. "Captain Geechy first, Montario, and then we see the rest of his crew."

"Of course, Nathan. Oh, I'm afraid we don't allow weapons inside the commune. Mr. uh... Cole was it? If you have any firearms you'll have to surrender them."

Nathan shook his head. "It's not Mr. Cole, it's just Cole and he doesn't go anywhere unarmed because I've asked him not to. He won't be disarmed."

Montario held up his hands again. "Nathan, I just want to ensure none of my people are harmed. Surely you realize you are safe here. The Children of the Apocalyptic Rainbow have been a peaceful organization since their founding. I assure you, firearms will not be necessary."

Nathan rubbed the back of his neck, growing impatient despite his claim that he would let things take as long as they took. He caught Celeste raising her eyebrows at him. It was sort of sexy when she did that. He stumbled over the memory and cleared his throat. "Celeste, why don't you lead the way to Captain Geechy and the rest of your crew while Montario tries to take Cole's gun away." He turned to Cole. "Catch up to us when you're finished, okay?"

Nathan took Celeste by the arm and started walking toward the door. "Which way?" he said and she pointed to the right, slightly bewildered. "Okay, let's go." They disappeared into the hallway.

"What are you doing here?" Celeste asked.

"That question has more answers than I'm comfortable with," Nathan said. "How have you been? Are you really holding up okay? Is your crew all right? You can speak freely now. No one else is around."

She smiled. "Well, I'm glad to see my ex-husband so what does that tell you? They've treated us fairly well but I had to deck one guy who thought the hard sell was the way to get us to join. They never stop recruiting for their organization."

"Yeah, about that," Nathan said. "They really don't seem like a cult or even a religion. Not like you'd think. It seems like they're more into partying and being janitors."

She smiled a bit. "I know what you mean. Instead of working toward a goal they're all about helping you be the best 'you' you can be, whatever that means. All I've seen are a bunch of university dropouts getting wasted and sleeping together so I guess this outfit is helping them do that as best they can."

Nathan chuckled. "It doesn't sound like a bad way to get by."

She raised an eyebrow. "I guess, as long as you have a trust fund to pay for it. In all seriousness, what are you doing here? Anyone could have brought that guy here."

Nathan shrugged. "We needed the work and Saji is paying us well."

"And that's it?"

"You being here may have had something to do with it," he said. "I couldn't just do nothing knowing you were in trouble." He sighed. "Sorry, that's pretty pathetic, isn't it?"

"Anyone who knows you wouldn't be surprised by you helping out a friend," she said with sincerity in her voice. She took one of his hands in hers. "And this is one old friend who is very happy you decided to help out. Now, my crew is right down this way. Let's check on them."

He smiled and patted her hand. "Of course."

— « o » —

Cole stood silently, eyeing Montario who looked completely confused. Things were obviously not going the way he planned and it was getting to him. Cole could see a little vein throbbing in his forehead. Montario looked at him.

"I don't know what's going on but you two…" he stopped as Cole took a couple of slow steps toward him.

They locked eyes and Montario held his gaze for a moment. There was some steel in there, Cole saw, but not enough to worry about. Not now, anyway. He walked past Montario, past the kids with the flowered wreaths, and went the same direction Nathan had gone. Frustrated, Montario hurried behind him.

— « o » —

It took ten minutes to ascertain Captain Geechy and his crew were safe and had been well cared for. He thanked Nathan for coming, expressed his apologies that his ship had been taken and told Nathan with a tear in his eye that Celeste had been just absolutely wonderful during their ordeal. The best first officer a man could hope for. Nathan shook his hand, assured him Saji Vy didn't hold him responsible for the actions of criminals and told him he would be free soon. Montario seemed to bristle at the word "criminal" but Nathan didn't care.

Montario led them to a large common room and he motioned to a large sectional sofa. Everyone sat except Cole, who stood behind Nathan with his hands folded in front of him.

"Nathan," Montario said, "now that you know the crew is safe, we really need to get the wetjack in here so he can get started on his part. I'm afraid it will take quite a bit of time and I don't want to hold things up."

Nathan held a steady gaze with Montario, raised a finger and shook it in front of him. "Assuring the well-being of the hostages was only one of my demands. Now I need to know their ship, the *Charon*, is space worthy. What can you do to prove it to me?"

Montario grimaced and looked at one of the young men. "Gary, may I have your tablet please?" A guy who looked like he should be in college stepped forward and handed Montario a tablet computer. He tapped the screen a few times and handed it to Nathan.

"I assume Saji Vy provided you with access codes to the *Charon*'s computer system?" Nathan nodded. "This tablet is keyed to the ship's comm system. You just need to enter the access code to see the telemetry from the ship."

Nathan sighed and reached for the tablet. He entered the code provided by Saji and waited while it loaded. When it did, he looked up at Celeste. "Can you come over here and validate this is correct?"

Celeste looked at Montario. He nodded and she got up, moved around the table, and sat down beside Nathan. She looked at the data for a moment, swiped the screen to show additional graphs, and then nodded. "It all looks good to me," she said. "Have you had people up there taking care of things?"

"We have," Montario said. "We have several people on staff capable of operating a starship. They have been taking good care of the *Charon* since it came into orbit."

"Since you hijacked it, you mean," Nathan said.

"No need to be unpleasant, Nathan," Montario said, taking back the tablet. "We've met your demands. Now please, call in the wetjack."

Nathan sank back into the sofa. It was leather, he noticed. No expense spared for the commune. "So, how do you envision this going down? Arulio comes in here, does his thing for you and then what? We load everyone up on my ship and shuttle them up to the *Charon*?"

Montario sank back into his seat as well. Nathan couldn't tell if it was because he was trying to seem calm or because it was one of those things you do when you notice other people leaning forward or sitting back and subconsciously do the same thing. "That's fine with me," Montario said. "Once I have what I need, I can give you the location of the *Charon* and everyone can go."

Nathan smiled a bit. It wasn't we anymore, he noticed. Now 'I' was slipping into the conversation where he used to refer to everyone. "Just so long as you understand, if any of this goes hinky, I'm calling in Protective Services. I'm willing to keep things quiet for Saji's sake but only up to the point where the life of my crew or the safety of my ship is imperiled. You understand me?"

"I do. You should know, however, that several members of the local Protective Services are members of our group."

Nathan smiled. "Of course they are. Okay, let's get it done." He rose from the sofa.

Montario nodded. "I have a group standing by your ship. If you let your people know it's all right they will be escorted in."

Nathan considered it. Up to this point Montario hadn't done anything too stupid so he was reasonably sure he could trust him to bring in Arulio and Kimiyo. That would leave Duncan, Marla, and Richie on the ship. "Okay, I'll make the call." He pulled his mobi from his pocket and sent a message to Duncan. He got an answer back a few seconds later. "They're on their way."

Montario nodded again and pulled an aide in close to speak with him. Nathan took the opportunity to look around. His eyes snagged on Celeste. She looked good, which was surprising since she had been with these people for almost a week. She smiled. His heart skipped a beat and his breathing quickened. He shook his head. He was too old to pine for women who didn't want to be with him.

— « o » —

On a landing pad a hundred meters from the one holding the *Blue Moon Bandit*, Caleb and a group of people were walking out to one of the shuttles parked there. He was on his way up to the *Charon* to manage the tech crew taking care of her systems. It was a crap job, one that Caleb didn't exactly understand. He understood they were providing hospitality to the crew of a stranded ship, but they had been here long enough to be handed off to the local government office. Assistance was one thing but these shuttle flights to ferry repair crews up and down cost money.

His bag dropped at the base of the ramp when one of the shoulder straps broke. He bent to pick it up and noticed a seam had also split. "Hey, Linda?" he called to the young woman ahead of him. "Can you tell them to hang on a second? I need to go back to my quarters for another bag. It'll just take a minute."

He turned to walk back in through the rain and noticed the ship on the next landing pad over. The rain had died down and was much lighter than the deluge that had taken place a few minutes earlier. First the rain held up their departure. Now it was this stupid old bag.

The ramp dropped on the other ship and Caleb saw Dean and Betsy, two fellow members who took care of housekeeping at the commune, wave to someone inside the ship. Caleb stopped for a moment and watched. A woman walked down the ramp and opened a large umbrella. A tall, lanky man with chalk white skin followed. It took Caleb a moment to recognize that this man was a wetjack. What was a human / computer interface doing here? Caleb turned back to Linda.

"Go on without me, okay? You're in charge."

She looked puzzled. "Why? I thought we were going to get some time together."

"I know," he said. "But I forgot about something with the new office on Olympia. It will just take a day or so to clean up. Then I'll be right along."

Her eyebrows crinkled. "You're sure?"

"I am. Just a day or so."

"Okay."

"Oh, one more thing, Linda? If Montario asks for me? Just tell him I'm tied up." He looked kind of sheepish. "I don't want him to know I screwed this thing up. Okay?"

She smiled. "Sure, no problem. I know how he can get."

He leaned in and kissed her on the cheek. "Thanks, honey. See you later."

Caleb gathered the remains of his bag and watched as the other party walked into the commune. He gave them another couple minutes to clear the doorway, dry off, and then followed them in.

He looked through the windows and saw the entranceway was empty. He walked into the commune, made a right at the corridor leading to the common room, and slipped down the hall quietly. The crowd in the room included Montario and more new arrivals. Caleb recognized the red headed woman as Montario's recent interest. The rest he didn't know. They all took seats on the large sofas. Caleb leaned back against the wall, out of sight, and listened in.

"Kimiyo and Arulio, Montario is the reason we're here. Whatever needs done, he can explain it to you."

"Thank you, Nathan," Montario said. "I want you to know I appreciate you all coming." He smiled, got up, and walked around to where Arulio sat with Kimiyo on the cushion beside him. Montario knelt down. "I know you've been wondering why I asked for you to come and I'll be happy to explain it to you." He paused. "But only to you Arulio."

"Oh what the hell?" Nathan said. "What is this nonsense?"

Montario swiveled his head toward Nathan. "This is for your protection, Captain Teller, you and your crew. What I'm going to talk to Arulio about is probably something you don't want to hear."

Kimiyo stood up and stepped between Arulio and Montario. "Please excuse me but Arulio doesn't go anywhere without me. I'm afraid that's non-negotiable."

Montario considered her demand for a moment. "That's fine, but just you and you don't get a say in what I tell Arulio to do. Understood?"

Kimiyo raised an eyebrow. "That's acceptable unless I feel Arulio is in some danger."

Cole leaned over to Nathan, "She can take care of herself."

Nathan held up his hands. "Fine. How much time do you need?"

"I don't think it will be long, based on what Milo told me about the test in the casino on Olympia," Montario said.

"Well get started. I want to be back in the air as soon as possible."

Montario gestured to a corridor. "This way please." He led Arulio and Kimiyo down the hall and out of sight. Nathan watched them go and walked over to where Celeste was sitting.

"May I sit down?"

She gestured to the cushion beside her. "Sure."

He sat down and folded his hands.

"You look good," she said, "like you lost some weight."

"Thanks."

"Cole looks really good."

He looked at her and she smiled. It was a good smile. "Everyone's good. Duncan's outside on the ship. He's happy."

"You think so?"

"What do you mean?"

"We keep in touch," she said. "I'm not sure happy is the word I would use. I mean, he doesn't seem unhappy but content maybe? Looking for a new challenge? I don't know. It's hard to read subtext in a message."

"Come on, he's married, doing well…"

She shook her head. "Still the same old Nathan. Not everyone has the drive to work that job as hard as you. Sometimes people need more, you know?"

He sighed. "Any time Duncan wants to go, he can go. You know better than anyone that if they want to get off the crew, they can go."

"Yeah and look where that gets you."

"Wait a minute," he said. "You were unhappy and you left. You sold your share of the business and you left me. And let's not forget that you left for something much better. You were piloting a cruise ship. I didn't even know you were flying the body barge."

"You're right," she said. "It isn't your fault but couldn't you have come with me? Do you even understand that I just didn't want to sit in the co-pilot seat of that junk heap for the next thirty years letting my ass get fat? You couldn't give it up, though. You just had to be the man in charge, captain of the ship. You had to be the boss. Well, I wanted a change and you didn't so I had to go. I didn't leave you, you chose to stay without me."

Nathan bit a knuckle, not wanting to fight but seeing how things were heading that way. "You know what, Celeste? Just sit tight. My crew and my junk heap will get you out of this. I've got it all under control." He stood up and walked to the other couch.

Cole leaned down close to Nathan's ear. "It's really something to watch a ladies' man like you work. I'm learning so much."

"I may leave you here," Nathan said. "I just want you to know I'm considering it." Cole smiled and walked away.

— « o » —

Caleb peeked back into the room. The big guy with the gun on his hip had almost seen him when he walked past the doorway but Caleb had snuck back down the hall. He had no idea what Montario was up to. One thing was clear; the starship in orbit wasn't having trouble at all. Somehow Montario had stopped the ship and had them brought here. There were only four pilots in the group currently occupying the compound. One of them had to have been involved. He hustled off to his room to call them.

— « o » —

A few more minutes passed in silence. Nathan stared at Celeste while she stared at her hands. Whenever she looked up, he swiveled his head and stared down the corridor where Montario had taken Kimiyo and Arulio. Finally, after what seemed like an eternity, they heard footsteps. Nathan stood and saw a young woman coming down the hall. He met her at the doorway with Cole behind him. She seemed surprised.

"Are you Captain Teller?" she asked.

"That's right. Did Montario send you?"

She smiled. "He did. He would like you to know that Arulio, wait, is that the right name?"

"Yes."

"Good. He wants you to know that Arulio estimates it will take about 30 minutes to complete the task Montario has requested."

"What is that task?" Cole said.

The young woman smiled again. "I'm sure I don't know. He simply wanted me to relay the message. Is there anything I can get you? Are you hungry or thirsty? I could get you something to drink."

"No thank you," Nathan said. "We're fine."

"I'd like something," Celeste said rising from the couch and shooting a look at Nathan. "I hate it when you answer for me." She addressed the young woman. "I'd like an orange juice, with ice."

The young woman nodded and walked off. Celeste went back to the couch.

Nathan turned toward her. "I'm sorry. I didn't mean to answer for you."

"Forget it," she said. "In another few hours I'll be back on my ship and out of your life. You don't need to apologize anymore."

"Fine."

"You were never very good at it anyway."

— « o » —

It took Caleb ten minutes to find the pilot he was looking for. It was an older man named Kenneth Bright. He was middle aged but a relative newcomer to the movement. All Caleb knew about him was that he had come to the Children of the Apocalyptic Rainbow after divorcing his wife. Caleb found him sitting at a table in the kitchen, a cup of coffee in both hands.

"I spoke with Tommy in operations," Caleb said. "He told me you took a group of guys up six days ago to meet a ship. He said you took the big shuttle."

Kenneth shook his head. "I don't know what you're talking about, Caleb. I haven't flown in a couple of weeks."

Caleb pinched the bridge of his nose and closed his eyes. "That's not true, Kenneth. You know it. I know it. Tell me what you did up there."

"Caleb, come on. I didn't do anything. I haven't flown."

"Kenneth, I need you to be honest with me. I get the feeling that time is running short and that something is happening. Montario has those people here for a reason. He took them off that ship for a reason."

"Come on, Caleb, it's a ship full of dead bodies being ferried back to Earth. Who besides the shipping line is going to care?" Kenneth took a sip of his coffee.

Caleb made a decision to trust Kenneth a little more, play friendly with him. "Look, Kenneth, I found something out about Montario. Something that isn't very good."

"Yeah?"

"That's right," Caleb said. "I have friends in Protective Services and they ran his DNA for me. Montario has quite a record. Mostly scams and petty theft. He's done some time, quite a few years in fact. I suspected he may be using a false name, but he wasn't. It was as if he didn't care if we found out."

Kenneth laughed.

"What's so funny?"

"Caleb, we're all here because we have failures in our past. We all need help. This organization exists for that very purpose." He took another sip of his coffee. "So what if he has a few busts on his record or did a little time. He seems okay to me. I don't see anyone around here worse for the wear."

"And those people from the starship he hijacked? Are they all right?"

The smile on Kenneth's face slipped for a moment. "I wouldn't worry about that, Caleb. I understand that situation is about to resolve itself. In fact," he looked at the clock on the wall, "I'd say those folks are on their way home right about now."

Caleb's eyebrows narrowed. "Right now?"

"Mmm-hmm." The pilot stood up and swallowed the last of his coffee. "You may want to let this one go, Caleb. In fact, maybe you should go open another office or something." He chucked his coffee cup in the recycler and walked out of the kitchen. Caleb's mobi beeped. He took it out, checked the message and the blood drained from his face. Anyone looking at him at that moment would have suggested he go see the nurse in the compound's infirmary.

— « o » —

Nathan was pacing the room with Cole, making small talk while they waited for Arulio and Kimiyo. "So," Nathan said, "you and Kimiyo, huh? What about your pawnshop lady back in Go City?"

"Betty? Nothing to worry about there," Cole said. "She's got a cop making house calls now. It was never too serious with her."

"She was very cute."

"Still is, but I think she wants someone with regular hours. Being on Earth six days a month makes it too hard."

"Everyone is on me about our schedule."

Cole stopped. "It's not all about you, Nathan. I know what I'm doing. I know what the risks and rewards are. I'm a grown up. If I didn't want to be here I wouldn't be. Besides, Kimiyo is kind of making me forget about Betty, you know?"

They heard a door close and footsteps move down the hallway. "Is that them?" Nathan said.

Cole saw Kimiyo round the corner with Arulio in tow. "It sure is," he said. "I hope they're done. I want to get off this rock."

Kimiyo and Arulio walked into the room with Montario behind them. The leader of the cult was smiling from ear to ear and had a large duffel in his hand. "Captain Teller," he said, "we are finished here. You can collect the crew of the *Charon* and be on your way." He handed Nathan a tablet. "Here is the tracking data on the starship. Thank you for your assistance."

Nathan turned to Kimiyo. "Are you both okay? Did anything happen to Arulio?"

She nodded. "We're fine. I would like to get going if that's alright with you."

"Thanks again," Montario said, "and please let Saji know that I'm glad he worked with us. I'm glad this went as well as it did."

"Yeah," Cole said, "I'm sure he'll appreciate that. You may want to look over your shoulder for the rest of your life. I understand he can hold a grudge."

"Believe me," Montario said, "that won't be a problem." He edged toward the door. "I guess this is goodbye."

A man burst into the room and pointed an accusing finger at the group. Nathan looked from him to Montario who had a puzzled look on his face.

"Caleb? You're still here?" Montario raised his eyebrows.

"What have you done, Montario?" the man named Caleb said. "You've killed us all."

Chapter 23

The room split in who they were looking at. Half turned toward Montario and the rest stared at Caleb. Then they switched, like it was a tennis match. Cole sidled around the room toward Caleb. Nathan looked from Caleb to Montario. "What's he talking about?"

Montario grimaced. "Caleb, this is not the time or the place. I'll talk to you in a bit."

"When?" Caleb said. "I can see that you're packed, Montario. I can see that you're leaving." He gestured toward Nathan. "Is this who you are leaving with? Are they in on it?"

Nathan put a hand up. "Hold on, buddy. We aren't in on anything and this guy isn't going anywhere with us. He is not our passenger."

"Then why are you here?"

"You'll have to speak with Montario about that," Nathan said. He turned to Celeste. "Get your crew together, we're leaving."

"Hold on," Caleb said. "No one is going anywhere. Not until I get some answers."

"I believe we'll do what we want," Cole said. Caleb turned and looked at him, noticing for the first time how close he was.

"Look," Nathan said, "We don't know who you are or what your beef is with this guy," he jerked a thumb at Montario. "Our job here is done and we're leaving."

Celeste was still standing near the couch, looking unsure. Her eyes flickered between Montario and Nathan. "Are we in danger?"

"You're fine," Nathan said. "But I need you to get your crew so we can take off."

Celeste looked at Montario. "Are we in some kind of danger?"

"No," Montario said.

"Why are you asking him?" Nathan said. "All you have to do is get your crew and your stuff and fly out of here with us. Let's get it done, okay?"

"No one is leaving until this is settled," Caleb said. "Your ship is locked down on the landing pad."

Montario dropped his duffel. "Come on, Caleb. Cut the drama, huh? All of this has nothing to do with you. This is business between us," he pointed at himself and Arulio. "Besides, we can't even lock down the landing pads."

Caleb walked toward Montario and smiled. "You know, I've always been amazed at how you ran this place but never really understood how anything worked. You just leave everything to the mid-level managers."

"It's called delegating."

"It's called being a lazy ass," Caleb said, his voice rising. "Of course you don't know the landing pads can be locked down. Did you know we have around ten thousand members on eight different planets and colonies? Did you know we are the leading business concern on this colony? Did you know we haven't paid a dime in taxes in more than twenty years?"

Montario stepped closer to Caleb. "What makes you think I care? I never had to know any of that. All I needed to do was point you or some other lifer at a problem and I knew you would take care of it."

Caleb took another step toward Montario. The space between them could be measured in inches now. Montario was slightly taller but Caleb was stockier. "Montario, do you really think I hung around here for twenty years because I like the program? Don't get me wrong, I like the girls and the work isn't all that hard but you're so shallow you've never really looked into things. Did it really never occur to you that me and the other lifers were here for a good reason?"

Montario threw his hands up. "Fine, Caleb, tell us why. What's the big secret that keeps you here when you could have gone off and done so much more?"

"Oh, crap," Celeste whispered.

"The money, Montario. I stayed for the gobs of cash that run through this place without anyone really looking too carefully.

You and all the other leaders just drop in, run things for a few years, skimming off a percentage while we do all the hard work. You all think you're so smart and all the while each of you have missed the big picture."

"What big picture, Caleb?"

"Nathan," Celeste said. "I want to go. Now."

Nathan held up his mobi. "We can't. I had Duncan check things out. This guy really does have the landing pad locked down."

"I really want to leave," she said. "I don't want to be here anymore."

He shrugged. "I have Duncan working on it. He'll get us loose. Just stay cool."

"The money, Montario," Caleb said. "It washes through this place like a river."

"Yeah, well we have a cleaning company, farming concerns, and a dozen other little service companies we use for fund raisers."

Caleb smiled. "Try money laundering, Montario."

The room went quiet. Everyone looked at Montario. Nathan spoke first. "Money laundering for who, Caleb?"

He spun toward Nathan. "Oh, now you're interested in talking to me?"

"What do you mean money laundering?" Montario said. "Who do we launder money for, Caleb? What are you up to?"

Caleb smiled and walked around Montario. He took a seat on one of the sofas. "I'm not up to anything Montario. Do you really not understand how all this works?" He spread his arms wide. "Laundering money is what this group has always been about. It's why we exist. This whole scam was started for the express purpose of being a front for organized crime."

Nathan sat down across from Caleb on one of the other sofas. "You mean organized crime? Like the Syndicate?"

"Hell yeah, I mean the Syndicate," Caleb said. "Do you know many other people who need large scale money laundering?"

Nathan turned to Montario. "Sit down, slick. We have a lot to discuss."

Montario picked up his bag. "No we don't. Our deal was you bring the wetjack to do something for me and I release the body barge and its crew. That's what we did. We're done and I'm gone." He turned to walk out of the room and Cole grabbed him by his collar and the waistband of his pants. He shoved the con artist hard into the conversation pit and threw him onto the sofa next to Caleb.

"You aren't going anywhere until this is settled," Cole said.

Montario started to get up but Caleb put a hand on his shoulder. "You really don't want to leave, Montario. You need to help fix this mess you made. In fact, you may be the only one who can."

"How did you know?" Montario said. "How did you know the money was gone?"

Nathan's eyes narrowed. "What money?"

Caleb turned to him. "You don't know? You hauled these two," he pointed at Arulio and Kimiyo, "all the way here from Earth and you didn't know why? Come on, you don't expect me to believe that."

Nathan sat back in the sofa. "This idiot," he said, pointing to Montario, "somehow managed to capture the body barge and its crew. His ransom was the services of a wetjack. We provided transportation for Arulio and Kimiyo. I assumed money was involved, or information, but until just now we didn't know what he wanted. So, if he's done something ridiculously stupid, like stolen from the Syndicate, I would just as soon take my ship, crew, and passengers and leave before they start asking questions."

Caleb held up his mobi. "It's too late to leave. I got a message the moment the account for the Children of the Apocalyptic Rainbow holding the laundered funds was accessed for more than one hundred thousand credits. That message blasted out to me and a dozen other people. I can assure you, they are on their way here right now."

"How much did he take?" Celeste said. She looked frightened. Hell, she sounded frightened. Nathan felt bad for her. The last couple years had seen her divorce, lose a cruise line job, pilot the body barge, get kidnapped and now, when freedom was near, she was wrapped up in this mess.

Caleb looked at her with a leer. "Sweetheart, this guy was trying to walk out of here with twenty-three million credits. I doubt you or your ship full of dead bodies is worth that."

Cole cuffed him on the back of the head. "Watch how you talk to the lady."

Caleb turned to him. "You think you're tough? Wait until my friends get here; then we'll see."

"Maybe we will," Cole said. He clearly didn't care about Caleb or his friends.

Nathan waved his hands. "Wait a minute. How does a cult come to have twenty-three million credits? There's no way you have that many trust fund babies running around here and I don't think cleaning services pay that well."

Caleb looked at Montario. "Tell him. Tell him how we came to have that much money on hand."

Montario sat quietly. "Well, I don't know exactly."

"Oh, really?" Caleb said. "That's shocking." He moved closer to Montario. "Let's face it, you're just a con man and you got this gig from the last idiot we let sleep in the big bedroom."

Montario held up his hands. "It was supposed to be a good gig. Skim a little off and enjoy the fruits of everyone's labors. Then…" He let his head drop.

"Then you found the big account," Caleb said. "The one you should never have seen."

"Yeah," he said.

"How?"

Montario shook his head. "Don't worry about it."

"Come on," Nathan said. "Let's hear it. This could be important."

"It was a girl, wasn't it?" Caleb said. "You've had a steady stream of them going through your room since you got here. One of them said something, right?"

Montario looked up and shot a quick glance at Celeste. "Yeah, it was Jennifer. She does the books and found a record for deposits in the account and thought it looked odd."

"And once you saw how much was there you just had to get your hands on it, didn't you?" Caleb said, his voice escalating.

"Well that wasn't nearly as important as I thought it would be," Nathan said. "How did you get the money, Caleb? How does a cult amass that kind of cash and not draw attention?"

Caleb gave him a sideways glance, like Nathan had insulted his mother. "We're a religion, not a cult. We do some good work here. People get their lives back together. People find a purpose here. They get cleaned up and start over. It's not all a scam."

Nathan sighed. "My apologies. Now, how did you get the money? Are you ripping people off on the cleaning?"

Caleb sat back. "I can't talk about it. Not with you guys. This has been a very profitable operation until now."

Cole cuffed him on the back of the head, harder this time. "Answer the question or I'm going to start using something other than my hand."

Caleb rubbed the back of his head and started to get up, then stopped when he saw Cole's face. "Okay! That's enough of that." He sat down and looked at Nathan who was staring calmly at him.

"You know how money laundering works, right? The basics?"

Nathan nodded. "You use a legitimate company to clean up illegitimate earnings. Funnel money earned through crimes into a business so it comes out clean on the other side."

"Right," Caleb said. "So, the Syndicate owns shell companies, lots of them. All designed to be legitimate. They all do real business; restaurants, manufacturing, retail, and wholesale supplies."

"Okay."

"Well, some of those businesses exist and some don't, see? Some just exist on paper, owned by the Syndicate. We bill those companies for cleaning services and hospitality services. Those companies pay us with Syndicate money."

"When I was a marshal we chased quite a few Syndicate guys who pulled scams like this." Cole said, "How does the Syndicate get their money from the Children of the Apocalyptic Rainbow?"

"The Syndicate owns a wholesale cleaning supply company. We buy all of our cleaning products from them. In order to get them their money we order twice what we really need, they deliver half the order. The wholesale company doctors the paperwork to make it look like they shipped us the whole order. They keep the credits for the supplies that were never delivered and the money is clean. They do the same thing with a hospitality company for linens and other supplies."

"That's incredible," Nathan said. "Does that really work?"

"It's worked for decades," Caleb said. "The balance in that account goes up and down as we bill nonexistent customers and buy nonexistent supplies. All Montario had to do was wait until the shell companies paid us and grab the money before we paid the wholesale company."

"Arulio?" Nathan said.

Kimiyo nodded. "He had Arulio hack into the bank and take the money."

"Then Arulio needs to put it back," Nathan said.

"Quite impossible, Captain Teller," Arulio said. Everyone looked at him. "The funds were transferred to ten other accounts set up ahead of time. The banks and investment houses are split between planets in two solar systems. Even I cannot hack into that many locations and retrieve the funds. Certainly not before this gentleman's business associates arrive."

"What about after they arrive? Perhaps we could cut a deal for time."

Cole shook his head. "No way will the Syndicate let us go, Nathan. We know too much about their operation. They'll kill us, torture Montario until he transfers the funds back where they belong, kill him after he's done, and probably do unspeakable things to Caleb for letting this happen in the first place. We need to get out of here. Is Duncan having any luck?"

"He's still working on it," Nathan said. He looked at his mobi but there were no new messages.

"Swell," Cole said. He shifted his gaze to Caleb. "Unlock the pad. You locked it down, you unlock it."

"No," Caleb said.

Montario looked at him. "Caleb, I have to tell you, you're not negotiating from a position of strength here. These Syndicate guys play rough, I know. I've had dealings with them before.

It's better to leave now and take our chances on our own than wait for them."

"My instructions were clear in this situation," Caleb said. "If the perpetrators could be delayed, I was to delay them." He looked at Cole. "I don't need to worry about the Syndicate. You do. You stole their money. I'm just helping to clean up the mess."

Cole looked ready to explode. "In their eyes you allowed this to happen. Do you understand that?"

"We'll see," Caleb said. He was smiling, smugly.

Nathan held up a hand. "Forget about him. Let's go outside and see what we can do to help Duncan." He turned to Celeste. "Go get your crew together and tell them we're leaving."

"Nathan," Cole said, "If these guys are really on their way, the landing pad may not be the best place to be."

"I'm not hiding in here," Nathan said. "We need to get away from here and figure out a solution. We need breathing room. The *Blue Moon Bandit* is our only shot at doing that."

Celeste was just standing in the middle of the conversation pit, still looking scared. Nathan studied her for a moment. "Celeste? You really need to get moving. Can you do that?"

She nodded but looked unsure. "I'll get Captain Geechy and the others and meet you outside."

"What do you want me to do with these two?" Cole said, pointing at Caleb and Montario.

"Do you have any restraints?"

"Sure."

"Cuff them and leave them here," Nathan said. "Let the two of them explain what they've done."

Caleb jumped up and moved away from Cole, trying to slide around a table in the middle of the sunken living room. Kimiyo slipped behind him and took hold of his wrist. She bent his arm back and pushed his hand up between his shoulder blades. Simultaneously, she kicked at the back of one of his knees and he dropped to the floor. She rolled him onto his stomach and dug a knee into the small of his back, immobilizing him.

Montario jumped up and Cole caught him halfway off the couch. He shoved the con man face first onto the floor and straddled him from behind. He had flexible restraints wrapped around his wrists in a few seconds. He got up, walked around the table, and smiled at Kimiyo. "Nice job."

"Thank you," she said. "I didn't want him getting away."

"He wouldn't have," Cole said, kneeling down close to Caleb's ear. "I would have shot him before he got out of the room." He slipped restraints around Caleb's wrists and left him lying between the table and couch. He got up and helped Kimiyo stand.

"All set here, Nathan."

"Good," Nathan said. "Why don't you escort Kimiyo and Arulio out to the ship. I'll help Celeste get her crew together because she still isn't moving."

Celeste seemed to wake up at that. "Yeah, okay. I'm okay. Let's go."

Chapter 24

The rain was light when Cole led Kimiyo and Arulio outside. The afternoon was still dark, though, with thick, slate gray clouds blanketing the sky. As soon as they broke from the cover of the Children of the Apocalyptic Rainbow temple, Cole scanned the area, moving his eyes from side to side. The *Blue Moon Bandit* was directly ahead on the launch pad. He could see heavy metal clamps anchored in the tarmac holding down the four landing gear struts. These were the landing pad lockdown devices. They looked remarkably solid.

Kimiyo was behind him leading Arulio by the hand. Her hair swayed in the breeze as she too swiveled her head from side to side, looking for danger. The landing pads on either side of the *Blue Moon Bandit* were empty. He remembered a shuttle being on one when they arrived but it was gone now.

Their footfalls made the only noise to be heard across the area, their boot heels echoing off the building behind them in the empty air. Cole's long steps were less pronounced than the staccato produced by Kimiyo's low-heeled leather boots. Cole didn't like being so exposed. The distance was less than a hundred meters but to his way of thinking it took too long to reach the ship. When they did, he stepped to the rear of the ship near the entrance ramp.

Cole pushed the intercom buzzer and the small screen set into it flickered to life. "Duncan?"

Marla's face filled the screen. "He's in the engine room, Cole, trying to figure out a way to bust us loose. Hang out there. He wants to talk to you. I'll let him know you're here." Cole nodded.

The back entrance ramp dropped and Duncan walked down before it even touched the tarmac. The big man was wearing gray workman's pants, a grease stained white t-shirt, a blue vest with a dozen pockets, and a wide tool belt. His heavy boots thudded down the ramp and he was perspiring.

"How we doing on these locks, Duncan? Nathan wants to get out of here. We've got some heat coming our way."

Duncan walked over to the nearest landing strut and knelt down. "Not too good. These are strong restraints, better than I would have expected out here. The lock mechanism is armored," he said pointing to a heavy metal box. "Very tough."

"Can you cut through?"

"Oh yeah, no problem there. I have a saw and a laser that will cut through them but it will take time. Do we have time?"

"Not really. We're expecting company sooner rather than later. The guy we came to see has pissed off some very dangerous people. What if I help you and Richie? Could we all take a strut and speed things up?"

"That would help. Individually it will take about a half hour per strut. We've got four altogether. Can you help too?" he said looking at Kimiyo.

She looked startled. "I'll do what I can but I've never touched a power tool."

"If you, Richie, and I all take one it will take about an hour," Duncan said. "The first one done moves on to the last one."

"I hate to even bring this up but could Nathan just hit the engines and bust loose?" Cole said. "Like we did with the *Martha Tooey*?"

Duncan looked shocked. "Really?"

"I just thought I would ask."

"Look, that kind of stuff is fine with other people's ships but not this one. If he did something like that with the *Blue Moon Bandit* he would likely rip the whole undercarriage out of her. I'm not sure we would still be space worthy."

Cole looked around. Nothing had changed yet. They were still alone. He was still calm. Their line of work often involved high pressure, low time situations, and they always came through.

He snapped his fingers. "Are these controlled mechanically or by a computer system?"

"Looks like either or."

Cole turned to Kimiyo. "Can Arulio hack this system? Cut us loose?"

She looked back over to the bottom of the ramp. Arulio still stood there, lost in the transmissions only he could perceive. "I don't see why not."

Cole smiled. "Go talk to him. See if you can get the process started. If he needs to go inside to keep from being distracted, take him in."

He watched as Kimiyo spoke with Arulio. After a moment she walked back over shaking her head. "He thinks he can do it but not for an hour. It will take him that long to purge the event logs from the last few days and he must do that before attempting any further tasks. I'm sorry."

"It's not your fault," Cole said. "Go ahead and take him inside and we'll take care of this. I'll be out here helping Duncan."

"How did it go in there?" Duncan said.

Cole sighed. "It was as terrible as I expected." He filled Duncan in while they pulled a saw from one of the ship's outside storage lockers. Duncan wrestled the large tool to the landing strut and Cole hefted the batteries.

"I knew nothing good was going to come of this," Duncan said. "I warned him that getting involved in anything like this was stupid no matter how good the money was. The fact that Celeste is involved only makes things ten times worse."

"Nathan told me you were all for taking the job before you knew Celeste was involved."

Duncan scowled at him. "Okay the money was good. Once we found out Celeste was involved I really did think it was a bad idea."

"Then why didn't you say something?" Cole said. "I told him how horrible all this was and you just sat there." He handed Duncan a charged battery.

The engineer shrugged his shoulders. "You know how he is. There are two things Nathan does not have a clear head about; money and Celeste. The minute Saji Vy offered him a wad of cash for this ridiculous job and told him Celeste was involved, he was going to do it. The real question is; why are we here?" He pointed to himself and Cole. "Marla and I would like to retire someday, and keeping the cash coming in is the only way to do that." He positioned the saw over the manacle holding the landing strut.

"Okay," Cole said, smiling slightly.

"What?"

"The two of you have been investing like crazy for the last couple years. You could have skipped this job."

Duncan handed Cole a pair of safety glasses. "So? What about you? Why are you here?"

"Every once in a while Nathan goes off the deep end and needs someone to look out for him, especially when it comes to Celeste. She has some crazy hold over him. I thought if I came along I might be able to steer him clear of whatever craziness ensued." He looked around. "I'm going to guess I failed."

Duncan grimaced. "Yeah, well, nobody's perfect. Besides, Celeste and Nathan together are a truckload of crazy." He pointed to a section of the locking mechanism. "Richie is bringing out the other saws. When he does, make sure you cut here." Cole nodded. "Let me know if you have a problem." Duncan brought the saw down on the manacle and sparks began to fly.

— « o » —

Nathan followed Celeste down the hallway to her room. He watched her walk, enjoying the way her hips swayed. It was futile, he knew, to think anything could ever happen between them again, but there was a part of him that enjoyed just being in her presence. Then she spoke.

"This is turning into a real cluster," she said as she opened the door to her room.

"Yeah," Nathan agreed. "This thing has certainly gone off the rails."

She snapped her head around looked at him and rolled her eyes. Then she grabbed a duffel bag and began shoving things in it. Clothes, a tablet computer, and various other things she had on the dresser top.

Nathan stood watching her. "You think this is my fault somehow?"

She stopped for a second. "What are you even doing here? Did you volunteer for this? I mean, I saw you walk in and

I couldn't even believe it was you. We're divorced. You're obligations to me are at an end."

Nathan laughed. "Don't worry, Celeste, I...I mean, we didn't come for you. We're here for the money. Saji's paying top dollar to get his ship back. I don't know if you remember, but that's sort of our thing. We do it well."

"That must be why we're running for our lives," she said. "Just like old times."

Nathan shook his head. "Come on, we rarely, if ever, got into jams this screwed up. You're exaggerating."

"Oh that's right, just like I always do."

He rubbed the back of his neck. It was amazing how fast they could fall back into these patterns. Maybe it was time to break the pattern. "You know what? I am here because of you." He pulled the chair out from the small desk and collapsed into it. "I admit it. I mean, I would have taken the job anyway because of what Saji is paying but once I heard you were involved, in trouble, well, that sealed the deal."

Celeste stopped packing and looked at him. "Oh, no. Come on. Don't tell me you still have feelings for me."

He held up his hands. "I don't know about all that but I have to admit that when I saw you outside, you took my breath away." He considered for a moment before going on. "You still look great."

She started jamming things into the duffel bag. "I'm not doing this. Not now."

"What do you mean? Do what?"

She pulled the drawstrings tight on her bag. "I am not going to start examining my feelings right now. First, this idiot kidnaps us, and now you show up to save us. I think I've had my fill of men for a while."

"I guess that's fair."

"Well I'm glad you agree." She swung her bag over her shoulder. "Now let's go get the captain and get out of here." She walked into the hallway and turned right. Nathan shook his head and followed her.

— « o » —

Montario and Caleb lay on the carpet in the conversation pit. Caleb turned his head to look in Montario's direction. "Did you really think you could get away with this? How stupid are you?"

Monatrio smiled. "I did get away with it. The money is mine."

Caleb rolled his eyes. He did that a lot and Montario thought it was probably his most irritating trait.

"Do you understand who is on their way here right now?" Caleb asked. "Do you know what they do to people who steal from them?"

"Quit nagging me," Montario said. "You're like every woman I've ever known. 'Do you know this? Do you know that?' Here's the thing Caleb, I know what the Syndicate is about, that's why I don't plan on being here when they arrive."

"Well you're doing a fine job of getting away."

Montario twisted himself around and pushed himself up to a sitting position with his back against one of the sofas. He huffed a little bit, out of breath from the effort.

"Where do you think you're going?" Caleb said.

"I'm not lying on the floor with my face in the carpet; seems a bit undignified."

Caleb looked up at him and started rolling around. With a great effort, he squirmed into a sitting position and pushed himself back against the sofa. "I don't think you are taking this as seriously as you should. You stole millions of credits. I mean, I've seen some dumb things in my time but this is light-years beyond anything else."

"Well, we can't all be middle managers in a vast criminal enterprise, eh?" Montario threw him a smirk just to rub some salt in the wound.

Caleb looked at him, eyes glaring. "Just wait. Just wait 'til they get here."

Montario smirked again.

— « o » —

Forty-five minutes later, Duncan and Richie were working together to saw through the last lock on the landing pad. The metal was tough but the two of them were making good time. Duncan was used to cutting ships free. In their line of work, someone was always coming up with new ways to hold onto their ship after they'd stopped paying for it.

Cole walked the perimeter of the landing pad. There was no one within sight. He caught a glimpse of faces at the windows of the temple. They pulled back when he caught them. He wished he could hear better but the saws Duncan and Richie were using made a high-pitched whine as they cut through the locks. The rain was now a drizzle, just enough to make someone miserable but not enough to be a real bother. Cole stared at the door to the temple and wondered where Nathan, Celeste, and her crew were.

A roar ripped through the air and Cole's head snapped around. He could hear it even over the sound of the saws. The *Blue Moon Bandit* was blocking the view of the section of sky Cole needed to see. He ran around the ship, ducking under the starboard engine housing. A ship was coming in fast, screaming down through the clouds. He watched it for a moment hoping that it was heading in the wrong direction but it wasn't. It banked slightly, burning off some speed and then it roared toward the temple. Cole grabbed his mobi from his pocket and sent a short message to Nathan and Marla as he ran for Duncan. He almost ran into an open equipment locker door and ducked around it. He tapped Duncan on the shoulder. The big man turned and looked at him, pulling his safety goggles down around his neck. He stood up and Richie took over the saw.

"What's up?"

Cole pointed toward the other landing pad. The other ship hadn't set down yet but he knew where it would be in a minute. "We're out of time. There's a ship on the way in and it's coming fast. How are you doing?"

Duncan looked down at the lock holding the landing strut. "I need another minute. Where's Nathan and Celeste?"

"Hell, I don't know. They're probably arguing about their divorce. I sent him a message. Do what you can. I'll try and buy you some time." Duncan nodded, pulled up his goggles, and moved to help Richie.

Cole walked back toward the rear entrance ramp and thumbed the lock on another equipment locker. It scanned his thumbprint and popped open. He reached inside and pulled out a rifle and a bandolier holding spare magazines. He loaded one into the rifle, racked a round into the chamber, and closed the locker door. From his vantage point he could see the next landing pad, but he had no cover except for the landing ramp. It was thin and offered little protection and everyone would need to use it in a moment. Drawing fire toward it seemed like a bad idea.

The ship circled the temple and landing pads, presumably getting a good look at the situation before they set down. Cole stayed back under the *Blue Moon Bandit*, making sure they wouldn't see him. Marla appeared at the top of the ramp.

"Do we have company?" she asked.

Cole nodded. "We sure do. The guys are just about finished cutting us free. How soon can we lift off once everyone is aboard?"

"I've already done the pre-flight checklist and started the engines so we're ready to go."

Cole noticed silence in the air and turned to see Duncan and Richie packing their equipment into cases. Duncan knelt, snapping the clasps on a large plastic case. Richie carefully placed a spare battery in his case and closed the lid. The restraints holding the landing gear were severed.

"The guys are finished. Where is Nathan?"

— « o » —

"My God, who gave him a bottle?" Celeste said. "The whole crew knows to keep liquor away from him. That's why the *Charon* is a dry ship."

Nathan looked at Thomas Geechy, captain of the *Charon* sprawled on the bed, passed out with an empty bottle of whiskey on the floor beside his outstretched right hand. The other crew members, all four of them, stood behind them, bags packed.

"It didn't come from the ship, Ms. Bezzle," one of the men said. "We search the captain's bags after every shore leave. We didn't find anything."

Celeste sighed. "Thanks, Chuck, but he obviously found a bottle somewhere."

Nathan's mobi buzzed and he pulled it from his pocket. He read the message. "There's another ship outside."

"That's got to be the Syndicate," Celeste said. "We have to move." She looked around the room but there was nothing helpful. "Okay, Chuck, can you guys carry him out to the landing pad? We have to catch a ride back to the *Charon*."

The material handler looked at her. "You mean to say the Syndicate is involved in this? That they're coming here?"

She nodded. "A lot has happened while we were locked up but yes, the Syndicate is part of it. They're on their way here. Please, carry the captain and we can all get out of here."

The men looked at each other. "We can move faster without him," Chuck said.

"Pick him up." Celeste ordered. "We aren't leaving anyone behind."

"Fine," Chuck said. "Come on Jeff, get his feet. We'll haul the old drunk out." They picked up the captain with a pair of grunts and the other two crewmen picked up their bags. "Let's go, Ms. Bezzle. The captain's not getting any lighter."

— « o » —

"Sir?" A voice whispered from the doorway of the great room leading to the kitchen. Caleb looked up. It was Gretchen, a young member of the Children of the Apocalyptic Rainbow and she was looking at Montario. "Are you all right?" She said as she moved into the room slowly, looking around.

Montario shot a warning look at Caleb and turned to the young lady. "Of course, my dear. I could use a bit of help though, if you don't mind." He turned his hips and showed her the restraints binding his hands.

"We heard shouting and then those people went down the hall."

"That's right, dear but if you could help untie me, I can put things to right. Can you do that?"

"Oh sure." She started back into the kitchen then turned back. "Are those people gone?"

"No, they aren't, dear, but no need to be apprehensive. Just go ahead and cut me loose and I'll take care of everything."

She nodded, said "Okay", and went back into the kitchen.

Montario looked at Caleb. "It was good you kept your mouth shut. I can get us both out of here. Give me a hard time and you can sit here and wait for your Syndicate friends."

Caleb was silent for a minute, doing the math in his head. What Cole had said earlier, about him being responsible for the theft had been worrying him. The Syndicate had little patience for failure and this was a screw up of colossal proportions. If he could trust Montario to help him run, he might have a chance. If he stayed put, he had a fifty –fifty chance of taking the heat for Montario's theft.

"What can you do for me?" he asked.

"Well, I'm a rich man. If you help me get out of here, I can set you up somewhere. You can go wherever you want and do whatever you want. What do you say?"

"Okay, let's get out of here, but I don't want to spend one more minute than is necessary with you."

"Just until we're free and clear," Montario said.

"You have a way out of here? One that doesn't involve catching a ride with Captain Teller?"

Montario smiled. "Oh yeah, I have a plan. Just follow me."

Gretchen walked back in, glancing around furtively. "Is it safe?"

Montario made a show of looking around. "It's all good Gretchen. Please hurry, dear."

She bent, cutting them free with a kitchen knife. Montario and Caleb stood up, rubbing their wrists. Caleb watched as Montario hugged Gretchen. "Thank you, dear. Now please run back to your room. I want you to be safe until these people have left."

She smiled and nodded, going down the hallway that led to the member's quarters. Caleb watched her disappear and turned back to Montario. The leader was looking directly at him.

"We're good?" Montario said. "You haven't changed your mind?"

"No," he said, shaking his head. "Let me grab a bag and we can go."

Montario grabbed him by the arm. "We can buy anything you need on the way. I'm guessing we're almost out of time."

The building rumbled as a ship flew close. They both looked up, realizing what the ship might be. Montario looked at Caleb. "I'm leaving now, Caleb. Are you coming?"

He looked toward the door leading back to the landing pad. If it was the Syndicate coming in for a landing, he could run out there and tell them what happened. Explain how it wasn't his fault. Sure, and maybe they'd set him up in another cushy gig like this instead of killing him. He looked back at Montario with nothing but hate in his heart, but his choice was already made. "Okay, let's get out of here."

— « o » —

The other ship circled the field once more. Marla and Kimiyo watched from the cockpit as the *Blue Moon Bandit*'s scanners tracked it. Marla let out a low whistle. "That's a LL-429 courier. Very fast. No wonder they got here so quickly."

"Faster than us?"

Marla wiggled a hand and gave her the half-and-half sign. "It's not all about speed. They're more maneuverable than us, for sure, but with the modifications my man has made to the *Blue Moon Bandit* we can outrun them."

Kimiyo looked back down the corridor toward the galley. Arulio was sitting there at the table, calmly staring into space. "Marla, may I ask, are there any more guns aboard?"

— « o » —

Cole watched as the courier ship hovered over the landing pad opposite the *Blue Moon Bandit* and slowly lowered itself. From his position at the bottom of the ramp, he saw the ship settle lightly on its landing gear. He had one hand on the strut support and a hand on his rifle. He glanced at the door to the temple and wondered where Nathan was.

A hiss of steam caught his attention and Cole looked at the other ship. It was outgassing, dumping coolant pressure from the ride in. After a few seconds, the noise stopped and the steam floated away, revealing a landing ramp. Before it lowered all the way to the tarmac, he saw boots and legs hurrying down. His breath caught in his throat and he said, "Oh shit."

— « o » —

"What the hell are they doing here?" Nathan said as he looked out a window at the rear of the temple. Atomic Jack, Kinty, and Bonto were stepping off the ramp of the courier. "We left that guy for dead back on Olympia."

"Which one?" Celeste said, moving to the window as the three men began walking across the landing pad.

"The one in the big pressure suit. The guy on his left," he pointed at Kinty, "shot him back on Olympia. He didn't have those bandages on his face then, though."

"They look pretty chummy. You sure they were trading shots with each other?"

"No, he shot him in the back. I don't have time to explain but this is very bad news."

"Can we make a run for it?" One of the *Charon* crew asked. "Maybe we could get to your ship before they get to us."

Nathan kept looking out the window. "Let me think a minute." He looked out the window toward the *Blue Moon Bandit* again and saw that Duncan and Richie had done a good job freeing the landing gear. Cole was standing at the base of the ramp, trying to keep as much cover between himself and the new arrivals as possible. He had a rifle in his hand and spare magazines strapped across his chest so Nathan knew the ex-marshal was expecting trouble. He was probably trying to cover their escape. He bit his lower lip and sized up the situation.

"Our best bet is to run for the *Bandit*," Nathan said. "Grab the captain and get ready to haul ass. If those jokers start to shoot, just run for the ship and get up the ramp. Cole will cover us. Try to stay out of his way. If any of you drop anything, besides the captain, leave it behind. We're only going to get one shot at this."

"What about Montario and Caleb?" Celeste asked. "We can't just leave them behind tied up like that."

"I really don't care," Nathan said. "They created this whole mess. I'm not sticking my neck out for them." He noted she looked back toward the common room. "We just don't have time, Celeste."

"We should have just gone through the common room on our way to the door. We could have cut them loose."

"They'll be fine. I imagine they've both had experience at getting out of scrapes. Besides, they wouldn't go back for you." He grabbed the handle to the door. "Okay, I'm going to open the door and we all run, okay? On the count of three; one... two...three!"

Nathan grabbed the door and yanked it open.

— « o » —

Cole watched as the three Syndicate guys surveyed the situation. They glanced toward the temple entrance and only gave a passing glance toward Nathan's ship. Atomic Jack was gesturing at the temple explaining something and he seemed to be ignoring the *Blue Moon Bandit*. That might work in their favor. If the message the Syndicate received was only about the money being stolen, they might not realize Cole and the rest of their crew was involved at all. Until something tipped them off, they might have a short window of escape. He moved slowly to get more cover behind a landing strut and the ramp, trying to reduce the angle at which they might see him. He glanced toward the temple entrance again and saw the door kick open. Nathan held the door as Celeste and four guys came running out. Two of them were carrying someone. They cleared the door and ran up the walkway toward the landing pad. Atomic Jack pointed at them and Kinty and Bonto started to move, pulling guns as they went. They clearly meant to intercept Nathan's group before they could get to the *Blue Moon Bandit*. Cole said, "Damn it", rolled around the landing strut and raised his rifle.

— « o » —

Nathan saw Cole moving and looked toward Atomic Jack and his crew. Kinty and Bonto were moving toward them, guns out. "We've got company coming, guys, move faster."

They picked up the pace but were slowed by Jeff and Chuck carrying Captain Geechy. The captain swayed between them as they ran, but they didn't stumble. They crossed the threshold to the pad as the two gangsters started running across the grass separating the two landing pads. Nathan ran toward the *Blue Moon Bandit* and gave his group even odds of reaching it in time.

— « o » —

Cole saw the two gangsters hit the grass and decided Nathan's group wasn't going to make it without help. Screw it, he thought. If they wanted to play with guns, he would show them how it was done. He sighted in ahead of them and let a long burst go from the rifle. The rounds kicked up dirt and grass in front of the two gangsters and they came to a halt, dropping, rolling, and raising their guns. Cole fired another burst and they threw their arms over their heads, slugs ripped through the grass all around them. Cole took a deep breath, calmly ejected the spent magazine, and loaded another. He stepped around the landing strut and hollered. "Just stay down you two. If you raise your heads, no more warning shots. We're leaving and if you try to stop us again, I'll put one right through your hearts."

He spared a glance at Nathan's group and saw them tearing across the landing pad. They were about twenty meters from the *Blue Moon Bandit* when the slug hit Cole square in the back and laid him out on the tarmac.

— « o » —

"No!" Nathan shouted. Cole's body sprawled on the tarmac and his rifle skittered away, coming to a rest near the landing strut he had been using for cover. Nathan ran toward him and another shot rang out from behind his ship. He pulled up short, unsure of where the gunman was. He didn't see anyone but clearly someone was in that direction. It was all just open grass past the tarmac's edge. Celeste ran up to him and said, "Nathan, look." She pointed at Kinty and Bonto who had been lying in the grass. They were up and moving toward them again, guns drawn.

"Just stop right there," Atomic Jack's voice boomed out from the other landing pad. It was amplified, of course, to reach across the distance between them. "Just stay where you are and no one else will be shot. We just want to straighten a few things out."

Nathan saw him moving quickly in his pressure suit, hustling across the open space.

— « o » —

Kimiyo watched from the top of the landing ramp as Cole went down. She rushed forward and Marla caught her arm. "Hold up, we don't want to get anyone killed."

Kimiyo shook her off. "You mean anyone else?"

Duncan came running up from the engine room corridor. "What just happened? Did I hear shooting? Did Cole shoot someone?" Richie was behind him with a bewildered look on his face.

"It's those idiots from the alley back in Go City and Olympia. The ones Richie owes money. They shot Cole."

"What?" Duncan said. "Is he all right? Where is he?"

"Bottom of the ramp but they don't want anyone moving. They say they'll shoot anyone who moves."

"*They* did not shoot Mr. Seger," Arulio said from the galley. He stood up and walked to Kimiyo. His red eyes were suddenly alive, blazing with intelligence and life where before they had been blank.

"What do you mean?" Kimiyo asked.

"It was not those three men that shot Mr. Seger. It was the man on the opposite side of the ship. I can hear the one they call Jack speaking with him on a radio. He's telling him to shoot anyone who moves."

Marla and Duncan moved to a monitor set into the wall to the right of the door. She called up a camera view under the ship. Duncan panned the camera around to where Arulio indicated. "Are you sure, Arulio?" Duncan said. "I don't see anyone."

"You wouldn't Mr. Jax," Arulio said. "He's quite invisible."

— « o » —

Nathan watched the two gunmen approach. They were walking more slowly now, more confident that they had things under control. He looked at Cole again. "I want to see my man," he said, raising his voice. "I need to see if he's all right."

"Stay put," Kinty said, close enough now to hear when he spoke. "You can check on him when we get there."

"Then quit taking your damn time," Nathan said. "I don't want him bleeding out while you mess around."

"Just sit tight. We'll get there in a minute."

— « o » —

"What do you mean invisible, Arulio?" Kimiyo said. "How is he invisible?"

"I noticed it after the other ship landed. There was all this buzzing, you see, creating interference in the spectrum, disrupting the signal flow. It took quite a bit of concentration to pinpoint it. The sensation was quite annoying."

"A shimmer suit," Duncan said. "The bastard is wearing a shimmer suit."

"What's that?" Kimiyo asked.

"Camouflage," Duncan answered, "turns you damn near invisible. If you look hard, you might see a ripple in the air like heat rising off a hot road but most times you wouldn't notice. Cole didn't see him."

"Arulio, where is this interference now?" Kimiyo asked.

"Behind the port engine nozzle."

She hefted the small assault rifle she'd been holding and chambered a round. Duncan saw she had two extra magazines, the high capacity ones Cole favored. "What do you think you are doing?"

"Please get ready to help Nathan," she said.

"With what?"

"Cole is a big man. He won't be able to lift him all by himself."

"Wait a minute..." Duncan said, but she was already through the door and moving down the ramp.

— « o » —

Nathan saw Kimiyo take three quick steps down the ramp and duck low. She had a rifle in her hand and aimed it toward the landing pad under the port engine nozzle. She laid down a continuous stream of fire in that direction and Nathan heard someone scream. Duncan ran down the ramp past Kimiyo.

"Nathan, grab Cole!" Duncan shouted.

They ran toward their prone crewman and Kimiyo turned toward Atomic Jack and his men, ripping off another burst in that direction. Nathan saw the mobster in the pressure suit moving faster now, probably as fast as he could in his suit. He was shouting at his men but Nathan couldn't concentrate enough to hear. He reached Cole at the same time Duncan did and both of them bent over their friend.

A shot ricocheted off the ramp near Kimiyo. She turned back to the port engine nozzle, surprised, and pulled the trigger again. She got two rounds off and the rifle clicked empty. She retreated up the ramp, trying to escape from whoever had a bead on her.

Nathan had a hand on Cole's shoulder to roll him over when Cole suddenly rose to one knee and drew his pistol from its holster. He snapped off two shots behind them before Nathan and Duncan understood what was happening. Someone in that direction screamed. Cole stood up fully and whirled back toward the approaching mobsters. They were no more than five meters away, pistols drawn.

Kimiyo stepped back onto the ramp, ducking low again, and provided cover. After a quite assessing look at Cole to make sure he really was ok, Nathan picked up Cole's dropped rifle and hefted it, staring at Atomic Jack. The mobster stared back. Stalemate.

Chapter 25

"You've got five seconds to explain what you're doing here," Jack said, his voice raspy and metallic. "I thought you were hunting that ship that carts dead bodies around. Tell me, or my boys are going to end this quickly."

"Anyone else behind us in a shimmer suit?" Duncan asked.

Cole raised his pistol to Jack. "So that's how you got the drop on me? Invisible men?"

Jack looked back, his fiery eyes drilling into Cole. "I have to admit; I'm less than pleased with their performance. They were expensive."

"The men or the suits?" Nathan said.

"The suits," Jack said.

"Anyone else in your vessel?" Nathan said looking around. "You have more guys?"

"I have everyone I need to take care of this," Jack said.

"That's not a straight answer," Nathan said.

"Well, that's the one you're getting."

Nathan looked back toward Celeste and the crew of the *Charon*. They were on the ground, either laying down or kneeling, like Celeste. She stood up and walked over, stopping behind Nathan. "I don't know what's going on here but my crew and I are leaving," she said.

"No," Jack said. "No one is going anywhere until my business is concluded. Don't worry, it won't take long."

"We know all about your business," Nathan said. "The money you're laundering through the Children of the Apocalyptic Rainbow. We know who took it and we know why you're here."

"How?" Jack asked.

"The people here took this woman and her crew hostage," Nathan said. "Their ship is the body barge. This cult stopped them and impounded the ship until their ransom was paid. My crew and I took care of that."

"That's why you needed the wetjack, wasn't it?" Jack said. "Your man with the purple skin, the one who bets on dogs, said you needed the wetjack to do something for someone, to get someone free."

"Yeah," Nathan said. "He told us how you tortured him."

"Well, he wasn't as forthcoming as we wanted. Anyway, our money is gone, you appear to be the people who took it and I need it back. Looks like you're my problem once again."

"No, we're not your problem," Nathan said. "See, we don't have your money. It's true that we played a part in stealing it from you, but we were coerced into doing it. You're looking for a man named Montario Dawson. He was the lead asshole around here until he got too big for his britches and decided to move into grand larceny."

"And I suppose he's long gone?" Jack said.

"You suppose wrong," Nathan said. "We left him tied up in the common room inside. Your man Caleb is tied up with him. By the way, don't be too hard on him. He did what he could, but he was outclassed."

Atomic Jack looked at Bonto and nodded his head in the direction of the temple. "Check it out."

"We've got an injured man," Nathan said. "We need to get him inside. I'm going to do that now."

"I'm fine, Nathan," Cole said.

Nathan knocked on his chest, producing a deep sound. "Duncan's bucky vest worked pretty well, huh? Nothing like carbon fiber."

"I still felt it but I don't think I'll even bruise. It was pretty easy to play possum."

"Anyway, the injured man is Captain Geechy. He's ill and I can't leave him lying in the grass." He pointed to the captain's prone form. He was face down on the ground, arms and legs splayed around him. "Besides, these people have nothing to do with this."

"Do what you have to," Jack said, "but if this ship moves, you all take a bullet and my pilot will shoot down your ship."

The crew of the *Charon* walked up the ramp, two of them carrying Captain Geechy. Nathan turned to Duncan, ducking his head and speaking softly. "Duncan, you go in too. Tell Marla to be ready for a quick take off. Help everyone get strapped in."

"She's ready now," the engineer said. "All we need is for everyone to come aboard. What about Kimiyo?"

"Leave her right where she is. For a caretaker she's a pretty good shot."

The crowd moved up the ramp leaving Nathan, Celeste, Cole, and Kimiyo facing Jack and Kinty. Cole nodded at Kinty. "The wrist looks healed. What happened to your face? What's up with those bandages? They look like they're covering up some nasty burns."

Kinty blew out a slow breath. "You're just making it worse, man. Things aren't over between us."

"I've heard that before. In the alley, at Sean's pawnshop. You like to talk. Must be a big part of your job, huh? Scaring people into giving up their money. You ever run into people who don't scare?"

"Let it go, Kinty," Jack said.

Cole shifted his gaze to Jack. "You ever forgive him for shooting you back on Olympia? Oh, wait, is that what the bandages are for? Did you burn him for what he did?"

"Yeah," Nathan said. "I've been wondering about that. How did you survive? I saw him put a couple rounds into you and your suit. You lit up like flare. How are you standing here?"

"He only popped the suit, not me," Jack said. "The regeneration unit in the suit and painkillers are doing their job."

"That is some amazing technology."

"It gets the job done." He looked at Kimiyo on the ramp. "Does your friend over there have any more biologic weapons? We're not being exposed to anything right now are we? No exotic virus this time?"

"She's got a rifle this time. I think you're safe."

Bonto came running out of the temple. He was moving fast, breathing hard, like he didn't do it very often. He ran up to Jack and held up a pair of plastic cuffs.

"They're gone, Jack.

"Where?"

"I found a girl who admitted to cutting them free. She said they ran off together, out the other side of the temple, toward that small town below."

Jack turned to Nathan. "You playing games?"

"He was in there when we left. That's all I can tell you," Nathan said.

"No one is leaving here until I get that money back."

"Can't happen, man," Nathan said. "It was taken from that account and transferred into lots of smaller accounts. When I found out who the money belonged to, I tried to have it transferred back. The wetjack couldn't do it before you arrived."

Atomic Jack looked at the temple and breathed heavily. Nathan could hear it through the speaker on the suit's helmet. "He had to have been planning this for a while."

"Obvioulsy," Nathan said.

"Was his plan to get away on your ship? Is he on there now? Are you playing me? Trying to make a fool of me?"

Nathan held up the rifle. "Calm down there, chief. We were hired to deliver the wetjack and escort the crew back to their vessel. Giving Montario a ride wasn't part of the deal. He had to have a plan for getting away, one that didn't involve us. There's no more shuttles on the landing pads either."

"I want to look on your ship, make sure he isn't hiding there."

"He's not," Celeste said.

"What would you know about it?" Jack said. "Weren't you being held hostage here?"

Nathan looked at her. "Did he say something while you were here? Did he say anything that would lead us to where he is going?"

Celeste blushed. "No, he didn't say anything. It's just that, earlier he was heading out the front of the temple when we saw him with his bag packed. He wasn't coming to the landing pad."

"I want to see inside your ship," Jack said.

"Not today," Nathan said. "We're leaving. I've told you who you're looking for and told you what went down. My people are out of here. Celeste, get aboard. Then you Kimiyo." Nathan lifted the rifle, pointed it at Jack, and said, "I'll hit more than just the suit if you try to stop us."

They heard a rumble then, the distinctive sound of a ship lifting off. All of them turned toward town. Atomic Jack stepped out from under the *Blue Moon Bandit* and Nathan followed, keeping the rifle pointed at him. A small ship was shooting into the sky, screaming as it shot through the atmosphere.

"That isn't coming from the regional spaceport," Nathan said. "The spaceport's on the other side of town. I saw it on the way in."

Jack fumed. "There was a private strip in that direction. We saw it when we circled the area."

"That's got to be your guy," Nathan said. "Looks like you have a choice to make. Are you going to keep screwing around with us or go after him?"

"Damn it!" Jack said.

"I don't ever want to see you again, Jack," Nathan said. "My crew and I are off your list. You want the guy who stole your money, go find him. We're going to go finish our job. Oh, and you're square with Richie."

Atomic Jack's skin flared orange as he breathed hard. He turned to Kinty and Bonto. "Get back on the ship." He pointed at the ship speeding away. "That's our man. Let's go."

They moved off toward their ship, running as fast as they could. Nathan watched them go, making sure they didn't pull anything as they left. Celeste and Kimiyo were aboard and Cole stood beside him.

"Are we going home, Nathan?"

Nathan nodded. "Yeah, let's go. I've had enough of this place."

He jerked a thumb toward the dead men at the rear of the ship. "What about Jack's guys? The ones we shot?"

Nathan looked at them. They were half visible, their suits in disarray after they were shot. "Let the Children of the Apocalyptic Rainbow deal with them. They weren't part of the job."

They climbed the ramp and closed it behind them.

Chapter 26

Marla had them rocketing skyward as soon as the rear landing ramp was closed. Nathan walked up to the cockpit and checked the course to the *Charon* and got an ETA. He made his way back to the galley and stood in the doorway. The room was crowded with his crew and the crew of the *Charon*. He saw Captain Geechy was awake and sitting at the table. He had a blanket around him and was sipping a mug of coffee. Celeste saw Nathan and she walked over to him.

"How's your skipper?" he asked.

"Sobering up," she said. "Duncan gave him a shot of something and that scary woman with the gun gave him some coffee."

"Kimiyo."

"Yeah, her." She looked over everyone seated around the table and standing in the galley. "This is a big crowd for this ship. I saw you go up to the cockpit. Do you have an ETA to the *Charon*?"

"Twenty-five minutes. We'll get you there and make sure she's spaceworthy."

She nodded. "I hadn't thought about that. I hope those kids took care of her. I have to tell you, the *Charon* is not the most well maintained ship I've ever served on. Saji Vy doesn't like to spring for a lot of new parts."

"I'll have Duncan and Richie help your crew. Cole and I will go first, though. That Montario guy said he had some people on board maintaining things. I want to make sure they don't give us a hard time."

She smiled. "Thanks. I notice you got Duncan a helper."

"He's needed one for a while and we're doing well enough now to bring someone aboard."

"That's good to hear," she said. "I was worried when I left that things would go south. Nice to see you've managed to keep things flying along."

"We're not helpless, you know. We are the premiere starship repossession company in Go City."

She smirked. "You're the only one."

Nathan shrugged. "It's a niche market. We fill a need."

Twenty minutes later Nathan and Celeste watched Marla match the orbital heading and velocity of the *Charon*. Celeste had been right about the condition of the ship, Nathan noticed as he looked over the hull. It was pitted and scarred with welds and rivets holding patches in place. He turned to Celeste. "You jump that past light speed?"

"Look, I've been through some stuff here, okay? You don't need to tell me how bad the ship looks. I fly it every day."

Marla turned to Nathan. "What do you think the *Blue Moon Bandit* would look like if Duncan didn't work as hard he does? Sounds like you and this Saji Vy have a lot in common."

"I'm getting ganged up on, here," he said. "Okay, Marla, swing us around the long axis. I want to see if anyone else is here."

Marla goosed the thrusters and they eyeballed the *Charon*. There was no shuttle docked with it. If the Children of the Apocalyptic Rainbow were aboard, they didn't have a ride home.

"Where's the best place to dock, Celeste?" Marla asked.

"There's a small loading bay but our shuttle is in there. Swing around over the top. There's a standard hatch amidships. We can go in there."

Nathan went back into the galley and grabbed Cole. "You ready? We're here."

Cole nodded. He hefted a shotgun. "Nonlethal rounds. You want one?"

Nathan shook his head. "I can't see where I would be any better of a shot than you. Besides, I think the kids are gone. I bet they got a call the moment we left the surface."

They felt their ship dock. Nathan turned to the crowd around the table. "Captain Geechy, we're going to inspect your ship. When we're satisfied it's secure, I'll call for you and your crew."

Geechy nodded. "Take Celeste with you as a guide."

"I was already going, Cap."

— « o » —

The inside of the ship smelled musty and the lights were low. Celeste accessed a control panel and called up the environmental controls. Fresh air began to flow and the lights grew brighter. "I don't think anyone has been aboard for a few days," she said. "I'll bet they were living on their shuttle."

"Given the cargo, I'm not surprised no one wanted to stay aboard," Nathan said. "What's the best way to search? Stern to bow?"

She nodded. "This isn't a complicated ship. Engines in the rear third, then the cargo holds, then the bridge and living quarters."

"Okay, then," Nathan said. "Let's have a look."

The engine room was empty. Nathan noticed it was in serviceable condition but nothing special. They passed the atmospheric generators and emergency batteries and then came to a door marked with a large black "A".

"What's in here?" Cole said.

"What do you think?" Celeste said.

Cole drew back from the door. Celeste laughed. "Come on you big baby. They don't bite." She pushed through the door and stepped into the hold. Nathan gestured to Cole. "You have the gun. Shoot anything that moves and isn't one of us."

"Right."

They moved in behind Celeste. She hustled ahead, moving at a good clip. Nathan looked around him. The hold was chilly, the temperature was probably around zero centigrade. A thermometer on the wall confirmed that for him. There were rows of coffins stacked neatly in custom shelving. The hold was arranged to hold bodies three high, each row was ten coffins long, thirty bodies to a row. There were five rows in this hold, Nathan counted.

"This is creepy," Cole said.

"Yeah," Nathan said.

"Two more holds to go, guys. Hurry up."

They moved to catch up to Celeste and moved through the second hold, marked "B". The last, "C" was almost empty. "You didn't have a full load this time out?" Nathan said.

"We rarely do anymore," Celeste said. "It seems like fewer people are opting for a burial back on Earth. It's expensive and it takes us a month to do a circuit so some families don't like the wait."

Cole moved ahead of them, pushing the door open. "Is this the door to the living quarters?"

"It is," she said. "There's another access corridor so you can reach the engine room without going through the holds but we needed to do the search."

"Well let's make sure we use the access corridor to get back to the hatch," Cole said. "I'm not going back through there."

"I remember you being tougher," Celeste said.

He pushed a cabin door open and looked around. "It's got nothing to do with courage. It's a bad luck thing. Those folks don't want me disturbing their eternal rest."

"Are you serious?" Celeste said. "Are you superstitious?"

"Think about everything we've done," he said. "All the scrapes we've been through, all the tight spots we've squeezed out of. You think that was all skill? Not me. I'm not getting my Karma all screwed up by disturbing the dead. Uh-uh. Those people earned their peace. I'm not disturbing them."

"Is he serious?"

"Sure is," Nathan said. "I'll tell you something else, right now I'm in total agreement with him. You may be used to treating the dead like boxes of vegetables, but I'll be happy when we're off your ship."

Cole nosed into a cabin at the end of the corridor. "This the last one, Celeste?"

"That's it. The bridge is just up those stairs." She moved to go up but Cole beat her to it. He climbed the stairs two at a time and went in. She followed and Nathan brought up the rear.

It was empty.

Celeste sat down at the controls and checked them. Nathan looked over her shoulder. "It's all automated," she said. "They set the auto pilot and it doesn't look like they messed with anything else." She made some adjustments and started bringing things back to manual control. "If you want to get Captain Geechy and the others we can probably be underway in an hour."

"I'll take care of it," Cole said.

"Is this where you were when you got boarded?" Nathan said.

"Yeah, it was my shift. Not a lot to do, you know. The ship pretty much flies itself. Even this ship."

"How did they do it?" he asked. "You were probably moving pretty fast. How did they make you stop?"

Celeste stared at the control panel and continued checking statuses. "I really don't know. The systems went dead, even gravity, and then we got pulled out to their shuttle."

"You didn't have to brake? I saw their shuttles. I wouldn't have thought they could catch a ship moving at speed."

"Well, they did," she said. Her shoulders hunched. "Look, it wasn't my proudest moment, okay? It was just another failure in a long list of failures. You know, I don't know what I'm going to do after this."

"What do you mean?"

"Flying this tub is the bottom of the ladder, Nathan. It's the end of the line. The list of pilot jobs available after you've been fired from flying dead bodies around is abysmally short."

"You don't know you'll get fired."

"You met Saji Vy. Can you imagine him keeping me on? Do you know how big of an embarrassment this incident would have been for him? There's nothing left but the termination notice delivered by a middle manager who is probably already hunting for my replacement."

"Maybe you could come back to work for me."

Her head drooped further. "I don't want your pity. Besides, you have an excellent co-pilot. Marla has great skills."

"I could ask around."

She shook her head. "You know what? Just give me a moment here, okay? Let me just deal with this."

He put his hand on the back of her seat, unsure of what to do next. Finally, he left the cockpit and went to check on the engineering crew.

— « o » —

The ride home to Earth took a little over two days. They kept things slow so the *Charon* could keep pace with the *Blue Moon Bandit*. To Nathan and Duncan's mutual surprise the body barge stayed in one piece during the transit through the warpgate back to the Sol system. They cleared Neptune, made a light speed jump, and arrived in Earth orbit fifty hours after departing Port Solitude.

Captain Geechy and his crew oversaw the unloading of the *Charon*. Grateful families were happy to receive their loved one's remains. The ship was only a couple days late arriving so nothing was mentioned in the press. Celeste offered to explain things to Saji Vy in person when she learned Nathan would be meeting with him. Captain Geechy asked her to stay aboard the *Charon*. "If anyone has any explaining to do," he said, "it's me. I'll be seeing the big man tomorrow. The meeting is already set."

Nathan and Marla took the *Blue Moon Bandit* back to the spaceport in Go City and landed in the berth Nathan leased. He left her, Richie, and Cole to do the post-trip work on the ship and called a taxi for Kimiyo, Arulio, Duncan, and himself. The van took them directly to Saji Vy's office in the downtown business district.

The building was impressive; about seventy stories tall, formed from dark, charcoal colored glass with a smoky tint, and chrome trim. It was different from the residential building where their first meeting had taken place but no less impressive. Nathan led the way in. It was afternoon on a Tuesday so business foot traffic in the lobby was heavy. Kimiyo produced an ID badge and whisked them past the security desk and up an escalator. The second floor held access to a bank of high-speed elevators and Kimiyo led them to one. She stopped a man in a suit from joining them by holding out her hand and saying, "Private car." Nathan noted the clean, pressed suit she had changed into after re-entry and realized she was at home in this corporate environment. She waved her badge in front of a reader in the elevator and pressed 70. The elevator raced up.

At the top, they stepped into a suite of offices that Nathan could only marvel at. His own store front office was barely a closet compared to Saji's digs. The décor was modern, tasteful, and didn't seem to reflect Saji's own eclectic tastes. He got the feeling Saji hired a decorator based on reputation and accepted whatever they said was a good look. A young woman who might have been a model was sitting at reception. It was a real girl, too, not a hologram construct like you saw in many offices. His musings were interrupted when a large security guard in a sharp suit stepped out to meet them in the lobby.

Kimiyo held out her hand, "Andre, how nice to see you."

"He's in his office, Kimiyo," the giant said. "Do you need an escort?"

She smiled. "Thank you but I know the way."

Kimiyo pushed through a door to the right of the receptionist desk. Nathan took a last look at the woman behind the desk and followed Kimiyo. She walked down a long hall to the double doors at the end. The doors swung open by themselves before she could knock. Nathan smiled at the little bit of theater and followed Kimiyo into Saji's office.

The billionaire was behind his desk seated in a large chair. He looked as small and shriveled as Nathan remembered. He gestured for them to sit down in the chairs on the opposite side of the desk. Nathan gestured for Kimiyo to sit first and then he and Duncan followed. Arulio remained standing.

The old man smiled. "Welcome back, my friends. I understand your journey was successful?"

Kimiyo nodded. "Very much so, sir. Captain Teller and his people recovered the *Charon* and its crew intact. The vessel is in orbit and its cargo is being delivered. All personnel are safe and accounted for. I've transmitted my report with the details for your review."

"Yes, of course, Kimiyo. I've reviewed your report. Very thorough, thank you. Top notch work as always. Tell me, how is Arulio?"

"He's right there," Nathan said. "Why don't you ask him?"

Kimiyo turned her head and shot him a look but spoke to Saji Vy. "Arulio is fine, sir. He's 100% operational although he does need to be debriefed and have his logs downloaded."

"You can take care of that when we're finished, Kimiyo." He turned his gaze to Nathan. "Captain Teller, I trust all is well with you? Your ship and crew are fine as well?"

"They are," Nathan said.

"You were somewhat reluctant to take on this particular assignment, Captain Teller."

"I was."

"Was it as bad as you thought?"

"The job went about as well as could be expected which is to say it was probably the worst job we've ever accepted."

"The worst? Surely not."

"Mr. Vy, there are a couple of dead Syndicate hit men back at Port Solitude who would disagree with you. There are probably officials on Olympia who want to speak with us regarding a shooting outside a diner. Oh, and the Syndicate will probably want to talk to all of us regarding the theft of twenty-three million credits that were stolen with Arulio's assistance. Believe me, sir, when I tell you this was our worst job ever."

Saji sat back in his chair and put his hands together, steepling his fingers. "Captain Teller, we knew this was going to be a difficult assignment when I offered it to you. That's why the payment is so generous. If you are unsatisfied, now is not the time to re-negotiate."

Nathan looked at Duncan and the two men smiled at each other. Nathan turned back to Saji. "I'm not negotiating, sir. The job is done and the invoice has been submitted. I'm sure you'll pay. I'm just letting you know that there could be trouble from the authorities and from the Syndicate. I'm sorry about that but it couldn't be helped."

Saji leaned forward again and the smile fell off his face. His eyes were hard and Nathan understood what it must be like sitting across from him, negotiating some deal, and how hard of a task that must be. "Captain Teller, I deal with the authorities every day. I'm not worried about them. As for the Syndicate, well, you don't grow the business I have without running into them once or twice. If they become a problem, I'll deal with them as well."

Nathan stood up and Duncan rose behind him. "Then I suppose we're done." He held out his hand and Saji took it. "Nice doing business with you, sir."

"And you. Can you find your way out?"

"We can," Nathan said.

Duncan shook Kimiyo's hand, "Nice to meet you. Stay in touch."

"I will."

The two men made their way to the door and Saji spoke. "Captain? One more thing."

Nathan turned. "Yes?"

"If you run into trouble with the authorities or the Syndicate, trouble you can't handle, because of this assignment, please get in touch. I have resources for dealing with these kinds of problems."

"Thank you. I'll remember that."

Nathan and Duncan made their way out of the building and walked into the afternoon desert sunshine.

Chapter 27

Three months after returning the *Charon* to Saji Vy, Nathan and his crew walked into a restaurant in a settlement on the Moon on the eastern slope on Mons Huygens. The mountain offered fantastic views of the impact craters of Mare Imbrium and the attendant lava flows. Tourists flocked to the settlement to hike and explore the local geography. Nathan was here for a different reason.

The rest of his crew, Duncan, Marla, Cole, and Richie took a round booth in a corner while Nathan moved to the bar. He ordered bourbon on the rocks and sipped his drink. He saw Celeste sitting on the other side of the bar. She was playing with her mobi and looked thoroughly annoyed.

The bartender walked over and refilled her glass with white wine. She took a sip and then spotted Nathan sitting in the corner. Her eyes fell. He got up, walked over, and took the stool next to her.

"What are you doing here?" she asked.

"Oh, you know how I like this place," he said. "It's nice, quiet, and the food is great. Remember how we used to come here?"

She sipped her wine. "I remember."

He swirled the drink in his glass. "See, what I remember is that we used to come here for meetings with people who needed a bit of privacy. You remember? Those couple times when a client would want privacy or was off Earth? This place was great for that."

"Is that why you're here? You're meeting with someone?"

"No. That's why you're here."

She looked around.

"He's late, isn't he?"

"Who?"

"Oh, come on. How long are you going to keep this up?"

She gave him a smirk. "Keep what up?"

"He isn't coming."

That stopped her. Her face grew serious and she drank a little more. "You don't know anything about anything."

"I know you're sitting here waiting your half of twenty three million and I know it isn't coming. He used you Celeste. You trusted him and he used you."

"Have you heard something or are you guessing?"

"I feel for you, Celeste, I really do. I know how things went bad for you on the cruise liner, about the captain of that ship and what he did to you, but this nonsense you've involved yourself in put us all in danger."

"You don't know anything," she said in a small voice.

"I don't know how you hooked up with him, but Montario Dawson is a con man with a record as long as my arm. From what I've been able to piece together, he was working a scam on those kids belonging to the Children of the Apocalyptic Rainbow. He was grifting off them and somehow figured out they were money laundering for the Syndicate. The two of you got together and cooked up a scheme to grab the *Charon* and get your hands on a wetjack so you could hack the account."

"You've been asking questions."

He nodded. "I have. What tripped you up is that the *Charon* was traveling too slowly for that section of space. Duncan and I saw in your logs that you had trouble there on prior runs with micro meteorites but you were moving way too slow. Just slow enough that a shuttle could overtake you. It was brilliant of you to keep working. I mean, it's so heroic after your hostage ordeal. You've made two more runs in the *Charon* and now you've taken some vacation time. I have friends in the travel industry. As soon as you booked a flight to this settlement on the Moon, I knew you would be meeting Montario. I also knew he wouldn't show up."

She had tears in her eyes now, big wet ones that were beginning to flow. She spoke in a whisper. "He should have been here an hour ago."

"What was the plan? You keep up appearances and meet later on? Let him establish new lives for both of you and then you just disappear?"

She nodded.

"That was a terrible plan."

"Why?"

"You can't trust guys like Montario. As soon as he had the money, he was gone in the wind. Hell, he took that guy Caleb with him but only because he had to. You were just a means to an end."

She was sobbing now, quietly and into a napkin.

"Don't feel too bad about it. This is what these guys do. They use people until they don't need them anymore."

"I really thought I could trust him."

"Let me tell you something. I had a very hard time getting over you after you left. I mean, a really hard time. I haven't had a decent relationship since you, and for a while I obsessed over you pretty hard. I've been seeing a therapist and I think I have my head on straight."

She shrugged her shoulders. "Well, as long as you're alright I guess everything is okay."

"What I'm trying to tell you is that you are a very remarkable woman. You just need to get yourself sorted out."

"You're offering to help?"

"Only with advice. I've learned that I can't be around you. If I start helping you now, out of kindness, it will turn into something toxic down the road. I just wanted to see you this last time, let you know that Saji's people have probably figured out what Duncan and I did. If you keep everything quiet, like you have, I think you'll be alright. If you quit your job and start looking for Montario I think you'll be in a world of trouble."

"Yeah," she said.

"Saji will punish you for using him and his ship and his wetjack. The authorities will throw you in jail, and the Syndicate will make you wish you'd been arrested. This is my advice; keep your job, keep your head down, and don't look for Montario. Living a straight life is the only thing keeping you out of trouble right now."

"It's not that easy to give up half of twenty-three million credits," she hissed.

Nathan got off his stool. "That's my advice, Celeste. As always, you'll do what you like."

He walked over to the booth in the corner and sat down just as Duncan was doing an imitation of him seeing Richie with his skin dyed purple for the first time. Laughter rang out, even from Richie, who was still a light shade of lavender. Nathan sipped his drink and relaxed in the booth, happy to be home with his crew.

ABOUT THE AUTHOR

Michael Prelee is an author from Northeast Ohio who enjoys good stories of any genre, sci-fi in any medium, and rooting for the Cleveland Browns

* * * *

If you enjoyed this book, please post a review.

Need something new to read?

If you enjoyed Milky Way Repo, you should also consider these other EDGE titles:

~ ~ ~

Beltrunner

by Sean O'Brien

As an independent beltrunner mining asteroids in the frontier of space, Collier South is a dying breed. Scrounging and cutting corners to work cheap, Collier isn't a stranger to lean times and make-do repairs; in fact his onboard computer hasn't had outside maintenance in years and its beginning to show its personal quirks.

When Collier finds an asteroid that shows promise, he thinks he's bought himself some time. But his claim is stolen out from under him by his vindictive ex-lover and her shiny new corporate ship. Powerless against the omnipotent mining corporations, Collier has always been too stubborn to give-up without a fight. Broke and desperate, Collier has one last chance to land a strike. If he doesn't come back with ore, he'll end up destitute and trading his own biologicals for his next meal.

What he discovers in the farthest reaches of the belt has the power to change his life and the fate of the entire system forever. That is, if Collier and his onboard computer can keep his discovery out of corporate hands.

Praise for Beltrunner

This is a fast moving book that leaves you breathless with hair-raising action and unexpected twists. The world creation is well-developed and highly creative. The interactions between Collier and Sancho are particularly entertaining - with Collier coming up with implusive dangerous plans and Sancho trying to talk him out of them. Highly recommended for action space lovers.
— Patricia Humphreys

Scavenging known space makes for a hard life, and surviving outside of the Corporations in the Belt makes it all the harder. It is not surprising that Collier and his unusual companion Sancho hit bottom, like many before them, until they make the discovery of their lives...or deaths, as it may turn out to be.

Beltrunner is a solidly enjoyable science fiction adventure, fast paced, and filled with the kind of characters that make you smile, break your heart, or just make you clench your jaw. I read it in one sitting and thoroughly enjoyed it. O'Brien builds a universe to get lost in that is as hard, gritty, and unforgiving as deep space itself. It is a well-written romp around space like many others, yet plenty of surprising elements give the story a depth and purpose all its own without the heavy strain of space melodrama. Read it because it is both light fun and thoughtful reading.
— A. Volmer

~ ~ ~

The Genius Asylum

by Arlene F. Marks

The truth is out there...

Earth Intelligence and Space Installation Security each think Drew Townsend is working for them. They're wrong.

Sent undercover to set up a covert intelligence operation on Earth's remotest space station, Drew Townsend finds himself managing a crew of brilliant mavericks, making friends with the most feared warriors in the galaxy, and feeling more at home in the controlled insanity of Daisy Hub than he ever did on Earth. Then he learns the truth about his mission there, and it's time to choose. In the coming interplanetary conflict, which side will Daisy Hub be on?'

Like the clues of a cryptic crossword, each book set in the Sic Transit Terra universe contains a puzzle – perhaps a riddle, perhaps a maze or an anagram – and in each case, the answer to the smaller puzzle brings the reader and characters one step closer to solving a much larger and more important one. The Genius Asylum is '1 Across' – it initiates a multi-book story arc that addresses one of the great mysteries of life: Why are we humans the way that we are?

Praise for The Genius Asylum

"The Genius Asylum starts out on Earth as something that looks like a crime story, but it then quickly describes a world of interstellar travel and alien alliances. After the first act concludes, the story's complexity starts accelerating and doesn't slow down, and you'll find yourself drawn into the world, needing to know what comes next. It is an excellently written story that provides the framework for the series that is to come, and I'm looking forward to reading the rest of it."

— Chris Marks, reviewer

I thoroughly enjoyed this Sci-Fi Brainteaser. Very well written with incredible plot twists and turns. We've got a very intelligent double agent as the main character and an intriguing support cast. I was thankful for the planetary history at the beginning as it was helpful in understanding the different organizations mentioned throughout the novel. The Author has a witty way of expressing viewpoints, clearly has put a lot of thought into the storyline and created edge of your seat suspense and mystery! Admittedly, I was confused about the title of the book until about halfway through reading it but it makes perfect sense now. I highly recommend this absolutely unforgettable installment and can't wait for the next.

— Stephanie Herman

~ ~ ~

The Salarian Desert Game
(Book 2 in The Unintentional Adventures of Kia and Agatha)

by J. A. McLachlan

What if someone you love gambled on her life?

Games are serious business on Salaria, and the stakes are high. When Kia's older sister, in a desperate bid to erase their family debt, loses the game and forfeits her freedom, Kia is determined to rescue her.

Disguised as a Salarian, Kia becomes Idaro in order to move freely in this dangerous new culture. When she arrives on Salaria, she learns it's a world where a few key players control the board, and the pawns are ready to revolt. Kia joins the conflict, risking everything to save her sister. As if she doesn't already have enough to handle, Agatha, the maddeningly calm and unpredictable Select who lives life both by-the-book and off-the-cuff shows up to help, along with handsome Norio, a strong-willed desert girl with her own agenda, and a group of Salarian teens earning their rite of passage in the treacherous desert game.

What can an interpreter and former thief possibly do in the midst of all this to keep the people she loves alive?

Praise for The Salarian Desert Game

I couldn't put it down! This exciting story had me reaching for my kindle in every spare minute I could drum up. Kia and Agatha are constantly in danger in this, their second space adventure.

Kia only cares about saving her sister. That's the only reason she agrees to alter her appearance and accompany Agatha to the planet Salaria. Little does she know, she'll be forced into participating in a barbaric coming of age custom, the Salarian desert game.

Will she lose herself in the game? Or will she be able to keep her wits about her, and stay focused on her goal?

Read The Salarian Desert Game, by JA McLachlan, and find out for yourself. It shouldn't take more than a single sitting, as long as you have five or six uninterrupted hours...
— Bridget Keller

Readers of The Occasional Diamond Thief will be delighted by the further maturation of the heroine Kia. The prickly, prideful and interesting protagonist journeys to a new planet and a bigger challenge in The Salarian Desert Game.

This is the sequel to the excellent first book, in what I sincerely hope becomes a series of adventures detailing the increasing complexity and maturation of this engaging heroine. Mindless bravery is not nearly as admirable as the true courage exhibited by a real character who is terrified - and does the morally right thing anyways. Will resonate with fans of Robin McKinley and Tamora Pierce
— Linda Stortz

~ ~ ~

Europa Journal

By Jack Castle

The history of humanity is about to change forever...

On 5 December 1945, five TBM Avenger bombers embarked on a training mission off the coast of Florida and mysteriously vanish without a trace in the Bermuda Triangle. A PBY search and rescue plane with thirteen crewmen aboard sets out to find the Avengers . . . and never returns.

In 2168, a mysterious five-sided pyramid is discovered on the ocean floor of Jupiter's icy moon, Europa.

Commander Mac O'Bryant and her team of astronauts are among the first to enter the pyramid's central chamber. They find the body of a missing World War II pilot, whose hands clutch a journal detailing what happened to him after he and his crew were abducted by aliens and taken to a place with no recognizable stars. As the pyramid walls begin to collapse around Mac and her team, their names mysteriously appear within its pages and they find themselves lost on an alien world.

Stranded with no way home, Mac decides to retrace the pilot's steps. She never expects to find the man alive. And if the man has yet to die, what does that mean for her and the rest of her crew?

Praise for Europa Journal

This book kept me guessing! It has an exciting start and keeps that same pace throughout the book. The building of the character personalities keeps a depth to the storyline and makes the reader feel connected to each character. The background information given through Europa Journal gives a great balance between the history, future and everything in-between! I love the mix of fact and fiction to create the story and inspire imagination. I'm excited to see what Castle comes up with next!

— Dianna Temple

With an action-packed opening, page-turning twists,a well-built world, and characters worth caring about, Europa Journal is like a bulldog - it grabbed me and wouldn't let go! It seamlessly blends breathtaking imagination with the gritty reality of survival, and beautifully blurs what has been with what might be. I love Dr. Who and grew up with Star Trek, but this book has broken the sci-fi mold in a wonderful way!

— Stuntwoman, Elisa Brinton

From the opening space shuttle crash landing to the stunning finish, Europa Journal is a real page turner. Ancient astronauts, the Bermuda triangle, WW II pilots, space shuttle crews – what else could you ask for? Mr. Castle keeps the story at light speed, with plenty of twists and turns before the awesome climax!

— James Wahlman, Firefighter in Alaska

~ ~ ~

Stranger King

By Nadia Hutton

They came. They conquered. We few survived.

Lena Greenwood is known as a "Daywalker", a select type of mercenary who has adapted to working in the deadly radiation of post-war British Columbia. When Earth is invaded by the Mokai, a hostile alien race, she and her company escape into the Canadian Rockies. Her last hope is to survive the harsh realities of a shattered world while the rest of humanity is culled or enslaved.

Thegn, a Mokai priest and a representative of the interspecies council who sanctions the Mokai, is captured and held hostage by a still free group of humans hiding in the mountains. It is his task to document and study the human species who he believes is sentient and worth protecting. When his interactions with the humans bring to light similarities between himself and his captors, Thegn must face the reality that to save those he learns to love, he may have to go against everything he once believed.

Stranger King is a story of love and conquest, of the patterns that immerge through the passions of love and war. It is the story of survival.

Praise for Stranger King

With Stranger King, Nadia Hutton has mashed together some intriguing ideas to present the reader with a well formed world populated by characters who are empathetic. We meet

Lena and she shows us her world as she begins her new job as a Daywalker. We get enticing glimpses of this near future world where Canada and the United States have had differences and some incident has left moving around in the daytime a hardship for most people. Then we are thrown into an alien invasion with beings who are well thought out and sympathetic in their own right. It's the kind of sci-fi that really engages the reader and covers well trod ground with a new perspective.
— Michael Prelee

The story is immediately engaging and almost impossible to put down. ... It is a tale of survival, loss and indominable will. Highly recommended as a science fiction adventure thriller.
— Patricia Humphreys

~ ~ ~

For more Science Fiction, Fantasy, and Speculative Fiction titles from EDGE and EDGE-Lite visit us at:

www.edgewebsite.com

——<<<>>>——

Don't forget to sign-up for our Special Offers

——<<<>>>——